HOW OUR HEARTS BREAK

L.K. REID

Cover Design by Seventh Star Art
Editing by Maggie Kern at Ms. K Edits
Formatting by Moonshine Creations

Playlist

Cold - Jorge Mendez
Nova - The Fallen State
Coming Back - Robin Loxley, Smudge Mason
Doomsday (Piano Reprise) - Architects
Everything - Lifehouse
Leave Out All The Rest - Linkin Park
Carry You - Novo Amor
Let Me Be Sad - I Prevail
Love - Nathan Wagner
Without You - Ashes Remain
The Sound - The Plot In You
Last Dance - Camera Can't Lie
One More Light - Jada Facer
You Said You'd Grow Old With Me - Michael Schulte
Hold On For Your Life (Acoustic) - Sam Tinnesz
Poljsko cvijece - Toše Proeski
Best Acquaintance - Mouth Culture
I Was Wrong - Sleeperstar
Love Song Requiem - Trading Yesterday
Someone Else - Loveless, Kellin Quinn
The Hardest Thing - Toše Proeski
I'll Be Fine - Parkwood, Christopher Vernon
Sun - Loveless

For survivors.

For fighters.

And for those that are no longer with us.

Foreword

I usually start this part with the list of triggers the book might have, so that you can be prepared. But this one is different.

How Our Hearts Break is not a dark romance. I think that I can't even classify it into the "romance" section due to its nature, even though it is heavily based on one relationship. The biggest trigger for this book is that it doesn't have an HEA. I don't exactly want to spoil the ending for any of you, but I need you to understand that tragic things happen in this book—things that none of the characters could prevent—and as such, it might not be for all readers.

I like to be transparent with all my books, and I don't want you to expect something that won't happen. This story is my passion project. It's something that came to me all of a sudden, and I just needed to write it.

I would also like to ask you not to spoil the book for other readers, so if you're posting reviews, try to do it without any spoilers.

Thank you for reading this story that took over my life, and feel free to reach out to me if you need to talk about it.

You said memories exist outside of time and have no beginning or end

Euphoria, Season 2 Episode 7

SOPHIE

SADNESS CAME IN WAVES.

It came out of nowhere and tapped you on your shoulder like an old, childhood friend whom you hadn't seen in years, and just like that, all those memories you'd tried to forget hit you in your chest, knocking the breath out of you. Some days, it was easier dealing with an avalanche of emotions it brought, but on the others, it hurt like an open cut, and you would start bleeding all over again.

That was the moment where you realize that you never truly healed, but that you were fooling yourself, trying to feel better, even if just for a moment.

My memories... They lived everywhere around me. Most days I tried to shield my eyes and ignore the whispers and that happy childlike laughter still bouncing off of the walls of my house. But today was not one of those days where I could pretend that I didn't remember the late nights spent beneath that willow tree behind our houses.

I couldn't pretend that his eyes didn't see everything I tried to hide. I also couldn't pretend that the boy I grew up with was nothing more than a stranger as he stood on the porch of his house, right next to mine, staring at me as if he had seen a ghost.

Sharpened claws scratched across the left chamber of my heart where he used to live when I remembered that I couldn't wave at him. I couldn't smile like I used to. I couldn't run down the three stairs and go over to his house, because he wasn't my Noah anymore. He made sure of it.

With all the strength I had in my body, I looked away toward the street where a car I knew all too well passed, stopping right in front of his house. I could still feel Noah's eyes on me, and I gripped the blanket wrapped around my body, holding on to it like a lifeline, because if I didn't, I knew my body would betray me.

I didn't want to give him the satisfaction of seeing the pain written all over my face. People often said that breakups were some of the hardest things they went through in their life, but what about breakups between friends? What about all the memories you made together? What about all those late nights when their eyes were the only light holding you upright?

What about words spoken and unspoken, the promises, the future we dreamed of? What about the small touches, hugs and kisses on your cheeks? How was I supposed to forget it all when he still lived in here, in me, in my chest, in every poem I wrote, in every new thing I did that I wanted to tell him about?

How could I forget that the boy that started as my friend turned out to be so much more, even though I never told him?

He was never mine, but losing him felt like thunder cracking through the sky, shattering the peace and quiet. He shattered my heart, and I couldn't exactly blame him— he never knew.

I could hear the voices coming from my left side, and I

gritted my teeth, pulled the blanket tighter, and got up to go back inside.

"Sophie!" *Goddammit.*

I kept my back to them. Even though it wasn't Noah that called out my name, it still had the same effect—my heart still cracked because his friends were not my friends anymore.

It felt as if an hour passed before I braced myself to turn around and face them, but in reality, it took a couple of seconds to take a deep breath and swallow down the sorrow and regrets dancing around in my throat. I knew I looked like shit—that was what I got after sleepless nights and eyes crying out tears I didn't want—but it was too late to pretend that I didn't hear Jared calling out to me.

I straightened up and wrapped the blanket tighter around my shoulders and twirled around with a small smile on my face. "Hey, J."

I trained my eyes on the tall, blond-haired guy who carried a smile wherever he went, instead of looking at the person every single nerve in my body was screaming for.

Jared leaned on the fence, and as he did, my eyes betrayed me and connected with the eyes colored like the bluest skies. He still looked the same, still looked like my Noah, but unlike all the other times, he didn't smile at me. He didn't move from the spot, his hands still inside his front pockets.

His shoulders seemed wider, his entire body taller, but that might have been my imagination because I did everything in my power to avoid him. I refused to go to hockey games. I refused to visit places he frequented because I didn't want to see his face. I refused to look at his house for the sole fear of seeing even a glimpse of him, because a broken heart could only take so much.

Noah was the first one to look away this time, ignoring

both Jared and me, and I bit down on my tongue when an involuntary whimper threatened to erupt from my chest.

"I haven't seen you in forever, dude," Jared continued, unaware of the awkward feelings lingering in the air. "Where have you been?"

Everywhere and nowhere, I wanted to tell him. I wanted to tell him what I found out—I wanted to tell them both. But as much as I loved them, as much as I missed them, especially Noah, they weren't my friends anymore. Losing Noah meant losing all these people I loved. When we stopped talking, when he forgot what we used to have since we were kids, his friends did too.

"Practice, you know? And school," I shrugged, keeping my emotions in check. If he really cared about me and where I'd been, he would've reached out. That was enough to cement what I already knew—his friends were never my friends, and it fucking sucked.

"I haven't seen you around the rink lately." Jared continued his mini interrogation. "I remember when you used to almost live there. Hell, you were there more often than any of us, including Noah." He straightened up and looked at him. "I'm right, aren't I? I could never go there without seeing her, and then boom, just like that, you were nowhere to be seen." He looked back at me with those words. "What happened?"

Something ugly unfurled inside my chest at the words so callously said, as if he didn't know what happened. As if he didn't hear how humiliating that night was, when the boy I believed to be my best friend threw me on the side as if I was yesterday's trash because I was embarrassing him. Because I was too much for him, his friends, and his girls that were flocking to him like chickens around the grains thrown on the ground.

What happened was that Noah's words hurt more than

anything else I felt before that night. What hurt even more was that he never apologized. It's been three months since that night at the carnival and he still refused to acknowledge what was said and done.

That night was the night where I knew that this friendship I was clinging to was a one-way road to destruction. I was the only one trying to make it work.

But that was also the night when I decided that there were more important things in life, and instead of scooting down to their level, I would be the bigger person. I could feel the familiar throb in the back of my head, and I didn't want them to see me in the state I became so familiar with.

"Nothing happened, J." I smiled while my heart cracked even further, but I looked at Noah instead of Jared as I spoke. "Sometimes the people you hang out with become just a habit, a familiar place, if you wish to call it that. I was never one to keep hanging around people when I wasn't wanted anymore."

"Wha—"

"I gotta go." I looked back at him, my heart beating a thousand miles per hour, ignoring the bane of my existence. I promised myself I wouldn't get angry anymore over the things I couldn't change, but it was getting harder and harder with each second that passed. His presence alone made me angry, and he was the least of my concerns right now. "I'll see you around. I hope you guys have an amazing game tomorrow."

I turned from them and started walking toward the front door of my house. With one last glance at my ex-best friend and Jared, I entered inside, shaking off the cold and headache slowly spreading through my skull. I knew it was only a matter of time before I wouldn't be able to move at all.

The picture of my parents, my brother, Andrew, and

me, hanging on the wall before the staircase, caught my attention, and the anger I felt before was nothing compared to the one I started feeling now. We all looked so happy, so content, in this picture taken just before Andrew went off to college. I never really understood the saying before, but time really passes quickly when you don't appreciate the small things in life, like the happiness of my family.

Now, this house that used to be filled with happiness, with laughter, love and a bright future, felt like a tomb— lifeless, depressing, dressed in gray colors of despair. I thought about all the dreams I had, the light shining in my eyes even on the picture, and then looked at myself in the mirror on the opposite wall. My once shining eyes were now dull, the bright green color dimmed, marred by every-thing that had happened. At least my hair was clean, tied up in a low ponytail, the sharp lines of my face more prominent this way.

I wanted to hide, but I knew it would bring me no good.

This morning when I woke up, I promised myself I wouldn't succumb to the same old emotions I'd been trapped with during the last month. But it was getting harder and harder fighting it, being brave, putting a smile on my face when all I wanted to do was scream and scream and scream until my throat went hoarse, and my voice died down in my chest.

All those things were mere wishes and if I wanted to survive all this, I had to bite down all these emotions clog-ging my veins and try to pretend that tomorrow, a brighter sun would shine through my windows.

"Soph." My brother's voice pulled me back from the dark and depressing thoughts running free through my mind. "Are you okay?"

I looked at him, hating myself even more when the dark circles he didn't usually have were the first thing that greeted me. He looked tired, sad, desperate, and I knew I was the reason. I knew he was here, away from his studies, because he wanted to be here for me, but I didn't want his life to end just because I couldn't handle my own shit right now.

"I'm fine, Andy. I think I'm going to go and lie down for a bit. My head's been throbbing, and I don't want it to get worse."

"Do you need anything?" I knew what he was asking. I didn't need to be a mind reader to know. Ever since he came home from college a week or so ago, he's been all over me, asking questions, begging me to tell him how I felt. How could I tell him when I didn't know how to describe this turmoil running through me?

I couldn't tell him that some days went better than the others, but that the dark cloud I'd been so desperately trying to run away from was getting closer and closer. My therapist said that it was normal, feeling like this, given the situation, but it was tiring going from being extremely happy to extremely sad, then angry, then sad again, then just numb.

"Nah." I forced a smile and stepped closer to him, wrapping my arms around his middle, letting the blanket fall off of my shoulders. "I'm all good." I squeezed as tight as I could when his arms wrapped around my shoulders, keeping me close to him.

His warmth was all I needed right now, and I hated myself for what all this was doing to him. It wasn't fair that he had to go through this.

I squeezed my eyes tighter, forcing the tears that threatened to spill to go back, to just stay still, at least until I moved away from him. I succeeded as I stepped away from him and lifted the blanket from the ground, shaking from the cold seeping through my bones.

"You need to eat something," Andrew said as I came closer to the stairs. "I don't remember you having breakfast."

"I had some cereal."

"That's not enough."

"Andy." I sighed. "I'm okay, and I'm not hungry."

"It's almost five in the afternoon, Soph. If you continue like this—" He stopped himself before he could say what was really on his mind.

If I continued like this, I would bring myself to the brink of death. That was what he wanted to say, but couldn't because we both knew what truly lay in front of all of us. We both knew that we needed to stay sane and collected if we wanted to survive what life threw at us.

"I'm sorry," he rasped. "I didn't mean it like—"

"It's okay, Andy. I know what you meant. I'm going to go to bed now. I promise I'll eat something once I get up. Sound good?"

A tiny nod was all I got before he disappeared down the hallway leading toward the living room. I wished I had something better to tell him to console him, to tell him that all these feelings running through him would one day be just a mere memory he wouldn't want to relive, but I couldn't because I feared that my own voice would betray me. Instead of me consoling him, he would be the one consoling me.

I watched him as he disappeared into the room, as the hushed voices filtered through the air—probably my mom —and started walking toward my bedroom, the tiredness already making my limbs heavier and my heart emptier.

I was supposed to be at practice right now, but I couldn't bring myself to go anymore. Figure skating used to be the one thing I never could get tired of, and now, no matter how much I loved it, I couldn't bring myself to drive to that ice rink, to put my skates on and just be.

Everything had changed, and I knew that nothing would ever be the same.

2

SOPHIE

I HOPED, prayed even, that with a good night's sleep, my
head wouldn't be trying to split open, but even the pills
that usually helped were useless today. It was as if the
universe was out to get me. After that horrendous Saturday
when I saw Noah and Jared, Sunday turned out to be even
worse, with me avoiding my entire family since everyone
was in a foul mood, and spending it in my bed because my
head decided to burst from the inside out.

At least that was what it felt like.

So here I was, on a Monday morning, my eyes trained
on the clock showing six-thirty in the morning, and I just
didn't want to get up. The two blankets covering me did
nothing to warm me up, and I knew that this kind of cold
wasn't coming from the lack of heating—our house always
felt like a furnace during the winter. This kind of cold was
coming from the inside, and if I could wrap my heart and
my soul in a blanket, I would. Maybe then I wouldn't feel
as if the ice was slowly taking over my body.

I slowly pulled myself up into a seated position and
turned off the blaring alarm that kept going and going on
my phone. I looked at the window where the soft morning
glow was just starting to trickle into the room.

I'd spent countless nights sitting in that window, talking to Noah. His window was just on the opposite side, and like a fool, I forgot to close my curtains last night. Now I knew that the first thing I'd see when I got up to look out would be him.

I knew him like the back of my own hand and judging by the time showing on the screen of my phone, he probably just came back from his morning run. I used to go on those with him—he'd be training for the next game and keeping in shape, and I'd be preparing my body for upcoming competitions.

It wasn't too long ago when we ran together for the last time, but these days, it felt as if it was years since the last time we shared space together. Since we last talked, laughed, hung out... Funny how these things work. You never know when the last time that the person you loved more than most other people in your life would become a stranger.

For an entire month after our fallout, I'd been wondering what it was that I did that made him so angry that night. I wondered if it was me or just him, and then I realized that no matter how much I break my head over these things, nothing would change.

In a few months, he would probably go to some college far away from here, no doubt getting a hockey scholarship, and I would never see him again. I just had to survive these next couple of months and that would be it.

Slowly, I stood up, pulling all the blankets with me, and walked toward the adjacent bathroom, flipping the light on as I came to the door. I preferred to walk around in the dark for as long as possible. I wasn't a morning person, and if I could spend at least a couple more minutes pretending I was still asleep, I would. The light from the bathroom illuminated my room, and as I walked in, I dropped the blankets on the floor, staring at myself in the mirror above the sink.

The dark circles around my eyes seemed better today, but I knew that I wouldn't be able to stand on my own by the end of the day if the pills I usually took in the morning did nothing but cause more nausea. I wanted to go through at least one day where I didn't have to worry that this thing I had to live with now wouldn't cause more pain.

The last thing I wanted today was to have to call Andrew or my parents to pick me up. I still didn't say a word to anyone at school and I begged my brother, my mom and dad to keep all this on the down-low. I still wanted to skate, and if I couldn't do it for much longer, at least I wanted to finish the last two competitions coming up.

This shit that was happening wouldn't be the end of me. I could still do things I loved. I could still live my life.

Taking a shower while freezing wasn't the nicest experience, but I knew I had to wash my hair and the remnants of the last two days from my skin. It was a new week, and I'd be damned if I started it on a shitty note.

Some days I went through motions—thanks to muscle memory and the years of doing the same every single day —but I was thankful that today was one of the days where my mind wasn't trying to disassociate from life. Even with the throbbing pain in my head, I still managed to go through everything in half an hour. Once I dressed up in the warmest clothes I could find, I pushed three notebooks into my backpack and started zipping it up, standing right in front of the window.

When I first met Noah, it felt as if this weird kind of electricity pulled me to him. Since that first day when we were in kindergarten, while he still lived on the other side of the town, I always knew where to find him.

And now, as I stood there, holding the backpack to my body as if it could save me from his inquiring eyes, I kept my eyes on the floor, looking at the small scratch on my Doc Martens boots, avoiding looking up.

But I was always a little masochist when it came to him, and I had to see him. I had to see if this separation hurt him as much as it hurt me.

I inhaled deeply, as if bracing myself for an impact, and looked up, a thousand emotions crashing into me when I saw him standing there, in front of his own window, shirtless, and looking at me.

Time stood still and nothing else existed but him and me. My heart violently beat against my ribs, bruising me, reminding me what he did, but nothing could deter me from looking at him. At that dark hair, those blue eyes, and those arms that always felt like home until he decided that he didn't want me anymore.

I always knew he looked at me as a sister and nothing more, but never would I have thought that he would so easily throw me away and forget everything we went through together.

My lower lip trembled as I remembered the first time I held him while he cried. His parents were going through a divorce, and for two nine-year-olds that felt like the end of the world.

If I remembered all these things, how was it possible that he forgot? How was it possible that all those promises we whispered to each other underneath the dark skies when the stars shone on us meant nothing to him?

I nodded at him without a smile, without a wave, and turned around, leaving him standing there like he always did. Sometimes I think that how I used to see him was just a figment of my imagination, because that version of him was the one I wanted to see.

13

Sometimes when you love somebody, you decide to turn a blind eye to all those bad attributes they had, because the good ones were the only ones you cared about.

I guess that I never really knew him at all.

Shaking my head as I exited my room, I went downstairs, only to find Andrew and my mom sitting at the counter, slowly drinking their coffees in silence. Both of them turned and looked at me as I entered the room, their faces betraying their emotions.

"Morning," I mumbled as I walked toward my mom, hugging her from behind. She smelled like cinnamon and apples, so soft and always accepting and supportive of everything Andrew and I wanted to do. I still remembered the first time I told her I wanted to do figure skating. Even though she feared for my life, she took me to the rink and it was love at first sight.

"You guys already ate?" I asked as I went to Andrew, hugging him as well. "What are those faces for?" The two of them were uncharacteristically quiet, staring at me as if I grew another head. "Is there something on me?" I looked down, trying to gauge if the sweater I put on in the room had a hole or a stain somewhere, but there was nothing. "Come on, guys. You're freaking me out."

"You're just…" our mom started, hiccuping as her eyes filled with tears. "You seem happy today."

"Because I am happy. And," I grinned, "I actually slept well last night."

"Headache?" Andrew asked from his spot while I took an apple from the bowl.

"A little bit," I answered, lying, and bit into the apple, letting the sweet taste float through my mouth. "But nothing major. I wanted to eat something before taking my pills."

Mom slid off of the stool and walked toward the

fridge. "I was thinking of making bacon and eggs. Would you like to have that?"

"Uh, sure." I didn't want to tell her that I planned on getting some cereal just to have something in my stomach until lunchtime, but the smile that overtook her face when she looked at me over the door of the fridge made me feel like shit. When was the last time she smiled like that? Two months ago, maybe?

She busied herself at the stove, cracking eggs and humming softly while the oil heated up in the pan. But Andrew looking at me told me that he knew what I was doing.

What? I mouthed at him, but he simply smiled and stood up, bringing his and Mom's cups to the sink.

"Are you going to the rink today, Soph?" Mom asked, her back turned to me. The sound of sizzling bacon filled the kitchen and as Andy started pulling out three plates, I realized how much I missed this. This normalcy.

"I might," I answered and threw the half-eaten apple into the trash. I knew if I ate any more of it, I might not be able to eat what she was preparing. I didn't want to disappoint her. "I'll text Coach Liudmila on the way to school to let her know I'm feeling better."

"Mhm," she mumbled, the unspoken words hanging in the air.

All three of us knew that I might never get better, but we all liked to lie to ourselves. Andrew looked at me while Mom kept flipping over the bacon and then putting it on the plate she placed on the counter next to the stove.

Tapping my fingers on the countertop table, I waited for one of them to say something. But instead of bringing up the topic I didn't want to talk about, Andrew started talking about college and his practice, while Mom finished preparing an omelet and bacon, putting the pan on the side and turning off the stove top.

One plate filled with more bacon than any of us could eat and one with an omelet was placed on the table. Without preamble, all three of us dug in, putting several pieces of bacon on our plates. Andrew cut the omelet in three pieces, taking the biggest one for himself.

"Hey." I laughed. "That's not fair."

"Sorry, Soph. I'm a growing boy and I need my nutrients."

"You're more of a hulk than a boy. What are they feeding you at college? Concentrate for cows?"

He threw a piece of bacon at me, which landed on top of my plate, earning a hefty laugh from me.

"Guys," Mom warned, but neither one of us listened to her. Between eating and laughing, pieces of bacon flew from me to him and the other way around.

I missed this. I missed laughing with my family. I missed having mornings filled with happiness instead of the dark sadness that filled our lives as of late.

"Where's Dad?" I asked, chewing the last piece of bacon from my plate.

"He has an early meeting, so he had to leave earlier," Mom answered without looking at me. I didn't have to be a genius to know that she was lying.

Dad was, how could I say this, lost? He was here, but he wasn't here. He avoided looking at me, at Mom, at Andrew, and it wasn't as if I could really blame him.

I just missed our mornings together, and the late nights when neither of us could sleep and we would sneak downstairs to eat ice cream from the tub. But, step-by-step as my therapist would say, I was positive that this thing wouldn't be the end for my family, and that we would come back stronger because of it.

"So, Sophie." Andrew grinned, and I knew that some kind of shit would come out of his mouth. "I saw Noah yesterday."

Fuck.

"You guys used to be really clo—Ouch!" he suddenly shrieked. "What the hell, Mom?"

I snorted and got up with my plate, taking it to the sink and rinsing off the crumbs. Of course, Mom would hit him. She was there that night when I came back from the carnival, crying my eyes out. I couldn't exactly tell her that everything was okay, when it was obvious that what he did would never be okay.

"Yeah, we used to be."

"What happened? Mom, stop hitting me."

"Then stop asking stupid questions," she replied.

"It's okay, Mom." I put the plate inside the dishwasher and turned to them, leaning against the counter. "We just… I don't know. We grew apart, I guess."

"You guess?" Andy asked, his eyebrow inching up. "You guys were inseparable. Hell, I always thought that he was in love with you, and that one day I would have to beat him up because no matter what, no one is good enough for my baby sister."

"Awww, you actually love me."

"Only on every third Monday," he snickered. "No, but really. I used to tell Mom that one day I would have to watch you get married to that little punk."

"Andy, he's not a punk," Mom scolded him. "He's actually really nice."

"Mom, every guy is a punk if he wants to be with my sister. That's a given. You already know this. You grew up with three older brothers."

"Well, thank God I only have one, because three of you would send me straight to an asylum." I laughed and

17

pulled my phone out when I felt it vibrating against my leg. "Oh shit."

"What's wrong?"

"I forgot Bianca was picking me up today."

I almost ran toward the other side of the kitchen, where my pills were neatly hidden in the cupboard.

"Slow down," Mom chastised. "You'll break your neck, rushing like that."

"Sorry, Mom." I pulled out the pills that should help with my headache, and popped two into my mouth, reaching for the bottle of water standing on the counter. "I gotta go."

"Sophie!" Mom called out, and I stopped at the entrance of the kitchen. I looked at her, again hating what I could see in her eyes. "Think about what we spoke about, okay? It's almost time to tell them."

I knew, dammit. I knew it was time to tell them, but I couldn't bring myself to do it. At least not yet.

"I know." I nodded somberly. "But not yet. Give me this month, please?"

I went back to her, hugged her, and dropped a kiss on her cheek, then Andrew's, and ran toward the front door, taking my coat as I went.

Freezing morning air hit me in my face as soon as I stepped outside. I pulled the coat on before rushing down the stairs, all the way to Bianca's car.

I could already see her face through the window, and she was anything but amused.

"I am so fucking sorry," I started as I opened the door and slid inside. Warmth of the car enveloped me almost immediately, and I thanked the person that invented heating inside cars. "I was having breakfast with my mom and Andrew and I completely missed the time."

I looked at her profile, the sharp edges of her face and

the pissed-off look. Fuck, I knew how much she hated me being late. "I really am sorry."

Her blonde hair was pulled into a high ponytail, accentuating her slender features.

"I'll buy you a coffee?" I tried again, but as she pulled the car away from my driveway and started driving toward the school, she still kept quiet, keeping her eyes on the road. "Come on, B."

I was ready to cry if that was what it took for her to finally look at me.

"Bianca?" I placed my hand on her upper arm. "Don't make me tickle you."

It was only then that she turned toward me and started laughing. "God, the look on your face is priceless. I'm fucking with you, dude."

"You little——"

"I literally arrived one minute before you came out, but I wanted to fuck with you."

"You are such an asshole." I laughed. "Here I was, apologizing——"

"A first for you."

"Shut your mouth."

"Come on. Remember the last time? You let me grovel for fifteen minutes, making me think that you were angry at me?"

"No, can't say that I do."

"Liar."

"I almost had a motherfucking heart attack, you fucker."

"But you still love me." She looked at me, grinning.

"Barely."

I switched on her radio and opened my Bluetooth to connect my phone to it.

"What are you doing?"

"What does it look like I'm doing? Playing some music."

"You know I don't let other people play music in my car?"

"Good thing I'm not other people then." In less than ten seconds, I connected my phone to her radio and played the song I knew she would love.

"No, you're my sister from another mister. I might forgive you for everything if you play this song every single day for me."

"Shivers" by Ed Sheeran blasted through the speakers and both of us started dancing in our seats when she stopped at the red light right before our school.

"So, coffee?" She looked at me.

"Is the sky blue?" I asked her, scrolling through my phone, trying to find the next song.

"Do you really want me to answer that question? Because if you look out, today looks like shit."

I did look outside, only to see a familiar black Camaro driving toward the school.

"It really does look like shit."

SOPHIE

BIANCA and I met in the fifth grade at the very end of the summer break, when her family just moved into White-brook Hill. It was love at first sight. She'd been threatening an eighth grader, telling him that she would make his nuts disappear if he ever looked at another kid in a bad way.

I was slowly passing by, waiting for Noah, when she looked at me and exclaimed, "You." I thought she was going to beat me up or something, but instead, she asked me to help her escort the kid, that was hiding behind her, home. On the way there, I found out that her favorite color was violet, not purple or lavender, but violet, and that she hated bullies.

I also learned that her parents recently separated, which was why she moved here with her dad.

We'd been best friends ever since.

She offered me on multiple occasions to go and beat up Noah for what he did and how he treated me, but I always laughed it off. I knew she would do it or something worse, like scratch his Camaro, and I really didn't want her to get into that kind of trouble.

Touching Noah's beloved Camaro was one thing that

could really make him pissed off, and he and Bianca never really got along.

"So, are you feeling better?" She eyed me while we walked through the parking lot toward the entrance door. "Or were you just lying to me while you were moping around, crying over an asshole that wouldn't know what he had even if you hit him in the face?"

I laughed at her exaggeration, but I would rather she think that I was moping around than that I was lying in my bed, unable to move because the headaches were getting stronger and stronger.

"I'm better, and I wasn't moping around."

"Mhm." She scoffed.

"I really wasn't. I've had a headache from hell for the last two days. I didn't even go to the rink on Saturday."

"Seriously?"

"Seriously. But I saw you-know-who."

"No."

"Oh, yes."

"And?"

"He'd been with Jared. That fucktard pretended that he didn't know about us not talking, and he asked me where I've been."

"Is he stupid or what?"

"I mean, all of us used to hang out, and now they're pretending as if I don't exist."

"Listen, boo." She stopped and turned me to her. "I truly hope that all of them get diarrhea during one of their games, but you don't need them."

I did need Noah, and he abandoned me when I needed him the most.

"Besides, you have me, you have Riley, and you have your skates and your ice. If Noah and his buddies can't see what a shining star you are, then they don't deserve you."

Her dark brown eyes shone with sincerity, but sometimes it was hard believing those words when that one person you thought would always be by your side, no matter what, decided to abandon you.

I had an amazing life. I had a family that loved me, friends that were always there. Noah wasn't the only person, but it still hurt like a fucking bitch that I meant so little to him.

"Yeah, you're——" But I was cut off mid-sentence, when a group I knew all too well caught my attention.

They were just behind us, walking in our direction, obviously going toward the front door of the school.

Out of all five of them walking and laughing, pushing each other, only one person caught my eye. Only one person could ever make my breathing slow down—Noah.

He was already looking at me, and I wondered how it was that we spent the last three months almost never seeing each other, to us seeing each other two times in the last three days. I was so careful, so obvious in avoiding him, and he never sought me out.

Did I expect him to, for the sake of our friendship? I fucking did. But hope was for fools, and I stopped hoping for him to talk to me over a month ago. I texted, I called, I tried to fix what happened, but he was the one that stopped talking to me.

He was the one that would look the other way every time he saw me in the hallway.

He was the one that told everyone that I wasn't worth it. That one was the one that hurt the most. Maybe if somebody just told me that, I wouldn't have believed them, but I saw that message with my own eyes.

So yeah, Noah Kincaid could fuck himself, for all I cared.

"Queen B," Jordan hollered as they came closer to us.

Noah still kept looking at me, earning a lifted eyebrow from me and a middle finger. "Whoa, you're feisty today, Soph."

"Bite me, Jordan."

"Gladly, but—" Noah smacked him on the back of his head, scowling at me. "What the fuck, man?"

"Shut your mouth, J."

Bianca looked from Jordan to Noah and then to me, confusion written all over her face. The confusion lasted for all of a second, when a wicked little smile appeared, and I knew whatever was going to come out of her mouth wouldn't be good.

"Bianca," I warned, but I knew it was too late. Whatever it was that she thought was going to bite us all on our asses, and I wouldn't be able to stop it.

"So, boys." She grinned and looked at Noah. "We've just been talking about an interesting little thing." Fuck. Me. "Sophie met this guy from college…" You know the sound of brakes screeching on the pavement? My face most probably looked like the driver's would, a second before stopping at the red light, praying to all saints that he or she didn't go through the red.

"And we just wondered, since all of you have so much experience with ladies, where should they go?"

"Oooooh, our little Sophie has a date." It was Jordan that started talking again, while my face went up in flames. I was going to kill her.

No, I was going to buy her a coffee with regular milk, just so that I could watch her lactose intolerant ass run to the toilet.

Motherfucker.

I refused to look anywhere else but at Bianca, who was still grinning like a Cheshire cat.

"You're what?" It was Noah this time, yet I still hadn't moved my eyes from B. "Sophie?"

"She's going on a date, dum-dum." Bianca answered instead, and I prayed for the ground to open up and swallow me whole. "But he's in Boston. She'll be visiting her brother soon, so they figured that it's much easier to just meet there."

"Sophie?"

I could feel him even though I couldn't see him. He radiated heat, and I hated my traitorous heart for beating faster as he came closer.

"Look at me."

If I looked at him, I would either punch him in the face or start crying. It felt like forever passed since we last stood this close, and the last time, he broke my heart in a thousand pieces, shattering all those good things we built together.

I understood then what Bianca was doing, even without her throwing daggers at me with her eyes, urging me to play along. Noah always had a problem with every single guy I would start liking, or every single guy that would ask me out.

That whole protective brother bullshit escalated that night when I was talking to one of the guys visiting our town, and Noah went ahead and ruined my night.

I pulled myself together and turned toward him, taking a step backward when I noticed how close we stood to each other. "Yes, Noah?" I thanked whatever was out there for how steady my voice sounded, curling my fingers into a fist.

"You're going on a date? In Boston?"

"That's none of your business."

"The hell it's not!"

"Lower your fucking voice," I seethed. "It stopped

being your business the moment you decided that you didn't want to be friends anymore."

"Sophie—"

"And yes, I am going on a date. And yes, it is in Boston, far away from here, far away from you and all your goons that would no doubt show up and ruin my night. Because that's what you do best, Noah, isn't it? Ruin my nights." I looked at Bianca and took another step away from him. "Let's go. I still need to catch Ms. Fiore to ask about that new assignment."

My hands shook as we walked away from them. I felt hopeful that maybe, just maybe, that silly crush I had on him was finally going away. We didn't manage to go too far, when he wrapped his hand around my upper arm and turned me toward him.

"Don't walk away from me."

"You walked away from me first." I shook him off and moved farther, seething. How dare he. How dare he come back like this, to start talking to me when he did nothing but hurt me. "What do you want, Noah? It's Monday. It's too early and I still haven't had my morning coffee. Standing here, talking to you, is doing nothing but increasing this already annoying headache."

"You have a headache?" I hated, fucking hated, the concerned look on his face.

"Cut the crap, buddy. What. Do. You. Want?"

He moved his weight from one leg to the other, looking at me as if he couldn't quite figure me out. And maybe he couldn't. The Sophie he knew was the Sophie that was never coming back.

"We need to talk," he almost whispered. "Please."

I scoffed and wrapped my arms around myself. "Wasn't that the same sentence I said to you almost three months ago?"

"Sophie—"

"Yet, you completely ignored me, deciding that I wasn't good enough to hang out with you."

"Please. I was an idiot."

"Yeah, you were. But guess what, Noah? The time for talking was three months ago. This, now," I pointed between him and me, "is just two strangers who used to know each other. I don't want to talk to you. I don't want to see you, and I don't want you to look for me. It was nice knowing you, but as far as I'm concerned, you're just my neighbor. I pray that after we finish school this year, I won't have to see you ever again."

"Sophie, please." *Goddammit, heart. God-fucking-dammit.*

I hated seeing the sorrow and pain in his eyes. I hated hearing those words and seeing how sorry he truly was. But he fucked us up. It wasn't me.

I had no idea why. I just knew that one day he woke up and decided to stop being my friend, and now that I was slowly getting used to life without him in it, he decided to come back to me.

I wasn't raised to be a doormat, no matter how much I loved the other person. I loved him with every single pore in my body, but sometimes... Sometimes love wasn't enough, and we just grew up to be completely different people.

"Don't worry, Noah. I'm not angry at you anymore. I will always love you, but this version of you is not the one I want to have in my life. I just... I'm done playing this game. I'm choosing me."

I wasn't going to let him hurt me again. I already had enough problems without Noah Kincaid being another one.

"Bye, Noah."

I turned around, leaving him there, while a thousand

emotions transpired on his face. Bianca looked like she wanted to high five me, but it would have to wait until we got inside. It would have to wait until I broke apart again, and I didn't want Noah to see it happen.

"Come on, B," I urged her. "I really need to get away from here."

She hugged me and started walking, through the main entrance and all the way to the place beneath the stairs in the North Wing, where I finally allowed my tears to come.

"I hate him," I sobbed. "I hate him so fucking much."

"I know, babe." She hugged me, dragging her hand down my hair. "I hate him too."

NOAH

Some stories were better left untold, and ours was one of them.

I could still remember the first day I met Sophie. I didn't remember the clothes I wore or what my mom made for breakfast, but I remembered her. I could never explain the feeling when my heart started beating faster at the sight of a petite girl, standing in the middle of the backyard of the kindergarten, washed in the afternoon sun, her golden hair glowing even brighter, rendering me speechless.

She looked as lost as I felt, and something… something told me to go and talk to her. Something pushed me in her direction. As I approached her, the most brilliant smile spread across her face, her eyes twinkling, two pigtails on her head bouncing when she moved her head from side to side. Nothing ever felt as good as her hand in mine. Nothing ever came close.

When she asked her mom to enroll her in figure skating classes held at the local sports center, I asked mine if I could start playing hockey, so that I would feel closer to her. After that first day, when my feet clad in skates I didn't know how to use hit the ice, I knew one thing—I found my one love thanks to her.

She was always there, on the sidelines, cheering for me, yelling and jumping, always, always with a smile on her face.

And now I'd lost her.

I'd lost the best thing I ever had, because I didn't want to admit to myself what was clear to everybody else around me. I was in love with Sophie Anderson, probably have been from that first moment I saw her. I was a jealous prick who couldn't stand seeing another guy talking to her, touching her, and making her laugh.

I couldn't stand to see his hands on her. Before those first words even left my mouth, I knew I was going to regret it for as long as I lived.

Three months, five days, and I didn't even know how many hours, but the image of her tear-stained face was etched into my mind as clear as day, and it was all my fault. I couldn't blame other people for what I said. I couldn't blame that guy for trying to win her over, because if I were him, if I were just a little bit braver, I would've done the same thing.

The moment she exited her house that night, wearing black, high-rise, skintight pants, her favorite Doc Martens boots, and a crop top sweater that revealed her stomach every time she stretched her arms above her head, I knew I was going to get into trouble. Instead of going to that motherfucking carnival, I should've taken her behind our houses, to our spot beneath that willow tree, keeping her with me. I should've taken her hand in mine and looked into her eyes until she finally realized what I felt for her.

I didn't want to destroy our friendship, and somehow by letting the jealousy eat me alive, I did just that—I destroyed us. Seeing her from a distance, watching her laugh and smile, watching her talk to other people when she wasn't mine anymore, it all ate me alive.

Wasn't it fucked up that we spent our entire lives already having everything we ever needed, yet we never saw it until we lost those things?

My words from that night kept bouncing back and forth in my mind, eating me alive, while I cursed myself for saying those things to her. I should've kept my mouth shut. I should've told her how much I loved her, how much I wanted her to be mine.

I should've told her that every time my lips landed on her cheek, I wished that I had enough courage and enough strength to just move them a couple of inches to the side, so that they would land right on top of hers.

I should've told her that she was my shining star, my past, present, and future. I should've groveled, begged, cried if needed, all so that she would look at me with the same adoration and love once again.

But as I stood here in the empty parking lot, waiting to see when she would emerge from the school, I knew that all those were just a lot of should-haves and none of them mattered when I never told them to her, and kept them to myself.

I'd spent years hoping that maybe, just maybe, she would be able to see through me and my act, because I didn't know how to tell her how I felt. I could say all these things a million times in my head, but words often failed me. Instead of just telling her that seeing her with that guy felt as if somebody pierced my heart with an arrow, I uttered the foulest words, putting that look of sadness and desperation on her face.

I couldn't remember my life before her, but I knew that the last three months felt like an eternity without her next to me.

Every single one of my good memories was somehow connected to her. I could lie to myself. I could lie to the

31

entire world, but the truth always laid in the depths of my heart that always beat only for her and nobody else.

I just hoped I wasn't too late.

She managed to avoid me today, just like she did every single other day since we stopped talking, since I stopped responding to her texts, her calls and knocking on the door. And every single time her name appeared on the screen of my phone, my lungs seized, my throat closed, and the pain I had never felt before started spreading somewhere from the center of my chest, through my veins, all the way to the tips of my fingers, like poison.

I looked up at the sky, the gray color decorated with white clouds resembling the sky from that day when I fucked us up. Beginning of March always felt more like winter than the near beginning of spring, and I buried my hands deeper into my pockets, trying to warm myself up.

The front door of our school suddenly flew open, the first students slowly trickling out with the cacophony of voices gradually filling the parking lot. But not a single one of them was her.

I was starting to lose hope, the dread dropping into my stomach, when her familiar blonde hair finally appeared on the steps, her eyes looking more tired than they did this morning.

Despite the cold, despite the violent air slamming into me from left and right, I felt warm, heated up, my blood singing, recognizing her for what she was.

Mine.

She was always mine, from that first moment when we were just kids, and I was an idiot for waiting this long to try and claim her. I should've done it years ago. I should've taken what always belonged to me.

She marked me on that first day, and I wasn't the same ever since. She stole my heart. She stole my memories, and no matter what, I would never want them back. If I had anything to say, she would never belong to anybody else.

I didn't care how many years it took, but Sophie Anderson would one day be Sophie Kincaid—my wife, my light, and my life.

She lifted her head at the same time as I strode toward her. Pinching her eyebrows together, a less-than-pleasant look passed over her face. "What do you want, Noah?"

"I told you already," I answered, trying to calm my racing heart. "To talk. To explain."

"Yeah," she murmured, lifting the strap of her bag higher on her shoulder. "And I told you as well—I am not interested."

I fucking hated myself for putting that look on her face —indifference. I hated that the smile and shining eyes were not directed at me anymore, that a whole world of pain reflected in her eyes. I fucking hated that she just passed next to me, heading toward the parking lot, without turning to look back at me.

Once upon a time, she told me I was a stubborn bastard who would do everything to get the things he wanted, and she was right. Only difference was—this time, it was her.

I ran after her, falling into step right next to her, earning another scowl from her.

"What do you think you're doing?"

"Following you, of course." I grinned. "I figured since you don't wanna talk to me, I'll follow you."

"Noah, please. I don't wanna talk to you. I don't wanna see you, and I definitely don't want to hear all the excuses I am sure you have already prepared so that I would talk to you again. Hell, maybe I would talk to you. Maybe we could be acquaintances, if nothing else, but we could never be friends again."

Her words hurt. They felt like a sledgehammer to my chest, but I didn't want to show it to her. I couldn't lose my cool this time. I knew I would have to be patient.

"Why not?"

"Are you fucking serious right now?" She raised her voice, suddenly stopping.

I whirled around, looking at her. "Dead serious, Soph."

"Well, where would you like me to start, Noah? Huh? Maybe I should start with the fact that for the past two years, I felt as if I was the only one trying to keep this friendship alive. Or maybe I should fucking start with that night at the carnival when you called me an attention-seeking whore?"

"I never said that," I gritted out.

"No, but you meant it. What was it you said?" She was fuming. "Oh yeah. 'You are so hungry for attention, Sophie, you would go with the first guy that showed you even a little bit of affection.' Did I get it right, Noah? Or would you like me to repeat it?"

Fuck, fuck, fuck. I wanted to rip my own hair out, because she was right. I hadn't been thinking. I had felt desperate, jealous, fucking angry because she wouldn't even spare me a glance since that guy had introduced himself to her.

He was Eric's cousin, only visiting during the winter, but none of it mattered to me. The only thing I saw was that I was losing her.

"Soph—"

"I'm right, am I not, Noah? So no, you don't get to barge back into my life just because you realized that you still wanted to be friends with me."

"I don't—"

"You know what's the worst of all, Noah?" Her eyes filled with tears, playing with my sanity. "I loved you so much. I would've gone up to the sky and back again if you'd asked me to. I would've done anything for you, because you were one of the most important people to me."

"Sophie," I choked out, unable to say anything else.

Tears fell freely down her cheeks, her pale skin luminescent from where they passed.

"But you didn't want me or my love. You obviously felt differently than I did, because our friendship was important to me. You were important to me."

"And now?" I managed to utter, asking the dreaded question.

"Now… Now you're just a boy wearing the face of a person I used to know. Now you're just a painful reminder that people we love, more often than not, don't love us in the same way. And that's okay, you know?" She sniffed. "Not everybody you meet will be worthy of your love, but I know better now. I know that I shouldn't be wasting my time on friends who want nothing to do with me, and on boys who could bring nothing but a broken heart and years filled with pain."

If she shot me, it would've hurt less than her words.

"So what you're saying is—"

"What I'm saying is that you can keep your words, and you can keep your apologies, because I don't want them. I don't want to be there at that place again where I wondered where I went wrong. I don't want to spend another sleepless night, trying to understand what was so wrong with me talking to that guy, what made you say those things. And the worst part, Noah… The worst part is that you humiliated me. All our friends heard what you said. All your groupies snickered while I cried. I waited for you to talk to me. I waited for you to tell me what happened, but you never did. I spent an entire month waiting for you, and you never came. You forgot about me. You don't get to just waltz back into my life as if what you said didn't rip my heart out."

"Please, Sophie. I'm begging you. I would—"

"No. You do know what that word means, Noah? Or did some other things change as well since we stopped talking? After all, you are the star athlete of our school, and I'm just an annoying little girl who isn't worth it."

Fuck. Me.

She saw that message. She saw that fucking message I sent in the moment when I missed her more than anything else, when the guys were talking about asking her out.

"I'm late for practice, Noah, but I truly hope you have a nice life."

She didn't wait for me to say anything else. She didn't look back. She just walked away, leaving me behind like I always feared she would.

SOPHIE

I was as familiar with physical pain as a kid was with their favorite toy. I knew how much a sprained ankle would hurt. I knew that the bruises on my thighs, my arms, and my stomach would slowly fade from that ugly purple color to the slightly red, until they finally blended with the color of my skin, leaving behind just a slightly darker patch until they completely disappeared.

I knew pain because I couldn't even remember how many times I fell and got up during my practices, and even my competitions. I could tell you that breaking my tibia a couple of years ago felt like I was dying, but even that pain was nothing compared to the one taking over my entire body.

Most of the days, the pain of missing Noah was more of a hum deep in my stomach, just a reminder. Today that pain felt like a hurricane set on a path of destruction throughout my body, and I wasn't sure if the urge to puke came from the pills I took earlier to suppress my headache, or because Noah managed to rip my heart apart all over again.

No matter how many times I promised myself I wouldn't go there, he still managed to make me feel so little, so irrelevant. All these feelings I'd been trying to push down and lock in a tiny box, suddenly escaped, coming up to the surface, reminding me every second of every hour how much it hurt losing your soulmate.

Hearts were fragile things. Easily lovable, but easily breakable as well. To make matters worse, they were trusting, forgiving, keen to open their doors again for the person that hurt them, that made them bleed.

I believed I stitched the wounds on my own heart when he stopped responding, when I decided to continue living my life as if he never existed, but in just one day, in just a couple of words, he managed to rip those stitches, and I was bleeding all over again.

I saw how sincere he was. I saw how much he wanted to talk to me, but how could I go back to what we used to be when I wanted so much more? A lot more than he was willing to give. I would rather live without him, than have just one-half of him, while some other girl, that maybe didn't even know him the way I did, got all of him.

I knew it was selfish, thinking like this. Maybe it was childish, but there was only so much I could take, and I wasn't willing to sacrifice my own happiness. Not anymore.

I knew my heart would survive. I just had to learn how to breathe again, how to live again, how to be happy without him.

I bent down and laced my skates, breathing through my mouth, my stomach cramping, fighting the nausea swirling in my stomach. I should've eaten something before coming here, but the food in the cafeteria didn't look appealing, and after the altercation with Noah, I just didn't feel like eating anything.

I'd spent that half an hour before my practice crying in an empty parking lot, hating myself, hating him, hating my own destiny. I kept myself together in front of Andrew because I knew he would go back and kick Noah's ass if I told him what truly happened.

Coach Liudmila would most probably ban me from entering the rink today if I told her that I didn't eat and that my head threatened to burst open from the pain that went from being dull to a full-blown force.

I placed my palms on top of my knees, squeezing my kneecaps, replacing the pain of my heart and soul with the bite of my nails into the skin over the leggings I wore. I couldn't stay here much longer and considering that my shitty performance in the first half of practice didn't make anyone happy, least of all me, I at least had to try to be better now.

I had a competition next week—one of my last ones— and I'd be damned if I allowed Noah to take this away from me as well.

I stumbled through the empty hallway, holding on to a wall, because whoever thought that walking in skates even with the blade covers was easy, was absolutely wrong. It felt like a mini earthquake with every step I took, but thankfully the entrance to the arena wasn't too far away from the changing rooms.

I could still remember the first day my mom brought me to the sports center. The Regional Championship was being held here, and for a five-year-old who dreamed of skating one day, seeing all those girls in their outfits, the music, the lights, and the crowd going crazy, was everything I ever wanted to have.

The first time I stepped on the ice, shaking, insecure, and a little bit scared because I had no idea what I was doing, it was like coming home after a long vacation. Everything was new, yet it was as if my soul knew it would always come here.

Mom thought I would get bored, that my fascination

would die after a month or maybe a year, but here I was, thirteen years later, still in love with this place. There were days where I thought that it would be best to quit, because my mind waged a battle against my body, and no matter what I tried to do, it wouldn't look how it was supposed to.

But nothing good ever came without a little bit of blood, and a lot of sweat and tears. The talent I had could get me only so far. *Practice, practice, and practice.* I could almost hear my first coach, Ksenia, yelling at us from the sidelines with her harsh accent, hair tied up on top of her head in a neat bun, and facial features rivaling those of a princess.

I could remember it all—every step, every win and loss, tears and laughter, days and nights spent here while my mom waited outside. And among those memories, Noah was in almost every single one of them. He was my biggest fan, my biggest supporter, and without him, I wasn't sure if I would've kept trying to reach the title of Regional Champion three years ago.

And now… Not only was he not here, but this, my second love, would soon be out of my reach.

"Sophie!" Coach Liudmila thundered from her spot on the ice, standing right next to a girl who couldn't have been more than eight years old. "You went all the way to Russia for the toilet or what?"

"No." I snickered slowly as I approached the rink. "I went to China but then they told me that they didn't have any toilets available, so I had to jump all the way to Australia."

"Smartass," she yelled out. "Come, come." She waved at me. "Maggie here wanted to see you do the triple axel."

I almost choked as I reached the rink.

"You're feeling okay to do it, no?"

No, I wasn't feeling well enough to do it at all but

refusing to do the move I'd been doing for the last four years would be a clear indication that something wasn't right. Coach Liudmila has been with me for the last five years, and I had a feeling that this little presentation she wanted me to do had much deeper meaning than I wanted to think about.

I was never one to miss practices, except that one time when I landed myself with pneumonia, confined to my house for almost a month. But with this new... revelation, I'd been missing a lot more practices. She knew that something was wrong.

I was too much of a coward to tell her the truth, because telling her what was really going on would mean admitting that there was nothing I could do to stop it.

"Sure." I nodded, praying and hoping that I wouldn't land on my ass, especially not in front of a little girl whom I'd seen around the rink, and who was always extremely nice to me.

I'd been having difficulty with balance, even while walking, which was why I tried not to do any of my usual jumps during the first half of my practice today. It led to Liudmila yelling at top of her lungs, asking me if I actually came to do a fashion show or to do some skating today.

Looking at this moment later, I wished I'd actually told her that I wasn't feeling well enough. I wished I hadn't tried to prove myself, because if I stepped back to reevaluate the situation, I wouldn't have landed on my ass, bruising my ego more than my skin.

The look on Liudmila's face told me everything I needed to know—she knew I was full of shit.

It wasn't until I went out of the complex, waiting for Andrew to pick me up, that an all-too familiar black Camaro caught my attention. Its door opened, followed by a body I knew.

He really couldn't take a hint, could he?

"I thought we both agreed to stay away from each other," I yelled out, stopping a few feet away from his car.

"No, Sophie. You talked, I listened. I've decided that you can pretend we would never be more than acquaintances for a little longer, but it doesn't mean I would stop trying, or that I would stop being there for you."

Damn him.

"I could always get a restraining order, you know?"

"You could." The bastard smirked. "But we both know you won't. You wanna know why?" The audacity of this guy.

"Why?" I rolled my eyes, dropping the bag on the floor.

"Because you miss me as much as I miss you. I know you're angry with me. I know you don't want to talk to me, but we don't have to talk in order to spend time together."

"That's bullshit, Noah." I hated that he actually had a point.

"Maybe, but it's the only option I have right now."

"You couldn't have waited until we were at school so that you could, I don't know, stand next to me or some shit like that?"

"Oh no, because Bianca would most probably kill me if I even looked at you there." He did have a point. "Besides, this way you won't be able to escape."

"I don't know what you're talking about. Andy is picking—"

"He's not." I could see him fighting the smug grin that was threatening to overtake his face, but he was failing.

"What do you mean?" My eye was already twitching, knowing where this conversation would lead. "Andy isn't coming?"

"Nope." He closed the door of his car and slowly came

closer to me. God, even at this distance he towered over me, making me much smaller than I was. "You're stuck with me, Soph, whether you like it or not."

I was going to kill Andy, or my mom, or both of them. Suffocate them during the night, something, anything, because I knew what this meant.

Noah wasn't giving up, and I secretly loved it.

"Fine." I huffed, too tired to fight with him. "But no talking, Noah. I swear to God, I don't have enough power left in my body to talk to you."

"Okay. That's okay. I just wanna take you home." And I wanted to rip out my own heart, because it suddenly remembered how much we loved him.

Stupid, stupid heart.

Didn't it know that he almost destroyed us once? Didn't it know that no matter how much I loved the cerulean color of his eyes, I would never be able to call him mine?

And I shouldn't, especially not now. Maybe it was for the best what happened three months ago. Maybe this way I could save him from the heartache later.

I picked up my bag and walked toward the car, ignoring the burning on the back of my neck from his stare. As soon as I slid inside, the smell of him enveloped me in the familiar hug—like cinnamon, coffee, and late autumn nights. I hated that my eyes immediately sought him, still standing there in front of the car, looking at the sky.

I hated that I actually wanted to tell him all about my day, and about what was happening lately.

I hated and loved that he was trying to fix this thing between us, when I would've been glad to know that he moved on with his life, forgetting everything about me. Because this, whatever he'd been trying to do, had an expiration date. I didn't want him to be yet another person with tears in his eyes where stars used to be.

After a minute, or maybe even longer, he slid inside, while I leaned to the side, pressing my forehead against the cold glass of the window, ignoring the fact that the tips of my fingers tingled from the need to touch him. I crossed my arms across my chest and closed my eyes, pushing myself to think about anything else but him.

"Soph," he started softly, almost apologetically. "I really am sorry, you know?"

"I do, Noah. I do."

"Do you think that you would ever be able to forgive me?"

A question with a million possible answers, yet only one bounced back and forth inside my head. I forgave him a long time ago, but it didn't matter anymore. It was best to keep things on the down-low with him. It was much better for him.

"Just drive, Noah. I wanna go home," I murmured instead, avoiding his question.

But that was what I did the best, wasn't it? Avoiding things I didn't want to think about.

SOPHIE

I WISHED I could tell you the exact moment I fell in love with Noah Kincaid, but I guess that it was much like everything else in my life—sudden and out of my control.

One day, he was just Noah, just my best friend, and the next one, I wanted to run my fingers through his hair, and his lips were the only thing I could think about. I could talk about a thousand other things I loved about him, but the one that was starting to make me really pissed was his determination to get things he wanted.

No one would ever say that he was a quitter, and as I exited my house two days after that day from hell, he stood there on our front porch, leaning against the fence.

"What in the fucking fuck are you doing here?"

He wasn't at school for the last two days, or at least I didn't see him. I thought that the whole "I miss you speech" was just a way for him to sleep better at night.

Apparently, I was wrong.

"I'm taking you to school." He said it matter-of-factly as if we did this every day.

We used to, I wouldn't lie, but it felt as if that happened in a previous life and not this one. On those days when he would take me to school, I would allow myself to pretend that the way he looked at me meant more than just friends. I allowed myself to daydream for those ten minutes we drove all the way from our home to reality, because I knew, somewhere deep in my heart, he would never be mine.

I'd spent countless nights crying myself to sleep, breaking my own heart over and over again, because the universe and I both knew that I would never tell him how I felt. It ate me alive. I'd mastered the art of pretending to be happy for him every time he brought a new girlfriend for me to meet. I'd mastered the art of a fake smile and a cheerful voice, while my heart broke into a thousand tiny pieces, only to be mended back together by itself, because I had no other choice but to be happy for him.

And every time he hugged me, I clung to him just a little bit longer, a bit tighter, because I never knew when would be the last time I would be able to do just that.

I guess I always knew that we weren't meant for happy endings. Some people had tragedy engraved on their bones, and no matter what, they could never run away from it. But somewhere between breaking my own heart, avoiding the truth, and smiling as if seeing him with other people didn't make me wanna cry every single time, I realized something else.

I would rather see him happy with somebody else, than sad and miserable with me. I would rather see him live his life fully, smiling, getting everything he deserved, while I watched from the sidelines.

But somewhere between all of that, all my wishes and dreams, I also realized that I wanted more. It wasn't his fault that his heart didn't hold the love I wanted it to feel. I knew he cared about me. I knew he loved me in his own way, but after losing him and after... Well, everything else, I understood why people said that every single minute we had on this earth was precious.

I made it seem like I didn't want to forgive him, but the truth was that I forgave him a long time ago. I just couldn't go back to what we used to be, because then I wouldn't be able to do everything I wanted to do.

I would go back to the old habit of waiting for him to wake up one day and realize that all he ever wanted, all he ever needed was right there in front of him. I hoped and hoped and hoped that one day, by some miracle, he would look at me and see the girl he could love as more than just a friend. And that there, ladies and gentlemen, was not a healthy relationship.

I would be hurting both him and me. I would be hurting him, because I couldn't keep these things inside my chest anymore, and I would be hurting myself because the things I always wanted to have would never be the ones I would get.

"I can drive myself to school, Noah." I wanted, *no*, I needed him to stay away from me. I needed to forget how it felt loving him, needing him, and looking for him in a room full of people.

I needed to train my mind and my heart to forget the fantasy I created in my head. I had to cleanse my system of him, and having him here, everywhere, was not helping.

One of my coaches once said that it takes twenty-one days to develop a habit of something, and I'd had fourteen years filled with him. Wasn't love just that? A habit.

When you get used to the person, when your days and your nights were filled with them, you don't really know how to rid yourself of all those expectations and all those things you wished you had.

"I know you can," he answered somberly, straightening up. "But I still want to drive you."

"Noah—"

"Please, Sophie. You don't have to look at me. You

don't have to talk to me. Hell, if you want to, you can scream at me and tell me how much you hate me, but please... just let me have this."

Invisible claws of despair wrapped around my throat, drawing blood as its sharp nails pressed against my skin. I didn't want him to see my tears. I didn't want him to see how much it hurt having him here, or how much I wanted to turn back time and instead of talking to him that day in kindergarten, I would have walked away. I would have kept to myself.

I also didn't want to slip out and tell him the truth. I didn't want him to know.

But I couldn't rob him of this time, when I knew that soon enough, we would have none left. He would be gone, and I would stay here, left behind.

"Fine." I exhaled, releasing the air I kept inside my lungs and took a step forward, toward him. "But you will then have to take me home as well. Bianca won't be able to, and I'm not wal—"

"Of course I'll take you home after school. I'll take anything you're willing to give me."

Goddamn him for the millionth time.

I always had a hard time telling him no, and it didn't help that he looked at me as if I hung the stars in the sky.

And friends don't look at each other this way. That annoying voice of hope inside my head reappeared again. That voice was the reason why I held on to hope for so long. I knew I had to ignore it.

I shook my head, attempting to clear it of all thoughts and passed next to him, going down the stairs. I could feel his eyes on me. I could hear his boots as he walked behind me all the way to his Camaro. Before I could open the door for myself, he stepped in front of me, taking a hold of the handle and opening it for me.

I looked up, our eyes clashing, the fire burning in his—the regrets, the need and sorrow, almost knocking me on my butt. There were moments over the years where I suspected that he felt the same way, but as soon as those hidden looks and small touches would happen, they would disappear as fast as they appeared, replaced by the look of indifference.

But this time, this right now… It felt different. He felt different.

He was like a magnetic field, pulling me in, calling me, and I wanted to answer. I wanted nothing more than to get lost in those cerulean eyes.

His chest expanded with every breath he took, making him seem larger than life. I always felt tiny standing next to him, but I also always felt safe.

Right now, I felt like Alice, falling down through the rabbit hole, descending into madness.

He leaned closer, his breath washing over my trembling lips. "Sophie." A murmur, a plea. One simple word holding so many different meanings.

I wanted to soak it in, to soak his heat and the need flashing in his eyes. I could almost see myself reflected in them.

He lifted his other hand and wrapped it around my neck, kneading the muscles on the back of it, pulling the strands of hair, and eliciting a whimper from me. I have never been touched like this by him.

I have never felt like this—as if my chest was going to burst open from everything I always wanted to tell him, but didn't have enough courage. All those words I kept close to my heart threatened to spill over my lips when he came even closer, closing his eyes.

"I've missed you so much, Sophie." My name on his

lips sounded like a prayer, like the prettiest word he ever uttered.

I stood there as still as a statue, afraid that even the smallest move would destroy the magic happening around us.

"I can't breathe without you, Angel. You're in every-thing I do. In every single thought, every single song. I've missed you more than the sun misses the moon."

I shuddered, closing my eyes, as the first tear betrayed me and slipped down my cheek.

"I will spend a lifetime apologizing for what I said, but please... I'm begging you, darling. Give me another chance. Let me in, Soph. Please, let me in."

I couldn't. I couldn't let him in, because letting him in would mean destroying him in the process. Letting him in would mean sentencing him to suffer with me, and I couldn't do that.

God, I wanted to. I wanted to so fucking much. I sobbed, fighting with my own traitorous body that wanted to do nothing more than to wrap its hands around his neck, to press these shaking lips that lied to him over all those years.

I wanted to see the world with him, to laugh and cry, to see us grow old together, but none of those things would ever happen. None.

"I can't," I cried out and took a step backward, hating, fucking hating the pain reflecting back at me. "I can't, Noah. I'm sorry."

"I really fucked up, didn't I?" he choked out, emotions washing over his face just like they did over mine. "I've lost you."

"Noah," I whimpered. "I can't talk about this right now. I can't."

"Then when are we going to talk about it?" he roared.

"I know I fucked up. I know, okay? But all I'm asking for is the chance to make things right. Because without you, Soph, nothing feels right."

I hugged my bag to my body, feeling the cold seeping from the inside out. The cold that had nothing to do with the weather or the freezing March air. This kind of cold was going to keep all those I love away from me, and there was nothing I could do about it.

"I'm sorry," I cried. "But I can't do this with you."

"You can't do this with me?" he asked, dragging a hand through his dark hair. "But you could do it with somebody else?"

"Noah—"

"No, it's fine. I get it. I messed shit up between us, and I'll spend my life trying to fix it if that's what it takes. But you don't get to decide that you don't want me anymore, Soph. You don't get to decide that the years we had together meant nothing, when we both know that what you're feeling isn't nothing."

"I don't—"

"Yes, you do, Angel. You feel it, I know you do. I'm not expecting you to just forget what I did, but cut me some slack, would you? I just want to get a chance to tell you why I said what I said. That's all I'm asking."

A minute passed, a minute that felt like an eternity, and neither one of us moved. His chest rose and fell with each breath he took and released, while I stood unmoving, trying to come up with yet another argument why taking him back into my life wouldn't work.

Just tell him the truth, my subconscious cried.

But if I told him the truth, I would break him. Noah didn't deserve to be broken. No matter what, I wanted him to be happy. I wanted to see him thrive.

"Let's just go, Noah. Please. We're gonna be late."

"Are you serious?" There it was—the anger.

I would rather him be angry with me, because then he might let go of me easier. I knew I wasn't strong enough to let go of him.

I stared back at him, gritting my teeth, trying to school my facial expression to as neutral as possible. "Deadly. Now can we go?"

"Unbelievable," he muttered, rounding the car, opening his door, and sliding in.

My throat closed, the tears I tried keeping at bay pushing to the surface, and the headache I thought I had under control, taking over my entire head. But I bit my tongue and got inside the car, closing the door with a loud thud.

This was all we would ever be now. Two strangers with too much history. Two strangers ignoring each other, because we were too late.

He was too late.

SOPHIE

TIME PASSED FAST when you knew it was limited.

I had a feeling that since that first day Noah drove me to school, I had just blinked and one week passed, making me wonder, where did all those days go? We were already in the middle of March, and the dreadful sensation of not having enough time was driving me with force, activating the anxiety I managed to keep at bay for months.

And Noah… Noah kept showing up every morning to take me to school and take me back home. No words, no looks, no more attempts to talk to me, but he was always there. Every practice I had, I could see him in the stands, observing my moves silently, as if he waited for me to make the first step now.

But I knew I wouldn't. Not because I didn't want to, but I couldn't.

I couldn't drag him into this, no matter how much my heart bled every single time he showed up in front of my house. My hands itched, wishing to touch him, to tell him how sorry I was, because we didn't have enough time.

I didn't have enough time to tell him everything I wanted to.

I didn't have enough time to tell him how much I wished to see the world with him, to go to Rome like we talked about so many times.

And worst of all, I didn't have strength.

Life was beautiful when you didn't know what was coming next, but when you did... nothing mattered anymore. Nothing but trying to fight as best as you could.

I knew I should've told him that he didn't have to wait for me anymore. I knew I should tell him to forget that I ever existed, but every time I tried to open my mouth, the words were nowhere to be found. Every time he played those fucking songs that made my heart ache, and my eyes tear up, something inside me told me to savor these moments, even if they were laced with misery dripping from our skin like acid.

My misery was etched deep into my soul, but his... His was written all over his face. It was ever-present in every song he played for me, in every look he sent my way, in the clenching and unclenching of his jaw, because just like me, he wanted to talk.

I knew Noah better than I knew myself, and sitting here next to him, pretending that we were virtual strangers, cut through me. Maybe it was selfish of me, pushing him away like this. Maybe it was childish trying to stay on my side of the lane when he so obviously wanted to patch things between us, but I couldn't bring myself to open up.

There was an endless well of forbidden emotions hiding inside my chest, covered by my bones, my ribs, and I wanted it to stay that way. If he didn't know, then it couldn't hurt him. Right?

But I couldn't erase the way he looked at me a week ago. I couldn't forget how fast my heart started beating, as if it was waking up from a deep slumber, shaking off the debris that collected on top of it. Ever since then, I again started thinking of things that could never be.

I started wishing for things I shouldn't be wishing for. My mind and my heart were not in sync, and no matter how hard I tried, Noah Kincaid would always have a place in my heart. Who was I kidding? He owned my whole heart even without knowing it.

The shades of gray skies cast shadows on our small town, and as much as I hated the lifeless state it was in, there was still something beautiful in death, just like there was something beautiful in life.

Seasons always reminded me of rebirth, of a new chance—a new opportunity to make things better. These past couple of months, I had to remind myself several times that endings were not forever.

Perhaps it was just my wishful thinking that death wasn't the end—it was just a new beginning. Maybe it was my way of coping with things.

But looking at the melting snow, people rushing to school and to their jobs, something shifted inside of me. Something profound, and it didn't leave me feeling helpless this time.

"I'm going to be here at three again," Noah started, gripping the steering wheel, his knuckles turning white.

I looked at his face, his handsome profile—the sharp jawline, those long, dark lashes I was always jealous of. It wasn't fair that a man had such eyelashes. My eyes moved to his ruffled, dark hair, to that little scar on his neck he got when he jumped from the swing that once used to hang on the weeping willow behind our houses.

He changed, yet he also stayed the same. Once upon a time, he used to be just the boy I had the biggest crush on. Somewhere in between then and now, he became a young man I fell in love with.

My other friends never understood what I saw in him, thinking that it was only these physical aspects of his that pulled me into his orbit, but Noah was so much more than what the eye saw.

The Noah I loved cried every single time a pet died in a movie or a television show. The Noah I grew up with held me in his arms when I had a panic attack, because I had no idea what I was doing.

He was the kind of guy you could call at three in the morning, and he would come to you—no questions asked.

My Noah was also an asshole, but only if you deserved it. He hated bullies, hated people shitting all over other people, and no matter what, he still remembered every little thing about those he loved.

Because of all those things, because I knew that what he said that night was not because he hated me, I had to let him go. I had to make him see that what he was doing here was not going to propel us back in time, so that we never fell apart.

I wished I had a time machine. I wished I could go back and change the things I so desperately wanted to change, but I couldn't. Life went on, just like seasons. It moved, whether we wanted it to or not. Sometimes life could be a mess.

Sometimes it could throw you a curveball, making you realize that none of those things you used to worry about mattered anymore.

"Noah," I croaked, my throat dry while nerves shook my hands. I pressed them between my legs, calming my breathing just enough to tell him what I needed to. What I should've done a week ago.

I never should've sat down in his car. I never should've accepted these rides. It wasn't as if I didn't have my own car, but something about being with him, even if it was only like this, made me feel better.

It made me feel less alone.

He turned slowly, those blue, blue eyes sparkling with untold emotions, with promises, memories, and unshed tears. There was so much regret there, so much pain, and I was the reason. I never meant to torture him like this.

I never meant for us to turn into this. He needed to know that I forgave him, but that sometimes, just sometimes, forgiveness and love were not enough to move forward.

Sometimes you had to cut the thread connecting you to the other person because you had to save both them and you.

"This can't go on, Noah."

His grip on the steering wheel increased as soon as the words left my mouth. His right eye got that familiar twitch that was only there when he couldn't, or he didn't, want to say things out loud.

"I don't know what you're talking about."

"This." I pointed at the two of us. "You and me. We can't go on like this." I took a deep breath, letting it expand my chest. "You can't keep driving me back and forth."

"Why?"

"Why?" I laughed. "Because I don't want you to. I-I," I stammered. "I can't keep seeing you like this. I hate that you're only here because you feel guilty."

"What's wrong with me feeling guilty, Sophie?" He turned toward me, unclasping his seat belt. "What's wrong with me wanting you back, huh? Of course I feel guilty."

"But you don't have to."

"But I do!" he bellowed, slamming his hand on the

dashboard. "Goddammit, I do need to feel guilty. If it wasn't for me and my stupid fucking jealousy, we wouldn't be in this situation right now. You wouldn't be sitting there, looking like you would rather go through fire than be here with me. I miss how we used to be, Soph. I miss seeing you smile. I miss us going through Spotify, finding new songs. I miss you telling me about all the things that happened to you during the day. I went to that weeping willow five times in the last month, only you were never there. Why?"

"Because I knew you might be." Because it hurt too much, seeing him at all those places we used to visit together.

Nobody ever tells you that when you lose someone who was still alive, it hurt more than if they were dead. No one ever tells you that seeing the person—your person—go on with their life, while you sit in the corner, all alone, wishing for time to go back, splits your heart in two.

Losing him made me realize how dependent I was on him. How much I needed him to tell me that things were going to be okay, even when they wouldn't. I missed hearing sugar-laced lies coming off of his tongue, because those lies were the only things that could get me through the day sometimes.

"Are you telling me that you would never be able to forgive me?"

"No." I shook my head. "I'm telling you that I forgave you a long time ago—"

"Then what the fuck is the problem?" He cut me off. "Why wouldn't you look at me? Why wouldn't you talk to me?" He wanted the truth, when all I could give him were lies, lies, lies, and some more lies, so that he would leave me alone.

"Because you're not my Noah anymore."

"Bullshit!"

"Excuse me?"

The grimace on his face was painted with sorrow and longing, pain and love. It was colored with everything I ever wanted to see from him, but not like this. Not right now.

Not when I had no idea what my life was going to look like in a couple of years. Not when everything hung in the air.

"No, excuse me. How can you say something like that? How can you sit there and pretend that the other day you didn't tremble for me just how I tremble for you? You can't tell me that all these feelings inside my chest, all these thoughts inside my head, are only a one-way street."

"Noah—"

"No! Don't look at me like that."

"Like what?" I recoiled.

"Like you pity me. Do not fucking do that."

"I'm not doing it deliberately, but you need to let me go. You need to stop doing this to me. You need to stop doing this to yourself. We will never be what we used to be. We will never be friends again."

"Friends?" He smirked. "You think I'm doing all of this because I want us to be friends again?"

"Well, uh, yeah?"

"You have no idea, do you?"

"No idea about what?"

Please, please, please, do not say it. I couldn't cope with it if he said what I thought he was going to say.

A deep rumble escaped from him as he dragged a hand over his face. "You know what?" He refused to look at me, making me loathe myself even more, making me want things I shouldn't want.

I wanted to wrap my arms around him. I wanted to

move from this fucking seat onto his lap, but I sat there, frozen, waiting for him to continue talking.

"Do whatever the fuck you want to do, Sophie. I'm done."

He was done.

He was fucking done.

He pushed his door open, leaving me inside, staring at the vacant spot he occupied mere seconds ago.

He was done.

It echoed inside my head, slipping all the way to my heart, dripping onto it like a black tar. Wasn't this what I wanted? I wanted him to be done with me. I wanted him to stop trying, because I knew that look on his face.

I knew he didn't want us to just go back to being friends. I understood now better than before why he said those vile words—because he was jealous. Because Noah felt something for me.

Because I wasn't all alone in this.

But it didn't matter anymore. None of it mattered.

I sat there for what felt like hours—unmoving, almost hearing the cracks spreading over my soul as minutes passed. My brain told me to move, to get out of the car.

To run away from his scent, from everything that reminded me of him, but my heart cried out every single time I tried moving.

My heart fought me, pushing, telling me to go after him. To fix this. To tell him the truth.

It wanted me to run out there, because the only place that ever truly felt like home was when he was with me.

Even when the raindrops started dropping onto the windshield, going from one to two, to three and more, I couldn't move. It wasn't until the knock from my right side made me turn around, seeing a familiar face standing there.

Pity was written all over her face just like the sadness was written all over mine.

Bianca was the only one that understood how much I loved him, but she couldn't understand why I kept pushing him away. She couldn't understand because for her, he was it for me.

I couldn't tell her.

It was only when her face turned into a grimace I knew all too well that I realized I'd been crying. I lifted my left hand, touching the cold skin on my cheek, feeling the wetness there.

She opened the door, letting the ice-cold air in, and pressed against me, hugging me, whispering that it was going to be okay.

"I lost him," I sobbed. "Oh my God," I cried out, shaking while she held me. "I lost him for good."

"Oh, Sophie."

"And it's my fault this time. Only mine."

"No, no, no. Don't say that. He fucked up as well."

I nodded against her shoulder. "He did, but he also tried to fix it. He almost told me—" I cut myself off, unable to voice it out loud.

He almost told me everything I ever wanted to hear from him, and I didn't let him.

"What, Soph?" She pulled back, holding my hands.

"He almost told me he loved me, B. A-and I… I didn't let him. I can't let him in again."

"Jesus."

"And now… He told me he's done, B. He just walked away."

"Well, what did you expect? You keep pushing him away. There's only so much he's willing to take, I'm sure of it. But, honey, I see the way he looks at you. I see the way you look at him. Why won't you let him in?"

Why? Because Noah deserved to have the best year of his life. He deserved to go to college, to play hockey as he always wanted to. He deserved someone who didn't have all these things happening in their life.

Not me.

Not anymore.

NOAH

THE VIEW alone should've made me feel better, but it did nothing to calm down my racing heart and my racing thoughts. Alkey Lake looked beautiful this time of the year —frozen, with the snow-covered forest around and the gray skies reflecting on top of it.

It was one of my favorite places to be, yet today, even being here, did nothing for me.

I tossed a small stone I found, letting it bounce off the surface of the frozen lake, wishing I brought my skates with me. Soon enough, the ice would start to melt, and I would have to wait another year to be back here, playing with my guys.

But hockey was the last thing on my mind right now. After one of the worst mornings in the past couple of weeks, I decided to walk away.

I would've given everything to have her here with me, looking at this beauty in front of me, but Sophie made her decision. I'd be damned if I pushed when it was obvious that she didn't want me. Maybe she felt something.

Maybe she loved me once, but after what I did, that love turned into ice. I fucking hated the detachment in her eyes. I hated the cold indifference with which she observed me, as if she was handling a wild animal and not talking to a person that was once her best friend.

It took me three months to realize that she was it for me, and it was obvious that in those three months, everything changed. She wasn't the Sophie I knew.

She wasn't the girl that made me do mud masks in the middle of the summer because she saw it on television. She wasn't the girl that cried when the Joker died in the last installment of *The Dark Knight* trilogy. Something changed, and there was a voice inside my head, telling me that it wasn't all about that night.

It was almost impossible to believe her when she said that she forgave me. And I wouldn't have, if it wasn't for that panic on her face, that sadness and those tears that threatened to spill over onto her cheeks.

But I wondered—was it possible that I imagined that look on her face the other day? Was it possible that the longing I saw there was actually something else, and what I saw was just my mind playing tricks on me because it was what I wanted to see?

No, it couldn't be.

But as I stood here, staring at the dark skies gathering above, casting shadows, I had to admit that maybe, just maybe, she truly didn't want me in her life anymore. Maybe it was true what they said—that people outgrew each other.

Maybe she and I wasted too much time pretending we were something else, when the girl I wanted to grow old with always stood right there. Maybe I was too late.

"I knew I would find you here." I turned around, seeing Jared in his red hoodie, looking at me with sympathy.

"What are you doing here?"

I was too short with him, too angry at myself and

everything that's been going on. I wished I could just turn around and go back to her. I wished I could shake her and make her see the truth—that I was in love with her.

I was in love with the girl that wanted nothing to do with me. I was in love with the girl that until recently was the only real person standing by my side. I fucked us up.

Why couldn't I have gained enough confidence to tell her how I felt before all this happened? Why did I wait so long?

"Bianca spoke to me." Of course she did. "She didn't tell me the specifics, but judging by that look on your face, I can only assume that shit went down this morning. Didn't it?"

"I don't wanna talk about it, Jared. I really don't."

"Fine." He lifted his hand in surrender and came closer to me. "We don't have to talk. We can just sit here in silence."

"I'm not interested."

"Well tough luck, buttercup. You're stuck with me. Whether you like it or not, I'm your friend."

Sophie was my friend as well and look what I did to us.

"You should take advice from Sophie, J. I suck at being friends with people."

"Nah." He put his hand on my shoulder, smiling. "You only suck at being friends with people you're in love with, and I definitely don't look like Sophie."

I almost chuckled at that. Almost.

"I mean, you do have some girlish features, bro," I teased. "Are you entirely sure you're actually not a girl?"

He pushed at my shoulder, laughing along with me. "Fuck off."

"And those eyebrows… Damn, are you plucking them?"

"I like to look nice, okay?"

"No judgment here, you know that. But seriously. Maybe if you put on some makeup, we could pass you for a girl."

"Oh, shut your fucking mouth."

My stomach clenched and unclenched as we laughed, momentarily wiping away the vision of Sophie this morning, sitting there in my car, looking so small. But joy, just like everything else in life, was a fleeting thing.

Just as fast as it came, this light feeling that encompassed my entire body, also disappeared, reminding me of things I wanted to have, but couldn't.

Both of us sobered up—me first and then Jared when he saw what was no doubt a grimace on my face.

"I really am sorry, you know. I know how much you love her. I can see it."

"Yeah." I swallowed, my throat tight. "But she apparently can't."

I turned around and sat down on the ground. I pulled my knees to my chest, resting my elbows on top of them. This place felt so peaceful, yet so tormented.

It was the memories that tormented me. The memories of us since we were kids. The feelings I had even then suffocated me, crawling through me.

"You did fuck up, you know."

"I do. But I also apologized."

I could hear him coming closer before his boots came into my peripheral vision. He lowered himself down and sat next to me. "Just because you said you're sorry, it doesn't mean that you deserve to get a second chance. Words are just that, Noah, words. Actions are what people need to see."

"Whose fucking side are you on?" I looked at him, ticked off by what he was saying. "You think she shouldn't give me a chance?"

"You know I will always be on your side. Don't look at me like that. I wasn't there that night, but if I had been, I would've punched you in your pretty boy face."

"What?"

"Man." He laughed. "If somebody said those things to my sister, I would've killed them, trust me. You took your friendship with her and threw it into a dumpster. Then, as if that wasn't enough, you took some gasoline, poured it on and set fire. What the fuck were you thinking?"

I ground my teeth, hating how right he sounded, hating myself most of all.

"I didn't." I exhaled. "I didn't fucking think because I hated seeing that guy with her. I didn't think, because for the first time in my life, she wasn't smiling at me. She was smiling at him."

"So you were jealous?"

"I was furious, Jared. And I wasn't even furious at her, I was furious at myself. The moment those words left my mouth, shame washed over me, but it was already too late. She left."

"Did you try to talk to her?"

I cringed and looked away from him. "No. She tried talking to me, but I never answered."

"You are a motherfucking idiot, I swear."

"I know."

"Why the fuck would you do that? She reached out to you when she had every right to be angry at you, and you still behaved like an asshole. No wonder she wants nothing to do with you right now."

"I know."

"Jesus Christ, man. I'm surprised she didn't try to kill you with one of her skates by now. I for sure would've if I were in her place."

"I know."

"Stop saying you know, you dipshit. You're lucky she even agreed to those rides with you."

I nodded, lost for words. It hurt to think back to that night when I fucked everything up, but Jared was right.

People could forgive, but it didn't mean that they had forgotten. Just because I apologized, it didn't give me the right to demand her attention when all I'd done was try for only one week.

"Then what am I supposed to do, Jared?" I turned my head and looked at him. "I have no idea what to say. I have no idea what to do to get her to see me. Hell, she's not even talking to me properly. Do I just go to her house and demand that she talks to me?"

He seemed to think about it for a minute, squinting his eyes, and chewing on his cheek.

"Grand gesture." I almost didn't hear him.

"A grand gesture? Seriously?"

"Yeah." He turned to me. "Seriously. I'm not saying that you should propose to her in front of the entire school, but you need to do something that's going to remind her of all those times you guys were happy, hanging out together. Then you can tell her what an idiot you were, and beg her, on your knees if you have to, to forgive you."

Sophie hated drawing attention to herself in public, unless she was on the ice, in her own element. She hated over-the-top things, and she was never a materialistic kind of girl that asked for expensive clothes, and shit like that. Her favorite birthday gift was a painting of the two of us I made.

"Grand gesture," I murmured again, pushing myself to think about things I could do to get her to take me back into her life. "You're a motherfucking genius, Jared." I threw my arm around his shoulders and pulled him closer to me.

"Whoa, whoa, easy there, tiger." He laughed. "I'm gonna start thinking that you might be in love with my girlish features."

"Shush."

"But yeah, I know I'm a genius. I don't know why you all think that I'm all looks and no brain."

"Uh, Jared, I hate to break it to you, but we don't think you're all looks at all."

"You mother—"

He tried to grab me, but I jumped up first, running toward the frozen lake. "You're more of an annoying little brother none of us wanted to have."

"I'm gonna drown you in this lake, Noah Kincaid," he yelled, running after me.

"You're gonna have to catch me first!"

I slowed down as I stepped onto the ice, slipping here and there as I moved farther away from him.

"Just you wait!" he hollered, going as slow as a snail after me, trying to balance himself on the ice. "I should have never told you that idea."

"Thank you!" I laughed, feeling lighter than I did before. "I'll make sure to invite you to our wedding one day."

"You fucking better!"

And I would. There was no doubt in my mind that one day, she was going to wear my ring. Nobody else would ever come close to her.

SOPHIE

"COME ON, Sophie. Lift that leg higher!" Coach Liudmila yelled from the sidelines, while I pushed myself further, blocking everything else.

Here, on the ice, was my happy place. It was the only place where it didn't matter if I felt good or bad that day, because the moment I put on my skates and stepped inside the arena, everything else faded away.

My pain, my worries, my anxiety, my love for Noah… Those things didn't belong here, because even the smallest distraction could cost me my life, and I couldn't afford that.

I remembered the first time I'd come here for practice, and how insecure I was on my skates. I'd spent two weeks holding the wall, because my balance fucking sucked. I remembered seeing all those beautiful girls, skating as if they were born on the ice, and I wished that one day I would be as good as them.

And I became that good—if not better.

My first coach once told me that talent has nothing to do with success. You could be the most talented person, but that talent you might be blessed with was only twenty percent of the whole package. Hard work, sweat, tears, and blood were those remaining eighty percent, and those were what mattered.

I was a competitive kid, not toward the others, but with myself. If I did something good in one practice, it had to be perfect on the next one. I drove my parents crazy, jumping around our garage and skipping dinners, because nothing less than perfection would be sufficient for me.

I'd missed birthdays, holidays, and going out with my friends, because my practices were far more important than those other things. Two years ago, I didn't even go to school for an entire week, because I'd been preparing for the Nationals.

I lived and breathed figure skating. I always knew that this was what I wanted to do. This was where I wanted to live and die. This was my place, my life, and nothing ever compared with it—except maybe loving Noah.

"Did you even eat today, Sophie?" Liudmila yelled again, and I both hated and loved that she always had to use my name with every single sentence. Liudmila and I met five years ago, when my previous coach decided to retire, leaving me all alone in the big, crazy world, thinking that I would have to do everything by myself now.

Of course, all those thoughts racing through my head at that time were nothing more than a product of an overly competitive teenage girl, who thought the world would end if I ever skipped practice.

I knew my parents didn't always agree with the way I went on about these things, but the older I got, the more they understood that there was nothing they could do to make me stop practicing. I was a girl who dreamed of the Olympics one day.

I was a girl who didn't mind having two practices per day. Ballet and figure skating went hand in hand. I didn't mind having only one day where I didn't have practice, or that all my friends spent all their free time just hanging around, playing, being normal kids.

My mom often joked that she gave birth to two sports machines, since both my brother and I lived for our sports —Andy with football and me with figure skating.

They were proud of us, but I knew that more often than not, they wished for us to spend more time just being kids, instead of competing on these levels. But there was no going back for me, especially after the first competition I'd won.

People often thought that what athletes did was as easy as breathing, and on some days, it did feel that way. But on most days, we felt like we had no idea what we'd been doing our entire life. I'd spent countless hours perfecting the simplest moves. I couldn't accept that they weren't flawless in execution.

I'd spent even more hours crying, because I thought I was failing myself and all these people that believed in me. And every single time, even though it now left a bitter taste in my mouth, Noah was there to shake those thoughts away.

He was my safety blanket, my perfect match. I held him up when he had a tough time, and he held me. Through good and bad, tears and smiles, we were always there for each other. He held my hand when I lost the regional competition two years ago.

He hugged me tight when I won the next one. It was messing with my head that all these memories I associated with my skating had him in them as well. It was fucking me up. Even though I wanted to leave all these things at the front door of our sports center, I couldn't.

Which was why I performed like shit today.

"Sophie!" Liudmila thundered. "For all that's worthy, just stop!"

And I did, hating myself more and more and more with each passing second. The regional competition was coming up in less than five days, and this close to it, I shouldn't be this distracted. I couldn't even blame it on my headaches or the fucked-up thing with my balance anymore.

I blamed this on Noah, and the constant stream of thoughts all directed to him. I couldn't stop thinking about him, about that morning from five days ago. I couldn't stop thinking about the look on his face, or the heartbreak screaming at me from his eyes.

I couldn't stop thinking about the pain in my chest when Bianca found me, or the fact that I couldn't even go through the entire day without a headache. Andy had to pick me up and bring me home. I had started puking somewhere around fourth period.

God, I had to put this behind me. He was finally done with me, and I got what I wanted. But even though I told myself that this was what I wanted to have, I couldn't stop thinking if it was the right decision to be made.

Liudmila skated closer to me, the thunderous look on her face telling me everything I needed to know—I fucked up. And not just a little bit.

"What the hell was that, huh?"

The worst part was, she had all the rights to be angry. I was angry at myself, but I couldn't exactly show it right now.

"Is there something going on that I should know about, *krasotka?*" she asked, making me flinch at the nickname she gave me on the first day we worked together. I wished I could tell her everything, but I couldn't—not yet.

"You've been sick a lot lately, is that it? Are you feeling okay?" God, I wanted to cry and scream, and throw something. Punch a wall maybe, get drunk, but none of those things would change the reality. None of them would change the inevitable things coming my way.

"No, I'm fine," I murmured, my voice small, barely audible.

"Then what is the problem?" Her accent was more noticeable now. It only came out when she became so pissed off that she couldn't contain herself.

Liudmila moved here with her parents, all the way from Novosibirsk in Russia, when she was barely eight years old. While her accent might have changed with all the years she spent in the United States, those hard *R*'s still tended to slip out whenever she was on the precipice between her infamous silent treatment and cursing in Russian.

"I fucked up, I know."

"Do you really? Because that looked like something one of the novice girls would do, not you. Where is your head, Sophie?"

Everywhere. *Nowhere.*

It wasn't in the right place, I knew that, but getting reamed by my coach was the last thing I needed right now.

I was my biggest critic, and at moments like these, it felt as if my entire world was collapsing.

"It won't happen again," I almost whispered, my head bent down, my eyes focused on the line made from skates on the ice.

"I know it won't, but it doesn't mean I'm not concerned," she said, softening her voice. "You never had a problem talking to me before, but you've been withdrawn lately. Quiet. Something's wrong, isn't it?"

God, I hated the fact that she knew me so well. This close to Regionals I was usually a bubble of bursting energy, ready to conquer the world. But as of late, all my energy was focused on avoiding Noah and going through the day without a headache.

Or when I did get one, I tried not to pass out. The pain was getting stronger and stronger.

"Nothing's wrong, I promise." I pushed a smile on my face, but judging by the look on hers, it probably seemed more like a grimace than a smile. "I'll be here early in the morning tomorrow, so that I can work on these. Okay?"

"Hmm." Her warm, brown eyes weren't buying what I'd been trying to sell, but at least she stopped pushing. "Fine. But please, for the love of everything, work on these at home today as well. I don't want you falling after your axels and getting injured."

This was the thing with Liudmila, which I appreciated more than I could ever say—she loved winning, but she never put any of us in danger because of it.

Once, long before her, one of our coaches pushed us to the point of exhaustion. I couldn't even skate off the ice. I hated that guy with a passion, and it wasn't long before my mom transferred me to a different coach.

But Liudmila, she wasn't like that. She was our friend, our ally, our second mother if you wished to call it that. She knew me better than I knew myself sometimes, and she never pushed, unless we wanted to talk about things.

"I get it."

"Mhm. Now go get changed and get out of here."

"But—" There was still a half an hour left of my practice.

"No buts, Sophie. We won't get anything done with whatever's going on inside your head. You know it, I know it. The rest of the people that just watched you drag yourself around the arena, know it."

I took a deep, deep breath and nodded slowly, hating to admit defeat, but that was what this was—defeat. I wasn't focused. I wasn't ready to do what was required of me, and I fucked up.

"Tomorrow, we will do your full choreography, so I expect you to be ready."

"I will be."

"Good. Now go and get something to eat. You're looking a little pale."

"Yes, Coach."

Two more competitions, I thought to myself as I skated back toward the gate. Two more times where I would get to do this, and then I'd be done.

Deflated, and less than happy with myself, I took off my skates as soon as I got off the ice, walking only in my socks to the lockers.

This late at night, I was usually the only one left at the arena, along with Liudmila. Noah hated me staying this late, but it was nothing compared to the wicked, crazy hours he used to pull at his practices. I knew he just worried about me, but even this reminded me of him, and I couldn't wait until I could get out of here.

Fresh air was all I needed.

Fresh air and an escape from reality.

10

SOPHIE

"I'm not doing it, Bianca."

"Yes, you are."

"No. Nope."

"Yep, yep, yep."

"You're fucking insane," I said as I walked away from her toward our table.

We decided to go out for coffee and drinks, which was loosely translated into a party in Bianca's vocabulary.

I knew that the hockey team had a huge party tonight, just down by the lake, but I didn't want to go. It'd been going so well, avoiding him for the last couple of days, and between my practices and school, I'd managed to see him only once in passing.

"We're going," she countered, sliding inside the booth.

"No, we are not."

"Come on, dude. This might be one of the last parties this year. Live a little."

"B," I moaned. "You know why I don't want to go. He's gonna be there, and I really don't want to see him. Besides, I have a competition tomorrow and I can't screw up."

True to my words on that day from hell when I fucked

77

up my entire practice, I'd managed to pull it together. I felt better, more secure in myself and the routine we chose to go with. All those pesky thoughts about Noah, and... other things, seemed to have evaporated. At least while I was on the ice.

Reality was completely different from my time on the ice. Every single night, I stared at my window, seeing the light coming through from his. Every single night, I battled myself and the urge to go to him, to talk to him. To apologize for pushing him away, when it wasn't his fault that I wasn't okay with myself.

"You're not going to screw it up," she argued, rolling her eyes at the same time. "You're a machine, Sophie. I've never seen anyone do those things on ice. It's like you're defying the laws of gravity."

"Stop it." I snorted.

"I know that even if you go to a little party, you won't fuck it up tomorrow. It's only seven right now. We don't even have to stay that long."

"Bianca, we both know that with you, we always stay late. I need to be in bed by ten tonight. I'm getting up at six tomorrow."

"Then we'll take your car instead, and you can drive home by yourself if you don't feel like waiting for me."

"And what? Leave you all alone?"

"We both know I won't be alone." She smirked. "Come on. It's been ages since we went to one of the parties, and you've been avoiding everything and everyone lately, including me."

"I have not."

"You so have, Soph. But I get it. Most of the people we hang out with are kind of mutual friends of both of you. I guess that you somehow decided that all of them belonged only to Noah."

"That's not true."

"Isn't it? When was the last time we all hung out together?"

The carnival was what popped into my head. That freaking night when everything went to shit.

"Okay, all right. You have a point, but I still don't want to go."

"Sophie," she groaned. "Please, please, please, please, please," she pleaded, taking a hold of my hands on top of the table. "I promise you, we don't have to be where he is. That lake is ginormous. You know that there are always several groups of people we could hang out with. Noah is not the only person in this town. Besides, there might be some other guys you could hang out with."

She wiggled her eyebrows, a sneaky look I knew all too well passing over her face.

"Bianca. What did you do?"

"Me?" She pressed a hand to her chest. "Nothing."

"B?"

"What? I didn't do anything."

"I'm gonna shave your hair in your sleep."

"You bitch. You wouldn't dare."

"Try me." I smirked. "What the fuck did you do?"

She pulled her hands back, putting them in her lap, and looked outside the window avoiding my eyes. She chewed on her bottom lip. I could see the wheels turning inside her head.

"Bianca!"

"Okay, okay." Her chest expanded with the breath she took before she turned her head toward me. "I did a thingy."

"Bianca," I groaned.

"But it's a teeny tiny thingy, and you can't exactly blame me. I did it for you."

"What. Did. You. Do?"

"Iinvitedsomecollegeguystothepartyand-toldthemaboutyou." She babbled so fast, the only thing I caught was the "college guys" part.

"You did what?"

"You heard me."

"I didn't, that's the problem. Did you invite someone tonight to be my date?"

"Maaaaaaaaybe." She grinned. "But he's super cute, and he's only nineteen, just started at college, and he's friends with my cousin."

I dropped my head to the table, hitting it with my forehead over and over again.

"Please don't kill me."

I might have to. I hated blind dates. I hated knowing that there was somebody waiting for me, when neither one of us knew each other.

"Why'd you do it?" I asked as I lifted my head. "You know I hate that shit."

"I know, and I knew you would be pissed, but, Soph... You were so sad. You broke my heart at least fifteen times since that day I found you in his car."

"So you thought introducing me to some random guy would suddenly cure me?"

"No, but I did think that it wouldn't hurt having a little bit of fun. I'm not asking you to marry him or anything, but just come along. It might be really fun."

I knew it might be fun. One part of me yearned for these normal things nowadays. But if Noah was going to be there, I didn't want to go. I didn't want us to get into yet another fight. Especially not in front of all these people we both knew.

"Pretty please," she begged. "Soon enough, we'll be

going off to college. God knows when the next time will be that we'll see each other, let alone party together."

When she put it that way... "You're killing me, Bianca."

"I'm not trying to, but just imagine us, a couple of years down the road, regretting it because we didn't go to this party."

"So now you're dishing out all those cards you've been holding."

"I never said I wasn't going to play dirty." She grinned. "Is it working?"

"Yes, dammit. It's working."

The light that took over her entire face could've blinded me, but something warm spread from my chest, through my limbs, all the way to my fingers and my toes.

"But I'm not drinking, and I'm leaving by nine-thirty."

"Deal."

"If you're getting wasted, I'm leaving you there."

"Agreed." She nodded again.

"We are also going to avoid Noah and his group of friends as much as possible."

"Absolutely."

"I don't give a fuck that you and Jared have some weird thing going on—"

"No, we fucking don't," she exclaimed. I lifted my eyebrow and tilted my head to the side, not believing a single word that just came out of her mouth.

Especially because her whole face went as red as a tomato, telling me everything I needed to know.

"As I was saying." I cleared my throat. "I will punch Jared in his throat if he even thinks about coming close to us."

"Pinky promise. There won't be any shenanigans tonight. You'll just go, have a nice non-alcoholic drink with a cute guy, maybe get a kiss, and then go home. Tomorrow, you will kill it at the regional competition, and we'll celebrate afterward. With alcohol," she pointed out.

"Fine." I huffed. "We're going, but I meant what I said."

"I know."

Sometimes what I wanted and what would happen were two very different things. If I knew then what I knew later, I would have gotten up and went home instead of going to Alkey Lake.

WE PASSED THE SIGN WITH THE *"VISIT US AGAIN"* inscription for our town a couple of minutes ago, and the nerves I'd been pretending were non-existent were pushing to the surface. I knew that in less than five minutes, we would be reaching our destination.

"Could you drive any slower?" Bianca complained from the passenger seat, drilling me with her eyes. "Best Acquaintance" by Mouth Culture was on full blast, filling the car, but I could barely hear the lyrics from the sound of my beating heart in my ears.

"It's dark outside, and this road is quite shitty."

"Oh, don't give me that bullshit, Soph. I think we've known each other long enough for me to know when you're lying. You're scared because he's gonna be there and you're going to forget why you decided to push him away, aren't you?"

"No," I answered too fast. The knowing grin from her told me she knew it as well. I was full of shit today, and my slow driving had nothing to do with the low visibility, and everything to do with the guy I both wanted to see and didn't want to see.

"You'll be fine." She placed her hand on my knee. "I can always kick him in his nuts if that's what you would like to see."

"No, you psycho." I laughed. "Why are you always so keen on kicking people in their nuts?"

"You mean, the same way that you're always saying you want to punch them in their throat?"

"That's different!"

"How the fuck is that different?"

"Well, a throat punch wouldn't leave any permanent damage."

"Except that the person could die."

"Oh, shut your face. It's not like I'm an MMA fighter. It would probably feel like a tickle to some of these guys."

"Mhm, if you say so. Just don't go around tonight, throat punching people."

"If they deserve it." I shrugged. "Why not?"

"I always knew that there was a little demon somewhere inside of you."

"Look who's talking." I snorted. "I swear, half of our school is terrified to even talk to you."

"That's because I have resting bitch face."

"You also have a mean mouth when you want it to be."

"I mean, my mouth is very good at some other things as well."

"Ewww, gross."

"I did not mean that, you little perv."

I was lucky we were already at the parking area of the lake because the way my shoulders shook from the laughter that erupted from me would not let me drive any longer.

"I can't with you." She huffed. "I can't take you anywhere."

"I'm sorry," I cried as I killed the engine, my parking skills long forgotten. I wouldn't be surprised if I actually parked across two spots instead of only one. "Just... The look on your face."

"Shut up." She snorted.

"I'm gonna pee myself." I let my head fall onto the steering wheel, and I had a feeling that the entire car shook from the force of my laughter.

"And you say that I'm the nasty one."

She opened the door, getting out first, letting me calm down all by myself. I loved Bianca like the sister I never had, and this was exactly why I knew that she was the perfect person for me to spend my evening with.

No matter what, she always made me feel better about, well, everything.

I wiped away the tears that spilled down my cheeks, still cackling, and turned around to take the hoodie I picked up from my house, from the back seat.

March was a freezing motherfucker, especially at night, and I wasn't going to risk getting the flu or pneumonia tonight. My immune system was already fucked up, and the last thing I wanted was to wake up tomorrow with a sore throat.

I pushed the door open and got out, letting my eyes adjust to the darkness outside. Two streetlamps in the distance cascaded their light onto the cars parked closer to them, and I realized that this party was not as small as I initially thought it would be.

Which, in a way, made me feel better about not running into Noah tonight. If I stuck to the shadows and avoided his group of friends, I could go through the entire night without seeing him. Maybe Bianca had a point in coming here tonight.

I could use some fun, especially right now. It wasn't like

I would get wasted. I didn't have to drink to have a good time.

"Who is coming tonight, do you know?" I asked Bianca as soon as I stepped outside, loving the cold breeze. Being here at Alkey Lake always brought up memories I tried so hard to forget, but tonight they didn't hurt as much as they used to.

Tonight, I could look at this place as a beautiful piece of nature, which we often used for parties and gatherings, and whatnot. The ice was going to melt soon, and I wasn't sure which view was better here—the one right now or the one during the summer.

It was just too bad that none of us would be able to see it fully tonight.

"What are you thinking about?" Bianca asked, looking in the same direction as I was.

"How beautiful it is here, no matter which season we're in."

"It really is. I mean, I've been here with you guys whenever you skated on the lake. I've spent countless summers here as well, swimming in that lake. It never ceases to amaze me how beautiful it is."

"Right?" I grinned. "It's like a small piece of heaven."

And if this was what heaven truly looked like, then no one should be afraid of dying.

"Shall we?" Bianca asked as she started walking in the direction where I could see a small bonfire going on. Our hockey team, Whitebrook Wolves, loved bonfires. It didn't matter what time of the year it was; they always found an excuse to have one.

The town people didn't really mind us having them here, as long as no one got hurt, which did happen from time to time, but nothing too serious.

I nodded and started slowly walking after her, my trembling hands by my sides. The need to run and hide was stronger than I anticipated, but I promised myself I would have this. I promised myself I would have one normal night that didn't involve thinking about Noah, about skating, or about things that I couldn't change.

The loud music we could hear as soon as we got out of the car started becoming louder and louder, until I started bobbing my head to the sound of the music, and the familiar song.

"Can You Feel My Heart" by Bring Me the Horizon was blasting in full force as we came to the area that led down toward the beach side of the lake. Teenagers roamed around, some in groups, some in couples, all of them with drinks in their hands, moving to the rhythm of the music.

The cacophony of their voices was smothered by the music, but I was sure that if it wasn't for that, we would be hearing all of them laughing, talking, and cheering each other on.

Bianca took my hand in hers, squeezing softly, as if she was asking me if I was okay.

I was. I didn't mind hanging out at places like these. I loved it, in fact, but I also didn't want to come face-to-face with the one person that had enough power to ruin my entire night.

I looked up at her, smiling, trying to convey that I was okay. That I was excited to be here.

She didn't wait for me to say anything. I knew that there were more things said in those two little gestures than any words could do.

We passed next to the two large groups, all of them people from our school. Some the same age as we were, some younger, but all of them seemed to be having a good time. A couple of girls in front of us started dancing as the song changed to one I couldn't quite recognize.

"There they are." Bianca almost squealed, pulling me along.

I tried to see who she was looking at, but there were way too many people for me to figure out who we were heading toward.

Some of the students nodded at us. Some ignored us completely as we squeezed between them, and I thanked the invisible forces of the universe that none of them were from the hockey team.

Every single one of them knew that Noah and I were friends, but most of them didn't know that we stopped talking. The memories of other parties where I showed up alone flickered through my mind, reminding me of all those times where people would tell him where I was without me realizing that they knew me.

I just hoped that none of these people that saw me would do the same.

"Brandon, Xavier," Bianca started, making me look at the two guys that would be with us.

Holy mother of all gods.

I had no idea which one was which, but I was surprised that they weren't tackled already by the girls standing around.

The guy standing on the left was slightly taller than me, with sandy-blond hair, and a blinding smile that looked brighter than my future. There was something boyish in him, something screaming boy-next-door, and I hated myself for immediately comparing him to Noah, and the obvious differences in them. His eyes weren't blue, but green with brown flecks around the irises.

His hair wasn't dark, he wasn't as tall, he didn't smell the same, and on and on and on, until I had to physically shake my head to lose those thoughts.

While the guy on the left looked like the kind of guy

you would bring home to your parents for a Sunday barbeque, the guy on the right side looked like the kind of guy our mothers warned us about.

Dark hair, and a chiseled jaw, he didn't smile at all. The leather jacket he wore did nothing to hide the fact that this guy screamed danger. His silver eyes were as cold as the ice trapping the lake right in front of us, but the way he looked at Bianca screamed of lust and nights you would never forget.

The tattoo on the side of his neck was a stark contrast to his skin—a crow with spread wings, and its head upturned.

"You must be Sophie," the boy-next-door one spoke, extending his hand toward me. "I'm Brandon." I gingerly placed my hand in his, shaking it as if in a trance. "And this is Xavier." He pointed toward Mr. Danger.

Xavier barely glanced at me, tipping his head down, then turned his attention back toward Bianca.

I was pretty certain that she wouldn't be coming home with me tonight.

"It's nice to meet you, Brandon. Xavier."

"Likewise." Even his voice sounded sweet like honey, but it did nothing to me and my insides like Noah's did.

"So, what brings you to our little town, guys?" I asked first, ignoring the eye-fucking that was happening right next to me.

"Just passing through," Xavier answered.

"Both of us are studying at Emercroft Lake," Brandon explained, pulling my attention back to him. "Xavier was born there, and I got a scholarship."

"That's nice. I've never been there, but a friend of mine told me I should visit. She said that the nature there truly is mesmerizing. Winworth is nearby, right?"

"Mhm," Xavier grunted. "But trust me, you don't

wanna go to Winworth."

"Why not?"

"Because," he finally looked at me, "they eat sweet little things like you for breakfast over there."

The sinister tone lacing his voice sent shivers down my spine. I had a feeling that this guy wasn't the type you would want to fuck with—both literally and metaphorically.

"O-kay. Then I won't go there. But where are you headed?"

"San Francisco." Brandon grinned. "Xavier has some business there, and I'm just tagging along."

"What kind of business?" I couldn't help but ask, which, judging by the look on Xavier's face, was the wrong thing to ask.

"I'm going to visit my new stepsister." He grinned, but there was nothing amusing or light in it. "I'm sure she'll love to meet her new brother."

Brandon chuckled, while I looked between the two of them, trying to decipher what all of that meant. Bianca just stared at Xavier, again, chewing on her bottom lip, when Brandon suddenly took my hand.

"Let's go and get a drink, yeah?"

"Uh—" He came closer, close enough to whisper in my ear.

"Trust me, let's just leave them alone for a while."

Okay then. I clasped my hand around Bianca's arm, willing her to look at me.

"Are you okay staying here with him?"

"Oh, absolutely. Go and have fun. I'll be okay."

Solemnly nodding, I let Brandon pull me away from them and all the way to the long table filled with both alcoholic and non-alcoholic drinks.

Fun, right? I was going to have fun.

11

NOAH

MEMORIES AND BROKEN PROMISES.

A thousand years filled with regrets.

Love, pain, sorrow, anger, all the emotions I shouldn't be feeling, but I did. I shouldn't have been stalking her like I did the entire night, pleading with the universe to push her in my direction.

She was smiling at him, looking at him as if she was really enjoying whatever the blond-haired idiot was saying. All those smiles, those little touches, her words like whispers on the wind, all of them once belonged to me, and I fucked it all up.

The alcohol in my veins did nothing to quiet down the vile thoughts rushing through my head. That she belonged with me. That she never should have been here with another guy.

He placed his arm around her shoulder, pulling her closer into his embrace, and as he did, the plastic cup I held crumbled in my hand, the remnants of the amber liquid spilling over the rim.

"What the fuck, Noah?"

I heard Jared's voice, but it never really registered in my head. As if a veil of darkness fell over my eyes, every time her lips moved, an arrow pierced through my soul, shattering me, piece by piece, one heartbeat after another. I never moved from my spot.

Shadows played around us, dancing with the fiery embers escaping from the bonfire, dragging their wicked little hands all over my skin, telling me to go, to run to her, to take her and show her everything she'd been missing.

Their caress felt both like a blessing and like a curse. As the wind picked up, bringing the feel of the cold evening air over our bodies, Sophie nestled closer to the stranger, letting him warm her up.

Her cheeks were flushed. Her sparkling green eyes filled with mischief and happiness, and it ate me alive. Her sandy-blonde hair cascaded over her shoulders and the red coat she loved the most, a contrast with the blue tips of her hair.

She once told me she wanted to be a mermaid, with crystals in her hair, pointed ears and colorful hair, but she never could color her hair fully because of skating. So this was the solution.

I was trembling, shaking to my core, my stomach recoiling, clenching and unclenching my fists, while the destroyed plastic cup still remained in one of them. He said something, making her laugh out loud, and I knew that look on his face.

He wanted her.

I couldn't let that happen.

Since that day I talked to Jared about what I should do, I'd spent every waking hour trying to think about things I could do to make her forgive me. I'd written countless letters she would never get to read because I was a coward. Because no matter what, I still didn't have enough courage to tell her that my heart burned for her.

I still fooled myself that what I told her already should

be enough, but somewhere deep inside of me, I knew the truth—Sophie needed more from me.

She was always the special one. The one that could understand me even when the words weren't said. Even when I held nothing but resentment toward my father and when the emotions coursing through my veins could not be contained in one's body, she still held me.

When I tasted pain, remorse, and sorrow, she still placed her hands on me, loving me when I didn't even love myself. And now she was with somebody else.

How many times have I sat in my window, looking at hers, willing myself to gather enough courage to tell her how I felt? Countless times. So many that I even stopped counting.

How many times have I reached for my phone in the last three months, my finger lingering on top of the call button, ready to call her just to hear her voice? But I never did call because I was a coward.

"Noah, man. You're shaking."

I was. I could feel it all the way to my toes, but it wasn't the cold that was eliciting this kind of reaction. It was the anger. Somebody else dared to touch what was mine.

I was tired of childish games and tiptoeing around the topic because I was too scared to lose her completely if she didn't feel the same. While her lips told the beautiful lies, her body told me she felt everything I felt too.

Her glazed eyes and parted lips, her delicate hands that were stronger than they looked—they all narrated the story she was not ready to say out loud.

I wasn't going to wait anymore until she came around. I wasn't going to wait while the best thing that had ever happened to me, walked around with a guy that wasn't me.

I broke my promises.

I tainted our memories.

But I was going to fix it whether she liked it or not.

This cat-and-mouse game was going to end tonight. Call me a fool. Call me a hypocritical bastard, but I was done standing on the sidelines, just watching her and wishing for her to be mine.

A slow song started, a song I knew too well. It was always my song for her. It would always be the one song that reminded me of her.

"Everything" by Lifehouse started playing, blasting through the speakers. The soft melody made everybody slow down, momentarily stunning them until they realized what song was playing.

Bodies moved. Faces filled with happiness as others looked at their boyfriends and girlfriends. Sophie looked lost. She scanned the crowd, her hair dancing on the wind, as if she could feel me in the crowd.

Maybe she could. I damn well could always feel her.

The fucker placed his hands on her shoulders and turned her around, gazing down at her as if she was the prettiest thing he had ever seen. And she was—I knew she was, but she was my prettiest thing. The most beautiful girl I had ever set my eyes on.

He pulled her hands up to his shoulders and settled his own on her waist. A fire that was nothing more than a flicker earlier was turning into an inferno now, and I tossed the destroyed cup to the ground before I could stop myself.

It was like watching an accident in slow motion. My heart hammered against my chest, hitting my rib cage that felt as if it was closing down on me. My lungs felt smaller, oxygen barely getting inside my body.

He lowered his head down, going lower and lower, until he reached his goal.

Her lips—*my lips*.

He clasped his hand on the back of her head, moving

them both in sync. My vision turned red. My hands fisted on the sides of my body, and like an out-of-body experience, I barely saw people as I passed by them, my legs carrying me toward them.

"Noah!" I could hear them yelling for me, begging me to stop, pleading with me not to do anything stupid. But all those words were a second too late. Deep down, I knew I was going to do something extremely stupid.

Something that she might add to the list of reasons why she couldn't forgive me, but I didn't give a fuck anymore.

People moved out of my way. Girls yelped as I passed. I could only imagine what my face looked like. It didn't take a genius to know where I was headed.

The motherfucker lifted his head just a second before I reached them, his eyes widening at the sight of me. His lips had that cherry gloss she always loved to put on, and my demons roared even louder, itching to remove even the memory of him from her mind.

He pushed her to the side just as my fist connected with his nose, the cracking sound not as satisfying as I thought it would be.

"Noah!" she screamed at me, but I was too far gone to stop now.

He fell backward, holding his face as the blood spattered everywhere. His weak whimper was music to my ears. The crackling of the bonfire and the wind felt like the push I needed to finish him up.

"You touched her," I growled, not even recognizing my own voice. "You touched what's mine."

"Noah!"

"Man, I didn't know she was in a relationship. She didn't tell me," he whimpered from the ground, trying to get away from me as I stalked toward him.

I dropped to my knees, caging him in.

He thrashed around, trying to escape, but the adrenaline pushing through me was enough to hold him down.

"You should've known," I murmured, leaning closer to him.

"Noah!" Sophie screamed again. "Stop! Somebody stop him. Jared!"

My fist connected with the douchebag's face, sending his head flying to one side, and then the other when my other hand connected with the other side of his face.

"What the fuck?"

"Stop him!"

I tuned them all out, focusing on the bloodied face in front of me and the anger urging me to push more, to punch harder, to show him what he did to my insides.

The way he looked was the way I felt—bloodied and bruised from the inside, bleeding and in pain.

I had no idea how much time passed, how many times I hit the guy, before they pulled me off of him. Strong arms wrapped around my torso, holding me while I tried to get free.

"Let go of me," I gritted out, trying to push those arms off me.

"Calm the fuck down, Noah," Jared warned, and I realized what I'd done.

"Fuck."

My blood still simmered in my veins, the adrenaline pushing onto the surface of my skin, while my eyes frantically searched the crowd, looking for a pair of green eyes.

"Where is she?"

"Gone. Where the fuck do you think she is?"

"Let go of me, J."

"Not until you fucking calm down. What were you thinking, man?"

"Let. Go." I pushed him backward and started running through the crowd. I saw her familiar figure climbing up toward the area where the cars were parked.

Oh no, you don't.

I was going to regret this tomorrow, but the pain from my knuckles was the least of my concerns. As I ran toward her, closing the distance between us, I prayed that I didn't destroy every single chance I had of getting with her.

"Sophie!"

"Leave me alone, Noah."

Her voice was clipped, her back turned to me. She didn't stop until she reached the even ground, walking toward her car.

Her hair was illuminated by the streetlamp. The crowd yelling behind me felt as if it was in another life. Without thinking, I grabbed her upper arm and turned her toward me.

"Will you just stop? Please?"

Anger and tears were never a good sight to see, but those were the only two apparent on her face as she glared at me. She shook me off and crossed her arms across her chest, suddenly looking much smaller than she really was.

"Soph—"

"What the fuck was that, Noah?" Her voice was calm —too calm for my liking—and she avoided looking into my eyes, focusing on my throat instead.

I wanted to reach for her, to touch her, hug her and kiss her. I wanted to wipe his lips from hers, to wipe these tears streaming down her cheeks, but I knew if I even tried, she would scream.

"Who are you?" she suddenly asked, her brows pulled together. "The Noah I used to know would never do such a thing."

She didn't know the Noah she used to know kept all

these feelings locked so deep inside, that all of them just started bursting out now.

I took a step forward and she took one back. I lifted my arm, trying to take a hold of hers, but she swatted me away, that crease between her eyebrows deepening.

"You don't get to touch me. You don't get to do anything anymore, Noah. We are not friends anymore."

"The fuck we're not."

"You said you were done!" she bellowed. "You fucked things up, not me, and now you expect that an 'I'm sorry' is miraculously going to fix everything. Well, news flash—it won't."

"I didn't mean to—"

"Just leave it, Noah. Just let me live my life in peace, far away from you, and I'll let you live yours."

"Angel."

"I don't belong to you, Noah! I never belonged to you." My eye started twitching at those words. "How many times did you say that you saw me as a sister, huh? Do you have any idea how much those words hurt? And now, what? You think that making me believe you have feelings for me is somehow going to let you waltz back into my life?"

"I'm not—"

"Just save it." She started moving back, away from me. "I will never be yours. I never was yours. I was just a girl waiting for you to see her as more than a friend, but you never did. You don't get to change your mind now. You don't get to put some crazy caveman claim on me, just because you feel like that."

"He kissed you!" I roared, needing to let it out. "He touched you."

"I let him, you motherfucking idiot! I let him because I wanted to forget the sound of your voice. I wanted to forget that you ever existed!"

"Don't say that," I choked out.

"I loved it. If you hadn't broken his nose, I would've let him take me to the woods to have his way with me."

"Stop."

"I would've let him erase the memory of you and everything we've done together from my head. You are nothing more than a painful memory. A reminder of a time lost."

"Please, Sophie. Stop."

"If I have to, I will let a thousand men touch me, to kiss me and fuck me, if it means that I will never see your face in my dreams again."

I wanted to give her space. I would've given her everything that she ever wanted, but not this. Never this.

My body had a mind of its own. I stalked after her, letting my instincts take over.

Mine, mine, mine, was on repeat inside my head, making me want to murder every single person that ever looked at her. These animalistic urges were not something I was familiar with, but I'd be damned if I tried to stop it.

Bending down, I wrapped my arm around the backs of her legs, and lifted her up on my shoulder, ignoring the screech that erupted from her as soon as her body went into the air.

"What the fuck are you doing? Noah!"

"Shhh," I soothed as I started walking toward the forest.

"Let. Me. Down." She slammed her hands against my back, hitting with all her force, but I didn't stop. "You're a psycho."

"Takes one to know one."

"I'm not the one kidnapping people."

"No, but you're the one that's keen on making me bleed out tonight with your words."

"Noah—"

"You're the one that's trying to erase everything we ever were, and that little glint in your eye told me that you loved hurting me just now."

A second passed, her hands pressed against my back, while I walked toward the area farther away from the beach, where they said the locals planted the trees more than thirty years ago, creating a small piece of forest right next to the lake.

"Where are we going?" she asked, trepidation evident in her voice.

"Farther away from people."

"So that you can kill me without any witnesses?" Seriously?

"No, so that I can talk to you properly."

Though, what I had planned, I had a feeling that there wouldn't be much talking involved. She said what she thought she wanted earlier, but she never heard me say what I wanted.

I wanted a future with her. I wanted us to grow old together. There was no one else I would rather have by my side when I'm old, gray, and unable to open a can of pickles.

"There's nothing to talk about."

"That's what you keep telling me, yet your body is telling me a completely different story."

"Noah, seriously? Stop playing this stupid game and let me the fuck down."

"Can't do that, Angel. You need to hear what I have to say, and until you truly do, I'm not letting you go. Hell, I'm never letting you go. I was an idiot for saying those things, and an even bigger one for never answering you or reaching out to you. I'm not waiting anymore."

"So, what? You got your head out of your ass and decided that I'm one of the last girls you never fucked?"

"No, Sophie." I stopped not too far from the entrance to the area where they planted the trees, and put her down. "I got my head out of my ass and realized that you are the only girl I ever wanted to be with."

She stumbled backward as soon as the words left my mouth, going deeper into the forest. "This is insane. You never felt this way about me."

"Didn't I?" I smiled. "I've been in love with you since we were kids, Angel. I just never wanted to let you know because I didn't think you felt the same."

"No." She shook her head. "Stop saying these things. Just stop."

"Why?" I crossed the distance between us, holding her face in my hands. "I know you feel the same way. I know that your eyes could never lie to me, no matter what."

"Stop it." She trembled. Her entire body shook as I dragged my finger toward her neck, pressing against her pulse point. "Please stop."

Her pleas were lost on my ears, because when her eyes fluttered and closed, I bent down and did what I should've done years ago.

Her breath fanned over my lips, the sweet smell of the cherry gloss she loved so much infiltrating through my nose, making me dizzy with need, lust, all these things I made myself stop feeling every time she was around. A thousand hours of longing, of feeling like I was going to go mad, because I wanted her and only her.

Faceless girls that could never replace her or feed the monster that made its nest inside my chest. A thousand nights where I held her, wishing that we were something much more than just friends.

"Do you want this?" I asked, wrapping my other hand

around her hair, pulling it back from her face. "Do you want me?"

"Noah," she moaned, the fight she was so full of before, disappearing into thin air.

Wind roared around us. The icy cold air should've made me shake, but my body burned from the need to be buried deep inside of her, until neither one of us knew where she began, and I ended.

Without preamble, without waiting anymore, I pressed my lips to hers, soft against hard. Sweet against sour, and took and took and took.

Our tongues clashed, our breaths intertwined, and my heart hammered, threatening to jump out of my chest. She pressed her hands against my chest, exploring with every moan escaping from her.

She wrapped her arms around my neck, dragging her nails across my skin, sending the small rivulets of pleasure straight to my core. My dick pressed against my pants, pain and pleasure, anticipation, while I devoured her sweet mouth, tasting her for the first time.

"You're mine, Sophie," I murmured against her lips, fighting for air, while she did the same. "Please tell me you're mine."

Her eyes glazed over as I sneaked one hand beneath the shirt she wore, finding my way to her bra. Beneath the cotton material, I found what I was looking for. Her breast fit perfectly in my hand, her perky little nipple standing up, waiting for me, begging for attention.

"Fuck," she moaned, closing her eyes as I squeezed and played, caressed and pinched until she started writhing beneath my hands.

"Tell me you're mine, Soph." I placed an open-mouthed kisses on her jaw, on her neck, all the way to her collarbone, pulling the shirt lower. My eyes feasted on the pale, luminescent skin waiting for me to be touched. "Tell me and I'll give you what you want."

"I'm yours," she admitted. "I have always been yours."

"Yes," I hissed, the roaring triumph inside of me pushing me to take more and more and more, until she was ready to do the same.

She owned every inch of me—every crevice of my body, my soul, my heart. I just needed her to see how much I burned for her. How much I needed her. I needed her to see that my days had no colors if she wasn't in them.

She took it all when she left that night three months ago—songs, colors, taste. She took everything that ever connected me to her.

I couldn't go near cherries because they reminded me of her. I couldn't listen to songs we used to listen to together, because every single lyric was meant for her.

I was born to be with her, and I was tired of constantly depriving myself of the one thing I truly wanted.

My hands strummed against her skin, and as I removed my hand from beneath her shirt, her eyes flew open, a whimper escaping from her mouth, protesting.

"Shhh." I pushed her coat off her shoulders, letting it fall to the ground. I'd wash the damn thing myself if it got that dirty.

The thin, black shirt she wore did nothing to calm down my racing heart. I could see every slope of her body.

"You are so beautiful, Soph." I leaned down and pressed a kiss to her forehead, holding her close to me. "And you're all mine."

I took a step back and removed my leather jacket, letting it fall next to hers. My shirt was next, and as her eyes widened at the sight of my naked chest, something broke inside of me. I pushed her to the tree behind her, plastering my body to hers.

I fisted her hair in one hand, while the other one played with the hem of the knee-length skirt she wore.

I hitched her leg up, wrapping it around my hip, letting the fabric climb up.

"Are you wet for me, Angel?" I asked between the kisses, while my hand roamed up and down her thigh. "Do you want my fingers inside of you?"

"Please."

"Tell me what you want."

"Please touch me." Her eyes were crazed, her cheeks flushed, and her hair looked beautiful wrapped around my fist.

"You want me to touch you?" I asked against her neck and then moved toward her ear, biting her earlobe. "Where, beautiful? Where do you want me to touch you?"

"M-My… My pussy."

God, my dick was painfully pressing against the zipper of my pants, ready to be released.

"Your wish," I bit her neck, soothing it with my tongue almost immediately, "is my command."

I dropped her leg and moved away only far enough to lift her shirt. The pale color of her bra looked so innocent, so pure, but we both knew that she wasn't the pure one.

"This needs to go." I unclasped it from the front, and she shimmied it down her arms, letting it fall with the rest of our clothes. "Perfect," I murmured as my hands took her breasts. A perfect fit for me. Perfect in every single way.

Her rosy nipples stood up, waiting for attention, and like a man starved, I dived and flicked my tongue against one of them, all the while twirling the other one between my fingers.

"Noah!"

"Do you want to come, Sophie?"

"Y-Yes."

"Do you want to feel me between your legs?" I asked as I took her hand and pressed it against my crotch. Her eyes widened, shock lacing her delicate features. For a moment, I thought she would step back and tell me that this was a mistake.

But I was wrong.

Instead of running, instead of shying away from me, a determined look entered her eyes, and she pressed against me before starting to run her finger up and down my length.

A groan erupted from me, rumbling deep from my chest. Before I could come like a twelve-year-old boy, I turned her around and hitched her skirt around her hips. Her panties matched her bra in color, but just like the bra, they needed to go.

I pulled them down. As she stepped from them, I lifted them to my nose, her scent driving me crazy.

"You feel like mine, Soph. You also smell like mine."

"Noah." Her voice penetrated through me. "Please, touch me."

I stuffed the panties into my back pocket and pushed her closer to the tree, lifting her arms in the process.

"Keep your hands where I can see them, Angel. If you move, you don't get to come."

"Noah," she protested.

"That's an order, Sophie. Keep your hands on the tree."

"Okay." She nodded, looking at me over her shoulder.

I dropped down on my knees and started pressing kisses on the backs of her thighs, caressing her legs, and her naked backside.

"God, you smell delicious."

Her pussy glistened as I spread her legs wider, her

juices slowly coating her inner thighs. "You're so wet for me, Soph. Tell me this is all for me."

"It has always been for you."

"Fuck." I buried my face in her pussy, inhaling her essence, inhaling everything that she was. I'd been waiting forever for this moment, and now that it was here, I momentarily didn't know what to do.

I didn't want to hurt her, but I also did. I wanted her to tell me everything she felt, even though I knew that she was never one for sharing emotions unless it was necessary.

But this was a necessity, wasn't it? I needed to know that she thought about me and only me. I wanted her to feel everything I felt.

My tongue lashed out, curling around her clit. An ear-splitting scream erupted from her.

"Noah! Fuck!"

She smelled like cinnamon and vanilla and my tongue tingled from the feel of her. As she started moving her hips in the rhythm of my tongue, I knew she needed more than this.

I lifted my hand and ran my fingers from her backside to her front, holding her hip with my other one. Slowly, carefully, I entered one finger in, earning a loud groan from her.

"More."

Her pussy fisted my finger almost immediately, and I curled it, hitting her G-spot all the while.

"Fuck. Me."

"Soon, baby." I chuckled against her pussy.

I started moving my finger up and down, increasing my speed, while she started pushing back, looking for me. Her juices glistened against her skin, and I moved my head, lapping at her thighs, then back to her clit, loving the sounds she made.

"God!"

"Not God, baby. Say my name."

"Noah," she moaned.

"Louder."

"Noah!" She screamed loud enough for half of the beach to hear.

"Has anyone ever touched you here?" I asked, entering her with a second finger, spreading her, preparing her for me. I almost had my answer, but I wanted to hear her say it. I wanted to revel in the satisfaction that I would be the first person that would get to do this, and if I had anything to say about it, I would be the last one.

"N-No."

Pride and satisfaction coiled inside of me, and I increased my pace, hitting that sweet spot inside of her.

"Have you ever touched yourself?"

"Y-Yes." Her voice was barely audible. Her body was not her own anymore, and I knew she was close.

"Did you think about me?"

"God, yes! Please don't stop!"

How could I, when I'd been waiting to see her like this my entire life? I'd spent countless nights fantasizing about her, fisting my dick to the point of pain, both hating and loving it because this was my best friend I was thinking about.

It felt wrong, but it also felt so right.

I was going to burst if I didn't bury myself inside of her soon, but I knew I would have to take it slow. I didn't want to hurt her, at least not yet.

I wanted her to enjoy this as much as I did.

"There!" she screamed. "Right there. That spot."

I added a third finger and focused on the spot that drove her crazy. I looked up, seeing her head turned backward, her face toward the sky, panting and moaning. Her back glistened with sweat, and I wanted to lick it off her body.

"Noah, Noah, Noah... Oh my fucking God!" She bucked against my fingers, and I dove, biting her clit with my teeth, then lapping at it with my tongue, and on and on and on.

"Fuuuuuuuck!" I felt it when her orgasm tore through her body, her pussy clenching against my fingers, holding me in. I never wanted to imagine a life where this wasn't a possibility.

Her body shook, the tremors rocking her. I had a feeling that if I wasn't holding her up, she would've been on the ground by now.

I slowly removed my fingers, earning another whimper from her, and smelled her on me.

I stood up, pressing my chest against her back, and pulled her hair backward, holding her neck in my hand.

"Taste yourself, baby." I pressed my fingers to her lips. "Taste how delicious you are."

Her makeup was running down her cheeks, her mascara ruined, and that cherry gloss smeared around her lips, but she had never looked more beautiful than she did now. Sophie kept surprising me tonight, letting me see this other side of her—a side I wanted to see more of.

She opened her mouth and lapped at my fingers, moaning as her eyes closed.

"God, I need to be inside of you. Right. Now."

Her response was to press against me, her ass rubbing against my aching dick.

I turned her around and wrapped my arms around her back—one in her hair and one around her waist—and dipped down, tasting her lips and her juices both at the same time.

Thundering in my ears quieted all the other noise, and in this moment, right here, it was only her and me.

"Are you okay?" I asked as I pulled back to catch my breath.

"Mhm." She nodded, smiling for the first time tonight at me. Her eyes were hazy, filled with lust, need, reflecting everything I felt as well. I could see the love there, swirling in those green depths, and hope blossomed inside of me, making me feel that maybe not everything was lost.

Blood was smeared across her cheeks, and I hated that I brought violence from earlier into this moment between us. But beggars couldn't be choosers. I knew that no matter what, blood or not, she was mine for good now.

"I need you to fuck me now, Noah. You're the first guy I've ever been with, and I want you to have it."

The heart was such a fragile organ, and mine hammered rapidly at her words, disbelief running through my veins.

"Are you sure?" I didn't want her to feel that she had to do anything she didn't want to do.

She looked at me and placed her hand against my cheek, a small smile forming on her lips. "Deadly."

I didn't want her to regret this—us—but I also knew that I was going to explode if I didn't do what she asked me to do.

Gently, I lowered her down on top of her coat and my jacket, and she pulled down the skirt bunched around her waist. I unbuttoned my pants, the instant relief running through me as my dick bobbed up when I dropped the material down.

"Jesus Christ," she exclaimed, her eyes frozen on my dick. That motherfucker loved the attention.

"You like what you see?" I smirked and bent down to retrieve a condom from my wallet.

"Uh, is that a real question? I mean, not that I know what the measurements are since it's the first dick I've ever seen in my life. Maybe when I see more, I will—"

I dove, cutting her sentence off with my lips on hers, the soft growl erupting at what she was insinuating.

"You are never going to get to see another dick, Sophie, because I am never letting you go."

She swallowed and nodded, lifting herself up to meet my lips as well.

"I'm all yours, Noah. I will always be yours."

"Good. Because I would go to the end of the world and back, looking for you, if that's what it took to bring you back."

I moved back and tore the wrapper with my teeth, rolling the condom on my dick. She lifted herself up on her elbows and observed my every move with wonder in her eyes.

"Is it going to hurt?"

"Yes." I didn't want to lie to her. "But I will make it feel better, okay?"

A small nod was all I got, before I came closer to her, spreading her wide open for me. I dipped two of my fingers inside of her pussy, her breathing hitching up as I stroked her walls, going back for that spot she loved.

"Fuuuck."

"You're ready for me. So ready, so tight, baby."

I pressed one finger against her clit and started rubbing it. She fell backward, her back arching off the ground. My mind and my heart were finally in sync, and gradually, I removed my fingers and pressed my dick against her center.

I started rubbing the head of my dick from her open-ing, up to her clit, coating myself in her juices, while she trembled on the ground, looking at me with wondrous eyes.

"This is going to hurt, baby. I'm sorry, but it'll pass."

"I trust you."

I gripped my dick at the base and guided it to her opening, stretching her bit by bit.

"Fuck," she cursed. As soon as the head of my dick disappeared inside of her, I stopped, letting her adjust to my size.

I bit my lip, calming myself down, her tight cunt pressing around me like a fist.

"Jesus," I panted, and closed my eyes for a moment, thinking about my grandma and that one time I saw her naked, so that I wouldn't come before I even managed to fuck her properly.

"Are you okay?" I gritted out, tensing as her pussy pulsed around me. "Jesus, you're squeezing the life out of me."

She tensed again, trying to pull back, and I leaned down, caging her between my arms.

"Hey, hey, hey," I soothed. "I'm here. It's okay."

"It hurts," she cried, tears slipping out of her eyes, mixing with the dark paint from her mascara that left traces on her cheeks earlier.

"I know, baby. I know it hurts, but it'll pass." I pressed a soft kiss to her lips, and pushed deeper, holding her head at her neck.

"Noah!"

"It's done, Soph. It's all done. Breathe for me, okay? Just breathe."

"Fucking hell."

Her hair lay wild around her head, her lips swollen from my kisses. As she looked up at me, I could feel the love shining from her eyes.

I moved my hand, sneaking it between us, and pressed against her clit, rubbing tiny circles in hopes that she'd relax.

"I need you to relax for me, Soph."

Her pussy squeezed around me again at the same time as a breath whooshed out from between her lips.

"That's the opposite of being relaxed," I groaned.

"Sorry." She chuckled. "This doesn't feel good to you?" She did it again, making my eyes roll to the back of my head.

"Fuck!"

"What's the matter, babe?"

"That feels too good. If you don't stop this, the whole thing will be over much faster than I intended it to be."

I pinched her clit, this time earning a moan from her, and moved slowly backward before slamming in again.

"Shit," she cried. "More."

I moved slowly, afraid to hurt her, but each and every stroke was pure agony while my blood boiled and the need to come drove through me with force.

"I need to go faster, baby."

"Please."

My fingers strummed against her clit, while my hips increased its pace, pistoning inside.

"Noah." I pressed my lips against her throat and bit down on the soft skin, just between her neck and her shoulder. I knew she was going to have marks tomorrow, but the beast inside of me didn't give a fuck.

I wanted to mark her. I wanted to climb Mount Everest and scream that she was mine.

Only mine.

"Fuck, Sophie."

"Faster," she panted, arching her back. My other hand

found her breast, and I started playing with the puckered nipple.

My hands looked good on her. As I looked down to where we were connected, the familiar feeling started spreading from my lower back and through my stomach, all the way to my toes.

Her chest rose and fell with every stroke I made, and she started closing her eyes.

"Eyes on me, baby."

Those green eyes, rounded by the darker circle, connected with mine, and I drove inside of her like a man possessed. She looked beautiful spread out like this—her lips open, reddening on her cheeks, and eyes glazed. She looked like a fucking goddess.

"Please, Noah. Please... God." She threw her head back, her hands going to her breasts. Seeing her touch herself like that, lost in lust just like I was, broke something inside of me.

As her body started spasming, her pussy clenching around me while I strummed my fingers against her clit, I let myself go.

An eruption, that was what it felt like letting go. My seed spilled into the condom as she locked around me, screaming for me.

My name, God's, and a string of curses echoed around us.

"Fuck." I collapsed on top of her, my dick still deeply rooted inside of her.

Both of us were trying to catch our breaths, and my hand wrapped around her hair, stroking through the tangled strands.

"My God." I almost moaned again as I pulled out of her, careful not to hurt her.

She winced at the motion, but the look that was there

on her face just mere seconds ago was suddenly replaced by the look of cold indifference—a look I saw earlier.

"No," I warned as I pulled off the condom, wrapped it, and threw it to the side. "Do not look at me like that."

"Like what?" she asked as she pulled herself up and reached for her bra.

"Like you regret what just happened."

"I don't regret it." She shrugged and pulled her bra on, clipping it at the front. "I just don't think it should ever happen again."

What did she just say?

"What?"

She stood up and started collecting her clothes. Her shirt was the first thing that went on, hiding her body from me. Her skirt followed. As she turned to me, I hated what I saw on her face.

"Look, it's been fun and all, but this is what we both wanted, right? Just to scratch the itch."

"To scratch the itch?" I repeated, dumbfounded.

"Yeah. This is what we both wanted. Now you can stop pretending that you wanted me for something more than this."

Anger, red, burning anger, ran through me.

"Thank you." She came closer and extended her hand to me, as if what we just did was nothing more than a business transaction.

I stared at her hand, then at her face, trying to find the girl I loved all these years, only to be met by a wall she built around herself.

"You can take your thank-yous and give them to somebody else, Sophie." I bent down and lifted my pants and pulled them on. "If what we just did meant nothing to you, fine. But remember that you were the one that threw us away. And when you're sitting all alone in your chair in sixty or seventy years, please remember that there was a guy that would've fought the entire world for you, but you didn't want him. I fucked up, I know, but you're the one that's destroying us right now."

I couldn't look at her. I couldn't stand there for another second, because looking at her when she behaved like this felt as if somebody kept branding my heart. I thought I knew what pain felt like, but none of it compared to what she just did to me—what she did to us.

Without another word, without a second glance, I lifted my shirt from the ground, followed by my jacket, and walked away.

If I had anything to do with it, this would be the last time I would ever try to fix us, to be what we used to be.

12

SOPHIE

My constant companions for the last three months were the tears I usually let out at night, when nobody else was there to see me breaking apart.

That first night when he broke my heart, I thought I was going to die from grief. I had no idea that pain like that could exist—but I was so fucking wrong.

Last night proved that.

After Noah left me there, and after I was sure that he wasn't coming back, I broke down, letting all these emotions I kept close to my heart come out. The grief over a friendship we had. The pain over the love I felt. The sorrow over what I just did.

I saw it there, clear as day—he wanted me. He really wanted me, and I pushed him away.

Noah didn't know the truth, and he could never know the truth. I knew what it would do to him, because I could see what it was doing to my family.

The devastation at such news was not something I wanted for him.

I had no idea how much time passed since he left me there, but eventually I picked myself up and drove home. I stopped three times when the tears became too much for me to drive, when my lungs seized so much, cutting off my oxygen. I couldn't forgive myself for what I just did.

I came home just before ten, but my body felt as if I'd just ran a marathon. For the first time in I didn't even know how long, I didn't go to sleep with a headache but without yet another piece of myself.

I just hoped that one day he would be able to forgive me.

I fucking hated mornings. I hated them even more when I slept for only one hour and when my eyes were so swollen that I knew I would have to put on ice packs to reduce the swelling. I loathed them because I knew that if I just looked through the window, I would see him there, even if he wasn't physically present.

But last night... Last night the light never came on in his room, and I couldn't help but obsess over his where-abouts and if he was okay. It wasn't his fault I pushed him away—it was mine. I hated myself for every single word that left my mouth.

I dragged myself out of the bed and into the bath-room. Instead of seeing the happy look on my face, which was what I always imagined I would look like after I slept with somebody for the first time, I looked like death dragged me back from hell.

My eyes were sunken and the dark circles around my eyes rivaled pandas'. I unbraided my hair and turned toward the shower, sick at myself and what I'd become.

Sick at seeing the pain in his eyes.

My actions had consequences, and if he didn't stop trying before, he definitely would now.

I slowly took off my shirt and my panties, and saw the streaks of blood on them—evidence of what happened last night. Proof that it wasn't just a dream. As I turned to the side to turn on the shower, my hair got in the way, and the scent still lingering on the strands almost sent me into another fit of crying.

My hair still smelled like him. My lips still vibrated, remembering how his felt on them, and my skin burned where he touched me.

But I knew that whatever he felt last night would be replaced by bitterness and anger, and while he tasted like sunshine as his lips pressed against mine, I was sure that the memory of mine for him would taste like poison.

I looked down and saw the bruises at my hips and as I turned to the side to look at myself in the mirror once again, I saw the hickeys lining up all over my neck, my chest, and on top of my shoulders.

I couldn't even be angry at him, because this was who he always was. Even when we both pretended that we were nothing more than friends, he always had a tendency to shield me from everybody else, always wanting my full attention on him.

Now I knew why.

I pressed the heels of my hands against my eyes, trying to erase the pictures clogging my brain.

Noah above me, his eyes shining with love, his words, his soft caresses. I knew I would never get any of those ever again.

Last night was my final goodbye. I just hoped that one day, maybe a couple of years from now, he would under-stand why I did what I did. Why I pushed him away and why I decided to stop this thing happening between us.

Or maybe he wouldn't. I couldn't know. The only saving grace was that he wouldn't have to go through all these… things, with me.

I wanted him to have a happy life, not one filled with sorrow and pain, and visits to the doctor.

I wanted him to have an amazing senior year, to get

that scholarship he wanted, and to get the fuck away from this town.

I turned the water on, pulling the tap to the hottest setting, willing myself to wake up enough to be able to compete today. It wasn't enough that my heart shattered into a million pieces last night. My head was an absolute mess, nausea swirling in the pit of my stomach, but I couldn't back out now.

I should have never gone to the party last night.

I should have gone straight home and to sleep, because then I wouldn't be in this position.

But I also couldn't regret what happened last night, because Noah was always the person I imagined losing my virginity to. He was the only person I ever loved, and it was only right that he got this last piece of me.

He would never know how much I loved him. He would never know how much I needed him, but it was okay… in a way. Not everyone could get their happily ever after. Maybe Noah and I were never meant to be together in the end.

Maybe life had something else planned for him, and I was fine with that as long as he was happy.

I stepped inside the shower, letting the water wash away last night. It washed my tears, my fears, my longing, but it couldn't wash away the love that lived inside of me. I wished it could. I wanted to get rid of this heavy thing sitting on my chest, but I knew that nothing could ever erase the years we had together.

As much as I loved it, I also hated it.

I hated myself for everything, especially now.

I knew that he wasn't going to be there today, standing in the bleachers, cheering me on. I knew he would do everything he could to avoid me like I avoided him.

If only I could wrap my arms around him one last time, I would be a happy person.

If only I could tell him things without uttering those words, I could live the rest of my life content.

I slid down the wall, hugging my knees to my chest as water cascaded over me, hiding the tears streaming down my cheeks.

We were both too late. We were too young for the things life threw at us. I could curse, I could cry, but none of it could change what was happening right now.

I fucked up.

But it was better this way. It would always be better this way.

I pressed my back against the wall, inhaling through my nose and exhaling through my mouth. I was going to be fine—with or without him. He was going to have an amazing life, and one day, I could tell others how I knew this magnificent man.

I could tell them that once upon a time, he meant everything to me. I could tell them stories of our childhood, and all those mischiefs we did. I could tell them about the nights and plans we made that we never got to do together, but I hoped he would do them by himself.

I could tell them about a love birthed from the friendship between two people who were two sides of the same coin.

I could also tell them that even though my heart hurt, my soul was happy because I had known him. I had him once, and that was more than some people had.

A lot of us went through life never experiencing love or heartbreak, and I was one of the lucky ones who got to have both.

I was so fucking lucky, because I had him, even for a while.

So I pulled myself up, holding on to the wall, careful not to slip, and got on with my day.

I might not have Noah anymore, but I still had things I wanted to do. Things I needed to do, and wallowing here in self-pity was not going to get any of those done.

I lathered my hair and washed it out, immediately feeling better.

As soon as I got dressed up, I collected my gear and went downstairs, where the smell of freshly brewed coffee and pancakes lured me into the kitchen. I found my dad sitting at the table and my mom at the stove.

"Daddy!" I ran toward him, dropping my bag to the floor. I hadn't seen him for a couple of days, both because he avoided being home and because he had to travel to New York. But he was here now.

"I missed you so much, my girl," he whispered as he wrapped his hands around me, holding me close.

He smelled like coffee and the cigars he occasionally smoked with his buddies. He smelled like home, like my childhood.

As I stepped back from his embrace, I could see the unshed tears in his eyes. I could see the regrets swirling there, but none of it mattered. What did matter was that he was here now.

"Are you coming to my competition today?"

Regional competitions were being held in the Boston Sports Complex, and the drive to there was around two hours from our town. In the past, he rarely missed any of my competitions, but taking into consideration the situation right now, I wasn't sure if he would be coming.

I could feel my mom's eyes on us. When Dad smiled, I knew I was going to like the answer.

"Of course I am. I took a couple of days off work, so

we can go to that ice cream place you like after the competition."

"Seriously?" I beamed at him. "Yeah, I would love that. Are you coming, Mom?"

"What do you think?" She wiped her hands with the washcloth and turned around to take the plate with pancakes. As soon as she placed it on the table, Andrew came strolling in, looking worse than I felt.

"Morning," he grumbled and went straight for the pancakes.

"Andrew Theodore Anderson, get your hands away from my pancakes." Mom hit him with the washcloth, while Dad laughed from his spot.

"I'm hungry."

"Then you need to wait for everybody else to sit down and eat."

"But Sophie always takes so long, and you and Dad are the same."

"I don't care," she grumbled. "Go and wash your face and your teeth and then come back. You can wait for five minutes."

"Seriously?" He glared at her, that sleepy look still evident on his face.

"Yes, seriously. Get going, chop-chop."

He grumbled all the way to the bathroom, and I almost felt sympathy toward him when he bumped into the shelf, cursing loud enough for us to hear.

"So, are you ready for today?" Dad asked.

"Yep."

"How are you feeling in general? Headaches, nausea, diz—"

"Dad." I placed my hand on top of his. "I'm fine, trust me. I know what I'm doing."

"I know you do. I'm just, you know, worried. I don't want you to push yourself too hard if you can't do it."

"We talked about this, Daddy. This is one of my last competitions, and then afterward, I can focus on other things."

He observed me for a second, but it seemed that he was happy with the answer I provided.

He didn't have to know that I couldn't wait for the pills I took to kick in, or that I wouldn't be able to eat more than two pancakes because my stomach felt as if it wanted to jump out of my body. Right?

SOPHIE

The Boston Sports Complex looked just as I remembered it—a white, round building, with several entrances. The building that gave me my first golden medal, and the one that had so many good memories.

Bitterness spread through me when I remembered that Noah wouldn't be here today, but I swallowed it down and focused on what was in front of me.

I could see people rushing toward the main entrance, hauling their huge suitcases and their dress bags with them. I loved this feeling. I lived for this feeling.

The adrenaline, the anticipation, this was always my favorite part of figure skating. It was also an opportunity to meet other people, to learn and learn and learn, because no matter what, even when you thought that you were at your best, there were still things you could do better.

Coach Liudmila stayed in Boston last night, and I was sure she was already inside, pacing from one side of the foyer to the other, waiting for us. She asked me to come with her last night, but I didn't want to let my mom drive by herself.

When I woke up today, I thought the day was going to

be filled with misery, but instead it was already going much better than I'd expected.

The nausea calmed down, my headache was almost gone, and it'd been such a long time since my family traveled like this.

Andrew followed us in his car, and as soon as we parked, I could see him walking toward us.

"You guys are extremely slow. I was worried she was going to miss the entire thing if you kept driving like that."

"Son, not everyone needs to drive like Niki Lauda," Dad said, placing a hand on Andy's shoulder.

"Come on, guys. I need to find Coach Liudmila, but I'll see you inside. Okay?"

"Go, go, go." Mom handed over my suitcase. "Good luck, darling." She hugged me and kissed both of my cheeks, handing me over to my dad.

He did the same, followed by Andy, who squeezed the life out of me.

"That hurts." I laughed.

"I'm proud of you, you know? So, so fucking proud."

"I know." I nodded and looked up at him as he let me go. "I'll see you inside, okay?"

"Yep."

This day was going much better than I expected. Now if only I could manage to find Coach Liudmila, it would be brilliant.

A couple of hours later, three energy drinks for Andy, a little bit of food for me, and a whole lot of nerves, I was warming up on the side, waiting for the current routine to finish so that I could go toward the rink.

I had hoped my headache would go down after some time, but I was so terribly wrong. Not only did it not go down, it hit back with a vengeance. Every single step felt as if someone was shaking my whole brain. My stomach clenched and unclenched, and I worried that what little food I had managed to consume today would start coming out.

I just prayed that it wouldn't happen during my routine.

I bent down, stretching my back, trying to reach my toes, when a sudden bout of dizziness hit me like a freight train, making me bend down.

Fuck. This couldn't be happening now.

I closed my eyes and started inhaling through my nose and exhaling through my mouth, but all I could hear, all I could feel, was the pounding of my heart in my ears. I tried pushing myself up, but every time I tried, my body felt as if it was going to collapse on the floor.

Fuck, fuck, fuck.

"And the next contestant, ladies and gentlemen, is the one that basically grew up on this ice." Jesus, it was my turn already. "One of the fan favorites, please welcome, Sophie Anderson!"

The crowd roared in unison, chanting my name, yet I couldn't lift my head.

"Sophie!" Coach Liudmila's voice came to me, and with the strength I didn't know I possessed, I managed to lift my head. "What are you doing?"

"Warming up," I answered. But even to myself, my voice sounded weak. God, I trained so hard. I couldn't back down now.

"Well, come on then." She came closer and pulled me

up. My stomach recoiled, and I bit down on my lip, trying to keep in the breakfast I'd eaten. "They already called out your name."

A couple of years ago, I caught the flu a week before the competitions, and the night before I spent puking my guts out. Did that stop me from competing the next day? Absolutely not. It turned out that I had pneumonia all along.

But this now… This felt ten times worse than what I felt back then.

Coach Liudmila brought me toward the entrance and helped me to remove the covers from my skates. It felt like an out-of-body experience as I skated on the ice, feeling the cold seeping through my bones.

The familiar feeling of belonging was nowhere right now as my body fought to stay upright. I knew this routine by heart, and I bit my tongue just as the song started.

Please, please, please, I pleaded with whatever force would listen. *Let this go okay. Please.*

My body knew what it had to do, thanks to muscle memory. As I went around the rink, closing and opening my eyes, fighting to stay upright, I knew I wouldn't be able to do what I came here to do. I could feel that my moves went okay, each and every step choreographed to the point where it felt like breathing, but my mind was far away from here.

I couldn't hear the cheering from the crowd. I could only hear the whooshing sound my skates made on the ice.

The staccato tones from the song ran over me, bouncing back off my skin, and my hips locked as I did one final circle around, getting myself ready for my signature move—the triple axel.

Doctors warned me to take it easy, that my body wasn't in the state to take this much, but I ignored their warnings.

If I was going to go through hell and back, I was going to do this even if it cost me.

But I should've listened to them.

Just before the last turn, the black dots started appearing in the periphery of my vision, and the ads strategically placed around the rink became blurry. I blinked and blinked and blinked, but with each passing second, my vision was failing me.

No, no, no.

I kept going, bracing my body for the turn, but it was at that moment that the pain, like no other, sliced through my head. I closed my eyes instead of keeping them open. I went up in the air, but as I opened my eyes, I couldn't see anything.

The crowd, the arena, everything was blurry, and I knew I should've stopped.

I should've slowed down.

I should've done a thousand things differently, but I chose this, and I would have to live with the consequences.

I landed on my foot, but instead of continuing, my body crumbled, unable to take any more. The last thing I saw was the blurry ice as I fell.

14

NOAH

Raindrops fell onto the windshield of my car as I drove down the street, not even five minutes away from home. Dark clouds littered the sky, casting a shadow over the town. I wouldn't be surprised if we ended up with a thunderstorm today.

It almost made me laugh, the fact that the weather behaved how I felt. Turmoil and torment kept me awake the entire night. After I left Sophie in the woods, I drove all the way to Boston, deciding to lick my wounds in private, in one of the apartments my dad kept for those rare times when he actually decided to show up.

Last night kept on replaying in my mind—her lips on mine, her soft body so pliant underneath my hands. Those forest-green eyes looking at me with love, need and lust, until she decided to hide herself from me again, tearing us apart.

I dreaded seeing her house. I dreaded seeing her, because I couldn't trust myself that I wouldn't drag her far away from here, just to make her talk, just to have her with me one last time. I couldn't understand why she would act the way she did last night.

I wanted her to talk to me, to tell me what was going

on inside her head just how she used to. But somewhere between that dreadful night when I let my tongue run fast and bitter, and now, something had changed. That little spark she always had in her eyes wasn't there anymore, and I needed to find out why.

I couldn't believe that it was all because of me. Maybe I was just another idiotic teenager who didn't understand how much words could actually hurt.

Her panties lay hidden in the glove compartment of my car. I knew that I would never return them. She gave me a piece of herself last night, and she couldn't be the one deciding that it would only be one time. I refused to believe that she didn't want this with me.

Hell, I would take her in any way that she wanted to give herself to me, even if it was in tiny pieces. Even if she decided that all we could ever have was sex, I wouldn't mind. At least not for a little while, because having her like that was better than not having her at all.

I parked my car right in front of my house, staring straight ahead, willing myself to get out, to look at her house. But loving her hurt. Needing her was an ache that only she could soothe, and she didn't want me.

My father once told me that if you wanted something, you needed to fight for it. But what if this wasn't just some silly game she was playing to punish me? What if she truly didn't feel everything I did?

How could I believe that when her eyes told me the story of a thousand promises she wanted to make? How could I sit here and believe that her body arched in lies last night, when I could feel her pleasure as if it was my own?

I was meant to move here with my parents, and she was meant to be mine. It was as simple as that. I believed in destiny probably more than most other things, and my gut kept telling me that she belonged to me and nobody else.

Some people spend their lifetime searching for that special someone, and I'd found her in the middle of the darkest period of my life. She was my beacon of light, my beginning and my ending. I couldn't spend the rest of my life thinking what would've been if I'd tried only a little bit harder.

I couldn't see it last night, too blinded by my own anger, but her fear was as palpable as the ice covering Alkey Lake. Instead of staying last night, making her tell me what was really wrong, I ran like a coward, too pissed off to talk it all out.

Did she make it home safe? Was she okay? Was she hurting today?

I never imagined that our first time would happen in a small forest overlooking the lake, but I guess that it only made sense that it happened there.

As children, we've spent countless hours skating there, dreaming of our futures. She wanted to be an Olympic medalist, and I wanted to play in the NHL. And unlike a lot of other people, unlike my own family, she never doubted me.

She never told me that my dreams were too big for a kid from a small town. She never told me that I couldn't do something. She was always the one pushing me to do better and better and better.

She never forsook me, and I wouldn't do the same.

With heavy limbs and an aching heart, I turned off the engine, determined to get this over with once and for all. Last night after texting my mom that I was going to the apartment in town, I switched off my phone, hiding from the rest of the world.

As I turned it on now, I knew I shouldn't have done

that.

Fifteen missed calls from Bianca and over a dozen from my mom greeted me as soon as the screen lit up. My heart clenched painfully, invisible hands of anxiety creeping through my bloodstream, and I knew without a doubt that something was wrong.

I looked toward Sophie's house, realizing that the lights were off. They should've been back by now.

She had a competition today. As much as it pained me not to be there for her, I knew that it wasn't the place or time to discuss what needed to be discussed. I stayed away, giving her some space to come to terms with what we were, no matter how much she tried fighting it.

With unnecessary force, I slammed the door of my car shut, and ran inside the house, my eyes frantically searching for my mom.

She wasn't working today, and I knew she was home.

I ran through the hallways, coming to a halt when I saw her hunched above the table in the dining room, looking smaller than she actually was.

"Mom?" My voice wobbled, too scared to hear what had happened.

She turned toward me, her cheeks flushed, her eyes red from crying, and then it started again. Her shoulders shook, her face contorted in pain, and without preamble, I crossed the distance between us, going down on my hunches right next to her.

"Mom, what's wrong?"

My hands shook as I placed them on her thigh, willing her to talk to me, to tell me what was wrong.

"Is it Dad?"

She shook her head, hiding her face from me.

"Is it Grandma? She sounded okay the last time I spoke to her." I tried pushing and pushing, but she continued crying, heart-wrenching sobs shaking her body. "I'm sorry I didn't answer my phone, but it was switched off. Is that why you're crying?"

"Oh, Noah." She suddenly turned to the side, toward me, and hugged me with all her might. "I'm so sorry, my boy," Mom said, squeezing me as tight as she could. "I'm so freaking sorry."

"Sorry about what?" I tried pulling back, but she wouldn't let me. "You're scaring me."

"I'm sorry." God, I wasn't sure if I wanted to know what was wrong.

"Sorry about what?" I finally managed to pull back and grabbed her hands instead. "Tell me what's wrong. Please?"

She pushed the loose strands of hair from my forehead, her eyes glistening with unshed tears, while her face as well as her neck had a crimson shade from all the crying.

"Did you watch one of those sad documentaries again?" I chuckled lightly, trying to change the mood. But that was the wrong thing to say, because her face again twisted with pain, and those crocodile tears started falling again.

"I-I love you so much. You know that, right?"

"Uh, I do. And I love you, too, but you gotta tell me what's wrong. Did something happen? Did somebody die?"

She pulled me closer to her, burying her head in the crook of my neck, wetting my shirt and my skin, shaking my body as well from the force of her own trembles.

"I will be here for you, okay? Whatever you need, baby."

"Mom." I pushed her away. "Tell. Me."

She stood up and with every passing second, my heart drummed faster, terrified of what was going to come out of her mouth.

Pacing the length of the dining room, from one side to the other, she turned to me suddenly, and I knew she was finally going to tell me what was wrong. Christine Kincaid was not a weak woman. She practically raised me by herself after my father decided that having a family was too much work.

She overcame the death of my younger brother and kept going forward. It took her a while to forget an awful night when their car went over the bridge, but she made it. Yet, seeing her like this scared the living crap out of me.

Pulling me up, I only then realized how petite she was, and how tall I was. With her hands wrapped tightly around mine, she sniffled before she connected her eyes with mine.

"It's Sophie, darling." What? "I want you to know that no matter what, we'll get through this together."

"What about Sophie, Mom?" My voice shook, my palms started getting sweaty. "What happened to Sophie?"

"Oh God." She placed her hand over her mouth, those tears free falling now.

"Mom." I took her by her shoulders, almost shaking her.

"You don't know, do you?"

"Know what?"

A heartbeat, two or three, maybe even a minute passed, until she said what I never imagined she was going to say.

"Sophie has cancer, Noah." *No. No. NO.* "She's dying, baby."

Her face blurred in front of me. Before I could understand what was happening, I was falling on my knees, chanting to myself as if that could change what she just said.

"No, no, no—"

"I'm so sorry, darling. I know how much you—"

"That's not true," I denied. "That can't be true."

Hot, angry tears rolled down my cheeks, connecting with my lips. My lips that not so long ago were devouring hers.

"It's true. I spoke with her mom a couple of hours ago. She's in Boston Memorial Hospital right now. She fell during the competition."

No. I should've been there. I should've been with her.

She couldn't be dying. She couldn't be leaving me.

We were going to grow old together. We were going to see the world together.

She was going to wear a white dress a few years from now, walking toward me down the aisle. She was going to have a round belly filled with our kids, while her eyes sparkled with joy. She was going to be my whole world.

How could my mom tell me that everything I envisioned was going to be just a foolish dream?

I was going to take her to Paris one day, and I was going to drop down on one knee right in front of the Eiffel Tower. She was going to say yes, because she loved me just as much as I loved her.

We were going to go to the same university. We were going to stay together forever.

Why? Fucking why was life this cruel?

"I don't believe you." My voice broke, my chest constricting, "I don't believe you!" I roared, planting my hands on the floor, letting the tears fall.

"Oh, Noah." My mom bent down and hugged me from above, but her touch was not the one I wanted right now.

"She can't be dying. She just can't." I looked up at her, begging her wordlessly to tell me that all of this was just a vile joke. "I can't lose her," I cried out. "I can't fucking lose her, Mom."

"I know, darling. I know," she cooed as she stroked my hair.

"I love her," I choked out. "And now I am going to lose her."

"She's still here. You can still make memories with her."

"But I don't want only memories!" I blasted out. "I wanted to have forever with her."

I wanted to have everything with her, but life had other plans.

NOAH

Life was just a series of fleeting moments; touches missed, happy little smiles, and painful tears. Some of them turned into memories that stayed with us forever, while others tended to fall into an abyss of dark onyx. But the worst part were the memories you had completely forgotten about, slamming into you full force, suddenly reminding you of those beautiful moments that somehow slipped away from you.

Moments that you took for granted because you didn't really know how important they were at the time they were happening.

And I took a lot of them for granted. I allowed myself to forget the beautiful sunny days when nothing else existed but Sophie and I, sitting beneath that tree, arguing over who was going to use the swing next. I always let her, because seeing that happiness on her face was enough to take me through the rest of those bleak days.

I allowed myself to forget about the crickets singing at night, while she sat there at her window, staring at the sky, trying to whisper so that our parents wouldn't find out that both of us stayed up after midnight on a school night. I forgot about that time she held my hand when her rabbit died, seeking comfort from me. That was the moment I knew—I would've walked through fire to make her happy, to make her smile.

Yet all I did over the last three months was make her cry. I made so many promises. I made so many plans, and all of them shattered like a house of cards as soon as those words left my mother's mouth.

Cancer.

Glioblastoma.

Terminal.

Terminal.

Terminal.

I gripped the steering wheel, my heart beating in the rhythm of the pouring rain as I drove through the streets of Boston, heading toward her. Words had the power to soothe and the power to hurt, but the ones I heard a couple of hours ago felt like a razor blade over my heart.

The end was never something any of us wanted to hear, and these tears falling down my cheeks fell for nothing. There was nothing I could do. I couldn't stop time, just to make the future I dreamed of come true.

I couldn't go back in time to tell her how much I loved her. Even if I could, all of this would still hurt the same. The outcome would still be the same even if I did things differently. It would still shatter my soul, even though I tried telling myself that it would've been better not knowing her at all.

But every single time those thoughts entered my mind, another sharp claw dragged over the left chamber of my heart, leaving a bloody trail behind. Guilt crept through my veins, because how could I think like that?

No matter what—pain, love, eternity, or just a blip in time—I would still choose her. If I had to go through the same thing over and over again, I would still choose to know her, to meet her, to love her.

As I parked in front of Boston Memorial Hospital, with my heart in my throat, and my soul lost somewhere in the past, I stared at the stark white facade and the darkening streaks from the top of the building, rain coloring it gray with its touch.

The hardest thing I ever had to do was to get up from that floor and accept that my mom was telling the truth. Wasn't that fucked up, huh? Sophie was barely eighteen years old, barely old enough to learn how to drive. She still hadn't seen anything.

She wouldn't get to live her life.

She would never get to have kids.

She would never get to travel all over the world like she always wanted to.

She would never become an Olympic champion.

And I... I would never get to hold her hand throughout it all. I just... I had no idea what I felt.

The tears that started when my mom told me what was going on hadn't stopped until now. I wasn't sure if I was angry or devastated. I wanted to punch something.

I wanted to climb on top of the hill and scream and scream and scream until my body couldn't take it anymore, because this... This wasn't fair.

It wasn't fucking fair, and I was helpless. I couldn't do anything. I couldn't suddenly cure her or give her hope. I didn't have to be a doctor to understand that terminal meant the end. I just never imagined I would ever have to face something like this.

I never imagined that the girl I loved would be going through something like this.

God, and here I was, sitting inside my car, while she lay hidden behind the walls of this hospital, probably scared, and I was paralyzed to get up and go to her. I wanted to be strong, but every single step I took, every mile I passed while driving here, every heartbeat, felt like a ticking time bomb. It was the time that we didn't have.

Mom didn't have enough information to answer all my questions, and I dreaded hearing those answers from Sophie. I dreaded hearing how much time we had left.

Life wasn't supposed to be lived like this, waiting for that expiration date to come. I knew it was ridiculous thinking like this because all of us lived and all of us died, but not all of us had to think about dying at the age of eighteen when we were just starting our life.

Not all of us had to think about the life that could've been if the disease hadn't come knocking at our door.

Not all of us had to imagine what her funeral would look like, and what color her casket would be.

I wasn't supposed to be sitting in front of the hospital, trembling from fear, because I didn't want to break in front of her. I was supposed to be knocking on the door of her house to beg her to forgive me. I was supposed to hug her and kiss her and show her how good the two of us would be.

This, all of this, just felt wrong.

I dragged my hand over my face and killed the engine, sitting in complete silence, gathering the courage I needed to go inside. My palm was wet from the tears, and when I looked at myself in the rearview mirror, my bloodshot eyes stared back at me, shining with anguish. I bent down to pick up the flower bouquet I bought as a knock sounded from my left side.

I turned around, holding the bouquet of sunflowers in my right hand. My eyes collided with Andrew's. Sophie's brother looked like he walked through hell and back as he stood there in the pouring rain.

Water dripped from the ends of his hair, the color a couple of shades darker, drenched from rain, and the pair of hollow eyes and his hollow soul seared through my own.

He knew why I was here. With a nod, he took a small step back, allowing me to open the door.

A gust of cold air enveloped me into its hug as soon as I stepped out, and I decided to leave the sunflowers inside, careful not to get them touched by rain. I had no idea how the florist even had them. As soon as I saw them, something squeezed around my heart, a melody so long forgotten, a childish laughter and the visual of Sophie running through the field of sunflowers located close to Alkey Lake, and I knew I had to get them.

"Andy," I croaked, letting the rain fall over me.

Silence greeted me as he stood there with his hands on his hips, just looking at me, as if he was measuring me. In a way, I guess he was, and I would too if I were in his position. I wasn't here to cause trouble, and the knowing look passed over his face.

His hug came out of nowhere, and I welcomed it with open arms, wrapping myself around his larger frame, grabbing a fistful of his wet shirt in my hands. I had no idea which one of us trembled, or which one of us cried, but we both shook with the unspoken words and the pain connecting us.

Andrew was the first one to pull back, shaking the rain from his hair, before I asked, "Is she inside?"

My voice didn't sound like my own, and this was exactly why I took my time to get here. I had to calm myself down. I didn't trust myself enough to walk in there and see her in the hospital bed, where she should've never been in the first place.

Andrew was just three years older than Sophie and me, but looking at him now, standing here like two idiots while rain pelted all over us, he seemed like he had aged ten years overnight. His eyes were tired, lines marring the soft skin around them, and the dark circles he usually didn't have threw a sharp contrast to his pale skin.

It wasn't so much about what he looked like right now, but what his eyes were telling me. Hollowness, pain, it was suffocating him. For a moment there, when my mom told me what was going on with Sophie, I only thought about myself and what I felt.

I thought about everything we would never be able to do, but I never, not once, thought about her family—about Mr. and Mrs. Anderson, or Andrew.

The problem with sickness was that it was never only one person that was affected. Families, friends, all those people that loved you, they all suffered together with you.

Andrew didn't speak. I had a feeling that he didn't trust himself any more than I trusted myself. With a somber nod, he indicated toward the hospital and started walking before I could ask another question.

The darkened sky cried as we walked toward the entrance, and the need to both run and stay was waging war inside of me. Fear like no other gripped my insides, sending my stomach into a turmoil. The strong smell of chemicals slammed into me as soon as we stepped through the sliding door, and seeing the doctors and nurses running all over the place froze me to the spot.

My eyes were stuck on a little boy, no older than ten, sitting next to an elderly woman in one of the chairs close to the reception. Tired eyes and a crooked smile were there while she talked to him, but there was no shine in either one of those.

His hair was shaven, or maybe it fell out, and the urge to run away started prevailing while this kid, much younger than me, turned around and looked at me.

God.

I didn't want to have this kid, who was probably going through hell, see me cry, but as my bottom lip trembled, a hand wrapped around my bicep. I looked to the side, only to see Andrew with glossy eyes and flaring nostrils.

"Don't stop, Noah. Trust me, you don't want to stop before we reach her room."

I wasn't sure if I nodded or if he just dragged me away before I could collapse right there at the reception area. I tried to tune out the noises, the kids crying, and the wailing of a woman hunched next to the wall.

Before today, hospitals weren't places where I felt like I was trying to catch my breath, but today... Today I saw what devastation looked like. A man stood by her, rubbing circles on her back while her body shook from the force of her sobs.

"My God," I said out loud, earning another sad look from Andrew.

"It's hard, isn't it?" he asked. "Seeing all of this. Seeing that all those things we usually complain about are nothing compared to this. The first time we brought Sophie for a checkup, I had to run outside, crying like a little baby. I cried for all these people fighting the battle that had no end. I cried for all of us—the families, the friends that had to watch our loved ones go through something like this—you know? I thought I knew hardship and pain, but everything I went through so far, dude, it had nothing on this."

"I—I just..." I trailed off, keeping my eyes to the front, trying to avoid seeing anything else. "I didn't know." My voice broke. "God, I didn't know."

"She didn't want you to know. Nobody knew, Noah. She wanted us to keep quiet about it."

"But why?" I asked, suddenly angry. Not at her, not at

the fact that she didn't tell me, but at the unfairness of all of this.

Why were some people destined for things like this? Why would destiny, a God, or whatever you believed in, take young people so soon? Where was the justice in that?

What was the fucking reason?

"Why, what?"

"Why wouldn't she tell us?"

"Because she didn't want you to look at her like she was dying." It felt as if he slapped me. "She wanted you guys to look at her as if she was more than this broken and sick person. She's still Sophie, you know. She's still the girl you love."

"I don't—"

"Don't lie to me, Noah. Something happened between the two of you. I don't care, but it's obvious that what you feel for her is more than just friendship. I don't look at my friends the way you look at her."

I had no idea what to say. I couldn't deny it, but I couldn't exactly tell him that I had wanted his sister for years. It felt inappropriate to talk about it with him.

"We're here," Andrew announced just as we came to the end of the hallway. "My parents aren't here at the moment. They went to the hotel to change and take a nap. She's sleeping, but you're more than welcome to stay as long as you want to. I have a feeling that you won't be going home tonight."

"I-I… Thank you." Words weren't enough to tell him how I felt, and even that simple thank-you felt like too little for what he just did.

"It's okay, Noah. I saw you sitting there in that car of yours, and I knew that look on your face. I looked the same when I drove all the way to the hospital after my mom called me. I wished that I had somebody with me, because it would've felt much easier walking through those doors and to Sophie's room."

"Does it get easier? Walking through that door?"

He stood silent for a second, turning his head to look at the ceiling. "I thought it would," he answered. "I thought I could be strong for her, strong for my family, but every time she's here, it feels as if the world around me suddenly lost all its light. It doesn't get easier, but I guess that in a way, you get used to it. You get used to this smell. You get used to the monitors beeping, children crying, and parents rushing out of the rooms, trying to hide their own tears."

My heart hammered with each word he uttered.

"Look, Noah… I've known you since you were a kid. We practically grew up together as well. I don't have to tell you that's my little sister in there. I like you, but I won't hesitate to punch you in your face if you make her cry again."

"Again?"

"You can be really daft sometimes." He chuckled. "Go inside, please. I'm gonna get myself some coffee. Call me if you need anything."

She was crying because of me?

Of course she was crying, you fucking idiot. What did you expect? That she was going to be happy when you broke all contact?

I shook my hand, showing an imaginary middle finger to my ugly subconscious mind, and took a step forward the white door with *Room 801* written in black, block letters.

The door seemed to grow with each passing second, and my breathing changed from the calm one I had just a minute ago, to a choppy, irregular one.

Goddammit.

I was a fucking coward. I was an idiot for thinking that I could be here for her when I was shattering on the inside.

But this wasn't about me. This wasn't about my pain, my wants, and needs. This was about Sophie.

My beautiful Sophie who was going through literal hell.

I swallowed the rising nausea and clasped my hand around the doorknob and pressed down, pushing the door open.

The beeping sound of the machine monitoring her heart was the first thing I heard as I entered the darkened room. Two lamps stood lit up on each side of the bed, casting a warm, yellow light over her face.

Machines I never saw in my life, stood on the other side of the bed, and the IV drip, already halfway finished, was connected to her right arm.

My eyes glazed over the scary machines, over the white walls and the television showing an unknown movie, and moved to her.

To the sleeping beauty.

Somewhere in the back of my mind, when my mom told me about her condition, my brain pushed these terrifying pictures that she wouldn't look like my Sophie anymore. I guessed that in order to understand what was going on, our brain pushed us in the direction where we couldn't see the person anymore, but only the disease eating them alive.

But now, as I stood here next to her bed, my hands shaking with the need to touch her, to see if she was still breathing, she still looked like my girl.

My fragile girl.

Her small frame looked even smaller in the massive bed, covered by a blue blanket all the way to her chest. The ashen color of her skin did nothing to appease the monster inside of me that wanted to save her and keep her far away from everybody else. And those dark circles around her eyes and the tubes connected with oxygen... They sent my anxiety into overdrive. Before I knew what I was doing, I was standing next to her right side, right where her arm was.

Unable to stand anymore, unable to keep the emotions at bay, I dropped down on my knees and took her hand into mine, brushing my thumb over her knuckles.

"I'm so sorry, Soph," I sobbed. The tears attacked me without a warning. The anguish that ran through me before felt like nothing compared to the sobs shaking my body now. "I'm sorry I didn't know," I continued. "I'm sorry I abandoned you when you needed me the most. Words aren't sufficient to explain what I feel for you, but I just hope you will find it in yourself to forgive me."

I looked up, craving to see those forest-green eyes open, to have them look at me, but she kept them shut. An angry-looking cut above her left eye stared back at me, and I remembered that she fell during her routine.

"I should've been there, Soph." I glared at the bandage around her head and the dried blood on her hair. This anger, it felt like a living, breathing thing. It was slowly spreading from my chest, through my veins, all the way to my head, but there was no person that I could throw it at.

Nobody was at fault, yet I blamed myself.

I blamed myself for the heartache I caused her. I blamed myself for being a shitty friend. I blamed myself for all those missed opportunities and years we had behind us, where we could've been much more than just friends.

If I were a braver man, I would've been holding her close to my chest a lot sooner, but I missed it. Now it was obvious to me that her tiredness didn't come just because of school or her practices.

I googled what glioblastoma was, and I wished I hadn't —headaches, dizziness, vision problems, and much more. I should've asked her, pushed more, but I retreated like the coward I was.

"I need you to open your eyes, Soph," I whispered, caressing her cheek. I dropped my head down, my forehead touching her arm. "I need you to tell me how you're feeling. You were always so vocal about the things that bothered you, and I need you to talk to me. Tell me to fuck off if you want to, but just wake up."

The rational part of my brain knew that she was only sleeping, but the irrational one—the one that feared that every single moment I spent away from her was a moment missed—wanted her to open her eyes. That part of me wanted to hear her voice, to see her smile, to have her yell and laugh at me.

I wanted to lie to myself for a little bit longer so that she didn't disappear right in front of my eyes.

"Noah?" came from my left, and with superhuman speed, I lifted my head, my eyes colliding with green ones.

"Sophie!" I jumped up while her eyes fluttered open and closed, her body fighting to stay awake. "Hey, hey, don't move," I warned when she started lifting her arm that was attached to the IV drip. "You'll fuck up your IV."

Confusion swirled in her eyes, as she struggled to keep them open, blinking rapidly. Not even a minute passed before the confusion disappeared, replaced by realization.

Her eyes connected with mine, her lower lip wobbled, and I could see it right there, staring back at me—she didn't want me to know about this.

"You know?" It was a question, a whisper, really. "God," she groaned and started pulling herself upward.

"Soph—"

"You weren't supposed to know," she cried out, avoiding looking at me. "I didn't want you to know." Anguish, anger, pain, they all sliced through me while she struggled to keep upright. "They weren't supposed to tell you until you went off to college."

"What?"

"I didn't want you to know, Noah."

I took a step back, my skin blazing as if she'd slapped me. But somewhere between the anger and the pain I felt, I understood.

"You didn't want me to stay." I didn't have to ask, I already knew.

She shook her head. "No." She looked down, locating the button I didn't know about, and the backrest of the bed started lifting, letting her sit as she intended.

"Baby—"

"I didn't want you to suffer, too," she cried out. "I didn't want you to see me like this, you know? I wanted you to remember me how I used to be, not this broken shell, getting eaten from the inside out." Her chest shook as a shuddering breath tore through her.

"Sophie." I came closer to her. "Look at me." She kept her head turned to the other side. "Sophie, please." My own voice shook with the plea. "I understand." I took her hand in mine again. "Trust me, I do. I'm not happy about it, but I understand."

"I wanted you to be happy."

"Darling, please look at me."

"Why?" She turned her head, keeping the tears at bay. "I don't want you here."

"I don't care. I'm not leaving you alone."

"I'm not alone," she gritted out. "I have Andrew, and my parents, and—"

"I. Am. Not. Leaving." I kneeled next to her bed and lifted her hand, pressing the back of it to my lips. "I'm sorry, babe, but you're stuck with me."

It felt like an eternity passed before she started talking

again, the only sound in the room were my breathing, her sobs, and the beeping of the machines.

"I'm scared," she muttered, shaking. "I'm so scared, Noah."

"Baby—"

"I never got to do anything. I wanted to live. I fucking wanted to live!" she yelled out. Those tears she was keeping at bay now free falling down her cheeks. "I wanted to see the world, to be in love, to have the life I always dreamed of, and now... None of those things will ever come to be." I had no words, because nothing I said would be enough to extinguish this anguish spilling over the edges of her soul. "I wanted to grow old, Noah. There were so many things I wanted to do, a-and it all got fucked up."

"Darling," I choked out, wiping the tears from her face. "You can still do them." I kept repeating to myself that I had to be strong, but seeing her like this—crying and broken—I could feel my resolve wavering. "We can do them together."

We both knew I was lying, because half of those things, just like she said, she would never get to do.

"I'm sorry I didn't tell you."

"I'm sorry I was an asshole," I said. "I'm sorry I wasted so much time without telling you how I really felt."

"I was such a bitch last night. God, I just didn't want you to see me like this. I thought it would be easier pushing you away, but I was lying to myself."

"Shhh, it's okay. I'm here now." I leaned down and pressed my lips against her forehead, hating how cold she seemed. "Everything is going to be okay."

"But it won't." She shuddered. I couldn't lie to her. I was trying to find a bright spot, just a little bit of light, but nothing about this situation was okay. "Will you hold me?"

She moved her head up and looked at me. "I-I just... I don't wanna be alone."

I blinked, then blinked some more, pushing these traitorous tears back. "Of course. Anything you need."

A tight-lipped smile appeared out of nowhere, and she started moving, scooting to the other side of the bed.

I bent down and untied the laces on the boots I wore, uncaring that the chilling air of the room started seeping into my bones through the wet clothes from earlier. But my own comfort would have to wait. I couldn't stop my heart from beating like crazy at the mere thought that I was going to have her in my arms.

I shook off the leather jacket, letting it fall to the floor, and lifted myself up onto the bed, positioning us so that her back faced my front. She kept the hand with the IV straight on the bed as I wrapped my arm around her waist, spreading my palm across her stomach.

She placed her hand over mine as a contented sigh escaped from her mouth.

"Better?" I asked, nuzzling her neck. "Let me know if you want me to move."

"Oh, Noah." She turned her head toward me and smiled. "I will always want you with me, no matter what. This is my favorite place. This is what I've been missing."

16

SOPHIE

Years ago, we had a dog my brother and I named Max. I could still remember the day we went to pick him up in the middle of rainy May, when the skies threatened to fall on us and when the thunders were the only things decorating the dome above us.

He was the most beautiful thing I had ever seen. A small, black body with patches of brown over his paws and his snout, and two brown circles above his eyes, and a tail that wiggled as soon as he spotted Andy and me. When our dad told us that we were finally going to get a puppy— a Rottweiler puppy—I spent days and nights trying to find out everything I could about their breed.

But nothing could ever prepare me for the amount of love I felt from that first moment I saw him.

While his brothers and sisters kept running around, hiding behind their mother, Max came all the way to the fence, wanting to play with us. I knew he was it. I knew he was supposed to come home with us.

He fell asleep in my lap while we drove back home. From that moment on, he and I were inseparable. I would wake up in the morning with him lying at the foot of my bed, waiting to start the day.

I would come back from school, and he would be there, waiting for me on the front porch, happiness radiating from his body.

But one morning... One morning Max couldn't get up to play with me. He couldn't even get out of my room, and that was when I knew. Even though my parents downplayed it after they took him to the vet. Even though Andy said that he just caught a small bug and would recover, I knew.

Three days later, I woke up and ran downstairs, wanting to hug him good morning, but he wasn't at his usual spot. Mom wouldn't meet my eyes, and Dad was already gone. They told me that they took him for a checkup since he seemed to be feeling better, but even in the mind of an eight-year-old, something sinister was whispering that it was the end.

That day, Max wasn't waiting for me on the front porch. His warm and friendly eyes weren't shining when he saw me, and when I saw the grim faces of my parents, the dam broke.

"*I'm sorry, darling,*" my dad whispered then, kissing my head, while the tears streamed down my cheeks and sobs racked my body.

"*He's not in pain anymore, bubba. He's in Heaven now.*" My mom tried to soothe my wounds, holding my hands.

"*But I just wanted him to stay with me. I wanted him to stay forever, Mom.*" I cried and cried and cried, but none of my tears could bring back my loyal friend.

"*Death is part of life, my love. We are born, we live, and we die. Isn't it wonderful that we get to go through this wonderful thing called life, even if it's just for a moment, huh? He's gone, but he will forever be remembered. He will forever live here.*" She pressed her hand against my heart. "*He will always be with us.*"

I didn't get it then. How could I when all I wanted, all I needed, was for him to come back?

But I got it now. I understood what my mom wanted to tell me. I understood because the death I hated so much for him was now coming for me.

Death haunted me since I was just a child, and now it had finally caught up with me.

"No, no." My mom shook her head, waking me up from the memory. She stared at Doctor Mathias with tears in her eyes. "Isn't there anything that we can do? Something—" Her voice broke.

"I really am sorry, but the area where the cancer is located is too risky."

"Please," she begged. "There must be something."

I turned my head to the side and looked at the old grandfather clock while the sobs from my mom filled the room.

"There's nothing, truly."

"She's only eighteen!" my mom suddenly roared. "Only eighteen years old. Oh God."

"Davina." Dad's voice tore through the misery, holding the edge of hollowness. "It's going to be okay."

"It's not going to be okay. None of this is okay."

The clock ticked and ticked and ticked, taking seconds and minutes away from me. Slowly, painfully, the future I planned was becoming blurry and every tick, tick, tick from the clock was just a reminder of it.

A hand gripped my own, and I knew it was my mom holding me. She wanted to comfort me, I knew that, but the ugly and sad truth was that she was trying to keep me next to her.

All of us in this room knew what the future held for me. We all knew that my body worked against me, that there was a ticking time bomb inside my brain.

Inoperable, was the first word Doctor Mathias said.

It grew, was the next thing he mentioned, while his eyes held sorrow so deep that even without him saying those words, I already knew.

We were too late.

I wanted to shake my head. I wanted to tell him to check his records again, to do something, anything.

Things like this couldn't happen to me. Impossible wasn't a word I had in my vocabulary. But as he went over the prognosis with my parents, I felt as if I was looking from the outside in. My body was here, but my mind… My mind was far away from here, observing all of this with detached feelings. What else could I do?

I cried a river of tears after they first diagnosed me. I cried some more when they sent me home with a bag full of medicine I didn't even know how to pronounce, in hopes that they would help with the shrinking of the cancerous cells. Those little, white pills still gave me hope, even when they made me sick.

Even when I wanted nothing more than to go to sleep and never wake up again, they gave me hope that I would be strong enough to beat this and live to talk about it.

But back there on that ice, where my past and future collided and where my vision started disappearing, some-thing deep inside me knew. It always knew, but I was too stubborn to see it in the beginning.

Hope is a dangerous thing in situations like these, and I used it like an addict. Hoping and hoping and fucking hoping for a miracle, but waking up in the hospital told me everything I needed to know—I was going to die.

I looked at the other side of the office, seeing all the diplomas and accomplishments Doctor Mathias had, and those invisible claws that were slowly coming closer to my heart finally reached their destination. They squeezed, pressing against my left heart chamber, pushing the blood out faster, and the first tear slowly escaped from my eye. Like a thief in the middle of the night, it fell silently, leaving a trail of broken dreams behind.

I would never get to see my diploma hanging on the wall like that. I would never get to stand on top of the podium at the Olympic Games, holding that golden medal. I would never get to see the gray hair on my mother's head, or to see Andy get married.

Maybe in another life, another me would get to live the life I always wanted to have. I looked at my mom, at her blonde hair pulled on top of her head, and my dad's hands firmly gripping her shoulders.

His lips were set in a thin line while his eyes shone with unshed tears, holding on by a thread. I never thought I would see the day where my parents cried over something like this. Looking at my mom, I only now realized how dark the circles around her eyes were. She was always so happy, so supportive, always there for us. Looking at this version of her now, she was nothing but a shell of the person she used to be.

I didn't want to listen to them. I didn't want to listen to the words spoken out loud, even though we all knew what they were. They kept going and going on repeat inside my head, but for some reason, they didn't feel as scary as they did the first time around.

"How long?" I turned to Doctor Mathias, cutting my mom off. I knew she wanted to save me. I knew she wanted to see me live, but sitting here and arguing with the doctor that was nothing but supportive from the very beginning would not miraculously heal me.

It wouldn't give me the years my mom was trying to hold on to, and wasting time was something I didn't want to do—not anymore.

"Sophie!" my mom exclaimed, while all three sets of eyes zeroed in on me, as if they suddenly remembered that I was here in the room with them. They kept talking and talking and talking about possible treatments, more drugs, more chemo, invasive techniques, but none of them asked me what I wanted.

"How long, Doctor?" I asked again, keeping my eyes firmly on his. "I have the right to know."

"Soph—"

"How fucking long?"

Doctor Mathias cleared his throat and closed his eyes. I bet that telling a person that they were going to die, or that their life had an expiration date, was never an easy thing to say, but he could do it. He wasn't the one sitting on this side of the table, waiting to hear when death was going to knock on their door.

"Four," he murmured. "Maybe five months."

"No!" Mom cried out and buried her face in my dad's stomach.

And me… I couldn't feel it.

Five months?

I maybe had five months to live if I was lucky.

Doctor Mathias's lips moved but I couldn't hear a thing.

Five fucking months and I'd be gone.

I had five months to do everything I wanted to do. I had five months to tell them how much I loved them. I had five months to be okay with the fact that I was dying before I even got to live.

"Sophie, we can do something. I'm sure we can." The grip on my hand increased. "We need to—"

"No, Mom." I looked at her, hating the hope in her eyes. Hating it because I would have to shatter it now. "I'm not doing any of those treatments."

"Sophie!" my dad thundered. "You can't just—"

"Give up?" I smiled. "I'm not giving up, but I also don't want to spend the rest of my time in a hospital bed. I want to run next to the lake. I want to go out and kiss the boy I liked. I want to see you guys at breakfast in the morning, and I want us to spend as much time as possible together. I don't want to be hooked on machines that can't do anything for me. I don't want to hope when it leads to nothing but more misery all of us are going to feel."

"Bubba." His lower lip wobbled. "We can still have all those things."

"We can't if I end up being paralyzed for the rest of my days when that brain operation goes wrong. We also can't if I keep vomiting fifteen times a day, unable to hold anything down. You know what this is, Dad. You know how it ends."

Silence greeted me, all three of them looking either at me or at the floor. I could almost see the arguments forming inside their heads, but I wasn't budging.

"I'm an adult," I argued. "I can make my own decisions, and this is the one I'm making now."

"Please, baby," Mom cried, pleading at me with her eyes. "We need to try."

"No, Mom." I placed my hand on top of hers. "We don't. I want to be remembered for looking like this." I pointed at myself. "With my hair, with my smile, and wickedly good at chess."

The first tear rolled down my father's cheek, followed by another one, until they all fell freely. He wasn't holding them anymore. He wasn't holding himself anymore.

From the moment they diagnosed me with cancer, he started pulling away. I didn't think that he did it consciously, but rather to protect himself in a way. I also knew that he tried to hide his tears from me, but now, as we all faced a dark future, he let it all go.

Now in the end, he finally understood.

Maybe I couldn't understand death back then, but I understood now.

My mom laid her head on my shoulder, her body rocking with silent sobs, stroking my hand with hers and murmuring soft, calming words to herself.

They couldn't accept it; I could see that. But back there between the ice and air, between past and future, between good and bad, I knew what was coming. I think I knew for a while, I just didn't want to believe that something like this could happen to my family.

I didn't think that something like this happened to young people like me, but death wasn't picky. Death and sickness did not have an age limit. They just took and took, and what was worse, they weren't only taking away lives.

They tore families apart. They left wounds that never healed.

They shrouded our lives in darkness, covered us with a veil of pain, laughing at the sorrow flowing through our veins.

"It's gonna be okay, Mom," I murmured and tapped her hand with my own. "Everything is going to be okay."

"Oh God. I'm supposed to be consoling you, not the other way around."

Dad took a step back and pulled one of the chairs from the back, settling himself behind us. One of his arms landed on me, hugging me from behind, while the other one wrapped around Mom. The two of them shook, cried, and cursed, while I sat there as still as a statue, unable to put these emotions into words.

"I'm going to—" Doctor Mathias started talking when

the door burst open, revealing Andy with two coffee cups in his hands.

His eyes landed on us, then on Doctor Mathias, then back on us. I knew that even if I left this world and never remembered who I used to be, I would remember the look on his face.

"No." He shook his head. "No, no, no." He entered the office and dropped the cups on top of the desk and came right to me. "Please tell me it isn't what I think it is."

Fear, as palpable as my pulse, was all around us— hollow sadness, broken souls, and an eternity of broken dreams.

"I'm sorry, Andy," I said as he dropped to his knees on my right side.

"How long?" Anger laced his words, but I knew it wasn't aimed at me. Just like my anger wasn't aimed at my doctors or at my family, but it was still there.

It was the worst kind of anger. The kind that came from a place deep within ourselves, that didn't have one concrete direction. It didn't have a person or an object you could be angry at. Instead of trying to find that one thing you could direct it at, you ended up being angry and snappy at all those people you cared about.

"Four months." I smiled. "Maybe five."

"That's fucking bullshit!"

"Andy!" Mom chastised from my left, but my eyes stayed glued to Andy.

His hair was disheveled, hours and hours of hands running through the dark strands. Lines around his eyes— lines that shouldn't be visible on the face of a young man.

And it was all because of me.

"I'm sorry, Andy."

I was sorry. Sorry for the pain they had to go through. Sorry for everything bad I ever did, for every foul word and every dark thought toward him. I was sorry for the life I was going to miss.

I was sorry for myself, for my plans.

I mourned the little girl that thought she could take on the world if she only believed hard enough. I mourned my childhood, my adulthood, my old age that I would never get to see. I mourned a young Sophie, the Sophie of this present and the Sophie of the future.

I was just starting to live. I was just starting to figure out things that I truly wanted to do. I was just gearing up for the amazing things I was capable of, but none of it mattered. Nothing mattered anymore.

Andy's fingers dug into the meat of my thigh, digging in deeper, as if he too was trying to hold on to me like my mom. He dropped his head to my lap, his shoulders shaking, his gargantuan size suddenly looking much smaller.

I placed my hand on his hair, dragging my fingers through the short strands at the back of his head. They needed this; this tiny moment of misery, because I knew that as soon as we stepped out of this office, they would try to pretend that everything was okay.

"I'll give you a moment," Doctor Mathias said as he stood up from his chair and started heading toward the door. At the last moment, he turned toward me, for the first time talking directly to me. "We'll discuss pain relief options for the months that are coming, but in the meantime, just think about what you'd like to do."

I would like to live, I wanted to tell him.

I would like to wake up from this terrible nightmare. I would like to pretend that none of this was happening, even if just for a moment.

I nodded. "Thank you. For everything."

"I didn't really do anything, Sophie. And I'm sorry I didn't. I'm sorry we aren't able to do anything about this."

I was sorry too, but most of all, I was sorry that my loved ones had to go through this.

It wasn't supposed to be like this.

It wasn't supposed to hurt this much.

I was supposed to die in sixty or seventy years in my sleep. I was supposed to have gray hair and a suitcase full of memories, not this tragedy.

I was supposed to be many things, but I wasn't supposed to die this young.

SOPHIE

It was so easy to forget that the rest of the world kept going as if nothing was happening, while my life was crumbling to pieces.

Three weeks after the competition where I got another seizure, ended up in the hospital, and where I had to face the hardest decision I had ever made, I was finally able to come back home.

Noah stayed with me for as long as he could, but he still had to go back to school and for his practices. I didn't dare to ask how many classes he missed or how much his coach was going to kill him, but it seemed as if he didn't give a fuck about the outside world.

Between those four walls inside the hospital, I felt as if I could breathe again.

And wasn't it fucked up that the place that gave me so much anxiety felt so safe? I knew why, though.

It was Noah and his calming presence. It was Noah and his smiles, and those eyes that still saw too much. It was Noah that didn't start behaving like I was a different person but kept talking about normal things.

We never discussed the elephant in the room, apart

from that first day when he just came, but I could see that he wanted to talk about it. I just wasn't ready.

I didn't think that any one of us was ready to talk about the fact that in a few months there was going to be nothing of us, but a tombstone and things we used to do. I couldn't tell Noah that every single day I woke up, I thanked whatever force there was in the sky, because it was another opportunity for me to live.

In the beginning, I blamed myself for not going to the doctor earlier. I thought I was just tired, or maybe I put too many things on my plate. Headaches, dizziness, lack of appetite, I pushed it all aside thinking they were nothing more but passing things.

I was so fucking wrong.

I still remembered the day when I collapsed on the ice for the first time. Two weeks after Noah and I stopped talking, I dragged myself to practice, already feeling like shit from everything combined. And there it happened—the first seizure.

First of many.

Rapid growth, the doctor said.

Stage four.

Terminal.

Months.

We are so sorry, Sophie.

I could still hear my mother's scream filled with anguish, and Andrew's face when he came to the hospital that day. I still remembered the tears in my father's eyes, and the abrupt exit he made when he couldn't hold them in anymore. It was the first time I saw my father cry. It was the first time my mom couldn't look at me, and the first time for Andrew to be unable to keep it together.

And me... I just lay that in that bed, still trying to

connect the dots and to understand the gravity of the situation.

I was dying.

Every day, every hour, minute, and second mattered. Movies never painted the real picture of what it felt like knowing that in a few months you wouldn't be walking on this earth anymore.

Anger was the first emotion that tore through my walls when we came home after the hospital. Scorching hot, like an inferno burning inside me, it spread through my body, tingling on the tips of my fingers and toes, and I wanted to shout, to kick something, to break things, because it wasn't fair.

It wasn't fair I had to go through this, even though I knew that a thousand other people went through the same. Statistics were there, I read them, and I wasn't an exception of a rule.

Cancer could find you, no matter how old or young you were. It didn't have a preference of gender, age, race or religion, it picked the first person, and like a silent killer, you wouldn't even be aware it was there until it was too late to do anything.

Why me? I asked myself so many times I became tired of those two words. I could ask and ask and ask, but the outcome would always be the same—I was still going to leave my loved ones.

But anger quickly got replaced by sadness, and before I knew it, I was unable to get out of bed. What was the point when I didn't have anything to live for? What was the point of going out, pretending everything was okay, when I knew that going to school, going for practices, doing any of those things was futile?

I would never go to college, and I would never get to go to the Olympics. So why should I try?

But just like always, its best friend slithered faster than I could recover, and numbness took over. I didn't take any of my meds. I didn't eat, didn't sleep, and I didn't care about anything.

While my mom cried, I stood there unable to feel anything. And I loved feeling like that.

There was no fear, no sadness, no anger, just a huge emptiness taking place inside my chest. I knew it wasn't healthy, I knew I had to process and cry and be angry, but I couldn't.

Every time I looked at myself in the mirror, I didn't see myself, but a girl who stopped fighting.

My therapist told me it was normal to feel like that, and when all those emotions I was suppressing came back, I was once again suffocating.

Even now, as I stared at my reflection in the mirror, it felt as if a stranger stared back. My cheeks were sunken, my eyes lost their glow. My shiny hair wasn't so shiny anymore, and even though I knew that all those were such silly things to think about, I couldn't stop myself.

Here I was, an expiration date stamped on my back, and all I cared about was my physical appearance.

"Soph," came from the door to my room, Noah's voice pulling me back to reality.

"In the bathroom," I called out and turned on the water to wash my face.

Just like he promised, he was the one constant in my life. Bianca came a couple of times, still angry and hurt that I didn't tell her about my condition.

Condition. I wanted to laugh.

When did I become a condition and not a person?

"Are you okay?" Noah asked from the doorway, his eyes searing into the side of my face. I stopped telling him to leave me alone on the third day when he held me down and pressed his lips against mine, effectively shutting me up.

I wished I could tell him to fuck off, to leave me alone, to go and live his life and forget about me, but I couldn't. I clung to him like a newborn baby to its mother, and I didn't want to let go.

He never asked questions I didn't want to answer, but I could see them dancing behind his eyes. I could see the exhaustion marring his face, but pushing him away wasn't an answer anymore.

"Just peachy." I smiled, lifting my head to look at him. "What are you doing here?"

Sundays were usually reserved for his games or practices. I picked up my phone and looked at the time.

"Shouldn't you be at the rink or something?"

"Well." He came inside the bathroom and closed the door behind him. "Coach gave us all a day off, and I was thinking." He stepped closer to me, his eyes hooded, his voice deeper. "Maybe we could do something together."

Just like me, Noah loved pretending that the cancer ticking inside my head didn't even exist. And I was grateful for it. I knew it ate him alive, but it was his choice to stick around.

"Like what?" I asked, suddenly breathless. His palms landed on the sides of my head, holding me in place. He stroked my cheek with his thumb and started lowering his head toward mine. My eyes landed on his lips, and I wanted, no, I needed him to fucking kiss me.

He touched me, stroked my skin, played with my body, but he didn't kiss me again. He didn't try to have sex, he didn't do anything I wanted him to do, and if these were the last months for me, I wanted them to be filled with good things.

I wanted him to have good memories that would one day overcome the bad ones.

"You remember how you said that you won't get to do all these things you wanted to do?"

I nodded. "Yeah?"

"I have an idea." He grinned. "I'm not sure if you're gonna like it or not, but still."

"What kind of idea?" I didn't like where this was going.

"Come." He grasped my hand in his much bigger one and turned around, opening the door of the bathroom. As soon as we stepped inside the room, I could see the rays of sun coming through the window, loving the much nicer April weather.

I looked toward my bed, seeing a notebook that definitely didn't belong to me.

"What's this?" I looked at him.

"It's for you."

"Me?"

"No, dummy, for Casper the Friendly Ghost." He snickered. "Yeah, you."

"But what is it for?"

He let go of my hand and walked toward the bed. He sat down and lifted the notebook, turning it toward me. "It's for your bucket list."

"My bucket list?"

"Are you just going to repeat everything I say today? Yeah, your bucket list. The things you wanna do."

"I don't understand."

"Soph." He stood up and dropped the notebook on top of the bed and walked toward me. "I know that you won't have enough time. Trust me, I fucking know. But I also don't want you to just sit inside this house as time passes. I want you to do all these things, you know? Maybe they

L.K. REID

won't be the same, but we can try. We can make new memories together."

And if I wasn't in love with him already, I would definitely be falling now.

"New memories, you say?" I grinned. "Is there space for some of these other things I have in mind?"

"What kind of things?" He bent his head, his lips hovering over mine.

"The things my dad would kill you for."

"Hmm." He pressed his forehead against mine. "I think that we can definitely fit them somewhere in there."

NOAH

I watched her as she walked down the street, right in front of me, wishing I could freeze the time so that this moment we were in right now would last forever.

But I couldn't.

Hopelessness was the worst thing that one could feel, and I was filled with it, consumed by thoughts that painted my life in colors of gray and black. Colors I wanted to run away from, but how could I, when the only person that held the keys to the bright shades was going to be taken away from me?

She put on a brave face for all of us, but I could see deeper than some of the others could—she was terrified. I always wondered what was there after the end—after the flatline. Was there going to be some kind of light, or was she going to spend her eternity trapped in the darkness, waiting for a better time to come?

Was she going to remember me, her life, her parents, and everything she wanted to do, or was she going to forget and become a floating soul without direction, without a purpose?

I never really thought about death. It was an omnipresent aspect of life, but I never had to deal with it.

169

All of my loved ones were healthy and safe. All of my friends were still here, and even the people that weren't part of my life anymore, were okay.

But now, as I kept staring at her back and at the white, puffy clouds gathering on the horizon, I couldn't stop thinking about it. Every single day since my mother told me what was happening with Sophie, I woke up with thoughts of death and endings. I went through my days thinking about it. My nights, my once pleasant dreams, were replaced by nightmares, painting the picture of a world without her in it.

Was she in pain right now?

Was she lying to us just so that she wouldn't worry us?

What was I going to do when the time came, when the clock stopped ticking?

Was this world our last destination or was there something else afterward?

The gravelly road, cutting this field in half, scrunched beneath my feet, my boots crushing the tiny rocks. Sophie's light hair wavered on the afternoon wind, her arms spread on both sides, as if she was flying.

She threw her head backward, laughing at whatever she was thinking about, yet I couldn't find it in myself to even crack a small smile.

I'd tried behaving as if nothing was really going on for her sake, but every single time I would leave her, it felt like a gaping hole the size of the Gibraltar passing took place inside my chest, tearing at the edges, spreading wider and wider, and I feared that I wouldn't be able to keep going on like this.

"Noah!" she yelled, pushing away the dark thoughts clouding my mind. "Hurry up!"

Her body was turned toward me, and I drank her up. I drank every single moment we had, storing them somewhere deep inside my mind for safekeeping, because I knew that soon enough I wouldn't be able to have them.

She didn't want to tell me what the doctor said after her last checkup just two days ago, but Andrew's face gave away all the answers I wanted to get.

Sophie didn't have long.

She decided to stop all the treatments, except for the painkillers, defying all of us and what we wanted for her. But I respected her wishes.

"I don't want to be a vegetable, Noah," she told me when I confronted her about her decision. "I want to spend my last months living, instead of fighting a losing battle. I know that I won't survive this, and trust me, this isn't me giving up. But I know, I just know."

And what was I supposed to say to that? I couldn't be selfish with her, no matter how much it hurt knowing that she wouldn't live long enough to see the next year. Grim faces, hollow souls, pain and anguish, they colored the walls of her house, and while her parents and her brother tried to do the same thing I was doing, tried to be strong in front of her, I could see the cracks in their armor every single time she wasn't watching.

Today, she wanted us to go for a walk. I wanted to stay inside, to keep her close, to hug her to me, to give her years of my life if I could, just so that she wouldn't disappear.

I quickened my pace, reaching her in less than five seconds, and wrapped my arms around her middle, pulling her to me.

"You're awfully slow today," she said, her eyes fluttering as she looked up at me. "Is this old age that's catching up with you?"

I pinched her arm and started laughing with her. "Smartass. I'm just admiring the view."

"You mean, you're admiring my ass?" She squeezed me tighter, pressing her chest against my own.

"Something like that," I murmured and lowered my head, pressing my lips against her own. I could still taste the honey and cinnamon she had for breakfast. Her scent of sweet vanilla filtered through my nose, reminding me of that night almost a month ago.

She opened her lips for me, letting me in, while her tongue darted out, shyly seeking out my own. I pushed all the bad and dark down into a box I made when I got the news, and tangled my fingers into her hair, holding her steady while I devoured her, inhaling her, engraving this moment into my brain.

Sophie gasped into my mouth and wrapped her arms around my neck, holding me imprisoned as much as I was holding her.

All these years, all this pent-up energy; need, want, love, all of them mixed together, driving me insane with desire.

"I thought you didn't like me anymore." She panted against my lips. "You haven't kissed me since that night."

"I was trying to give you space."

"I don't want space, Noah. I want you."

"Soph—"

"I'm not fragile," she whispered. "I'm not going to break. Trust me on this. But if you don't touch me again, I might break you, and I don't think you'd like to see that."

I was standoffish after her time in the hospital, because it was hard separating the fact that she was still here, still breathing, still living, from the fact that she had the poison spreading from her head through her body, killing her slowly. It was hard remembering that these would be our last months together.

It was terrifying thinking about the "after."

But my girl wanted me just as much as I wanted her. I'd been pushing these thoughts away, but as she gazed at me with fire burning deep inside her eyes, with her lips spread and her cheeks rosy, I couldn't stop thinking about the way she felt beneath me.

About the way she took me in, or how it felt like finally being home.

She was always mine, it just took my brain some time to catch up with the rest of my body.

"I know you're not breakable." I pressed another kiss against her lips. "I just… I don't know. I didn't want to push, because this," I grinned, "is not just some passing attraction, or an itch to scratch."

"Oh really?"

"Really." I smiled and pulled her head onto my chest, holding her tight. "I remember the first time I realized that what I felt for you was a lot more than just friendship."

"Wanna tell me about it?"

"Oh, you're going to laugh at me."

She pulled away from me while the brightest smile decorated her face. "No, I'm not. Tell me." She pouted. "Please?"

"Fine." I exhaled. "About four years ago, during the summer, you came out in these tiny shorts and ran toward your bicycle, while I waited for you in front of your house. Remember? We were going to the lake."

She nodded. "I do. You were awfully cranky that day."

"No, baby. I was awfully horny that day. And you kept talking to Sean at the lake, completely ignoring me——"

"I was not ignoring you."

"Oh, you so were. And that bikini you wore did nothing to extinguish the fire rising in my body. I almost ran home and jerked in the shower, so fucking pissed at you."

"It was not my fault." She crossed her arms on her chest and glared at me. "You were such an asshole that day."

"I know. And no, it definitely wasn't your fault, but there I was, barely fourteen years old, fantasizing about my best friend. Man, I had a boner almost every single day for two years back then. And you just kept smiling at me. You just kept going on as if nothing was happening."

"Was that why you started going out with so many girls?" I hated the look of sorrow passing over her features, and I wanted to kick myself for putting it there.

"Hey, hey." I reached out for her, pulling her back into my embrace. "I was trying to forget you, okay? I was going insane, Soph. I wanted you so badly, so fucking badly, but I didn't want to fuck up our friendship. I didn't want to do something that would end up in the two of us never talking again. I was afraid of losing you, but I never realized how much I was hurting you."

"I understand." She sniffled. "It doesn't make me feel any better, but I understand. I just wished we didn't waste so much time hiding how we really felt."

"Maybe we would never be able to get back what was lost, but we will always have now, Sophie."

She nuzzled her face between my pecs, rubbing small circles over my back. "When did you become such a poet?"

"When I fell in love with you."

My life before her felt like a black-and-white movie. I was going through the motions, but there was nothing extraordinary I would remember it by. But now that I had her, now that we could be honest about how we felt, it was as if a splash of color fell over me, and everything made sense.

I didn't want to think about the impending doom

waiting for us. I wanted to live in the moment, right here with her, with her arms wrapped around me.

"It's getting late, Soph."

"It's only afternoon."

"Yeah, but we promised your mom we will be back before four, and considering that you still wanna spend time by the willow tree, I say that we need to get moving."

"Fine." She huffed. "But you're gonna carry me there."

It took me a moment to realize what she meant, when she jumped up, wrapping her legs around my waist, holding on to me like a spider monkey.

"You know, this position could be used for other things as well," I said, placing my hands on her ass. "You're just giving me ideas now."

"Hmmm, are you gonna tell me what those ideas are?"

"Later." I bit her neck, earning a sudden moan from her. "It's gonna take us quite some time to reenact all these fantasies I stored over the years."

And while I loved doing this, carrying her, playing around, I knew the real reason why she wanted me to carry her. I knew without a doubt that she started feeling exhausted, but I didn't comment on it.

I would let her have this. I would let her lie to both of us if that's what she wanted. Sometimes, in order to survive, white lies were a necessary evil.

Years ago, after we just moved into the house next to Sophie's, she woke me up at eight in the morning and dragged me out of the bed to *"go and see her favorite place."* Truth be told, after my parents divorced and after they threw all the nasty words at each other, all I wanted to do was sleep for a year and forget that those months even happened.

But there she was, an angel in disguise, trying to cheer me up. Even back then I could never say no to her, and begrudgingly agreed to go out. It was the same period of the year, just how it was right now. Early April morning, still cold but not cold enough to wear a coat. Fresh morning air and the birds singing for the start of a new day.

Her small hand was tightly wrapped around mine, pulling me in the direction behind our houses, and if I wasn't as sleepy and as cranky as I was back then, I would've been able to enjoy the sight in front of me a lot more than I did. But it didn't take me long to realize why she loved it so much.

"Fairies are dancing here, but we can't see them, Noah."

Grass was still covered with a layer of frost, and the cool breeze kept sending chills over my body, but when she started dancing around me, pulling us closer and closer to the weeping willow, I started forgetting about what was happening.

There she was, this beautiful girl, my best friend, trying to cheer me up, and I almost told her to fuck off because I was too angry at the rest of the world. I was glad I didn't let my mouth run free that day, because I would've never been able to share this imaginary world she created for herself.

The area looked like it came out of a fairy tale. The weeping willow stood all by itself in the middle of the meadow, overlooking a small pond that was there for as long as the people that lived here could remember. Nobody knew if it was man-made, or if it got created by nature itself, but Sophie loved thinking of it as a portal to another dimension.

"*What if we jump in?*" she asked me once, staring at the pond as if it could give her all the answers. "*What if we jump and we go out to the other side, where elves and fairies ruled, and where people could live forever?*"

Even as a child I could understand why she asked those questions. Her grandfather died and she couldn't deal with the reality of the situation. The tears in her eyes as she asked all those questions stayed seared into my mind, and I hated that I couldn't do anything to stop them.

"Noah?" She stirred in my arms just as I stepped beneath the tree. The swing we placed on one of the branches was still here after all these years, and as she slowly lowered her legs down my body, I helped her onto the swing. "What happened?"

"You dozed off." I smiled, my chest constricting because the words I wanted to say out loud echoed loudly in my head.

You dozed off because you're getting exhausted by a simple walk now.

But I couldn't tell her that, even though she knew. Of course she knew.

"Oh. I guess I shouldn't be staying up again until three in the morning just to watch reruns of *Supernatural*, huh?"

"No, you probably shouldn't."

I sat down on the grass in front of her, my front facing the pond. She placed her hands on my shoulders and leaned down, hiding her face in my neck.

"I don't want today to end," she murmured, her breath tickling the short hairs on the back of my neck.

"Me neither." I turned my head to the side and caught her cheek with my lips, closing my eyes as a tremor ran through me. "If we could stay frozen in one moment, just one, which one would you want it to be?" I asked as she pulled back, threading her hands through my hair.

"One moment?"

"Just one."

Time ticked slowly while she played with the strands of my hair, goosebumps erupting all over my skin.

"The day we first met." She smiled. The smallest, saddest smile that held so many emotions that I couldn't even start to decipher which one was which. "I think it's one of my favorite days."

"You wore that purple shirt with a unicorn on it."

"It was my favorite." She laughed. "I drove my mom mental, because I didn't want to take it off, even to sleep."

"You wore that thing everywhere. Literally, everywhere."

"I know." Sophie chuckled. "You had that *Star Wars* shirt on."

"Oh yeah, and I never even saw *Star Wars*."

"It was so funny when kids started talking to you about R2-D2 and you just stared at them blankly, just nodding at whatever they were saying."

"I had to seem cool, okay?"

I leaned back right between her legs, and wrapped my hand around her ankle, hating... Fucking hating how cold her skin was. The wind started picking up and when I looked up, I could see the gray clouds pushing away the white ones I saw earlier.

"It's going to rain, isn't it?" Sophie asked, looking toward the sky as well. "I wonder if it'll rain wherever it is that I'm going."

If she slapped me, it would've hurt less.

"That is, if there is anything after, you know?"

"I do," I answered, my voice wavering along with the wind. "Do you remember those stories about fairies you used to tell me? The elves, their kingdoms and beautiful lands?"

"Oh my God." She started laughing. "I was so lame."

"Nah. I wish that land really existed, you know? I wish that we could just jump into the pond and travel somewhere far away from here, where we could live forever."

"Noah—"

"I wish life turned out differently, Soph. I wish snowflakes truly could be in the colors of the rainbow like you described them once, and that sickness and death never existed over there."

"Baby," she whispered and hugged me from behind as she came down onto the grass, sitting right behind me.

"Right now, I would give anything for all of that to be our reality, and not this."

"But it can't be, Noah." She put her chin on my shoulder. "Unfortunately, fairy tales are just stories for little kids, and we are far too old to believe in those things."

"I know." I nodded. "I just... I just wish things were different, you know?"

"I do. I can't tell you how many times I wanted to wake up from this terrible nightmare I was going through, but every morning was still the same. That bottle of pills was still on my nightstand, and the headache was still tearing through my brain. Dreams are for people that have a future, Noah. They're not for me. Not anymore."

"Sophie." I turned around and placed her legs over my own, pulling her onto my lap. "That's not true."

"But it is." A sad smile played on her lips. "I have months to live, if I'm lucky."

"No, don't say that." I could feel my eyes tearing up, but there was nothing I could do to stop it. "Please, don't say that."

"I'm sorry, Noah. You have no idea how sorry I am

that you're here with me, going through all of this. But we have to face reality. We have to start preparing."

"Stop it."

"Noah." She placed her palms on my cheeks, wiping the stray tear cascading down my cheek. "I need you to be ready, okay? I don't wanna talk about this any more than you wanna listen about it, but I have to. On my last checkup—"

"Please don't." I hugged her. "Don't say it."

"You need to know. You deserve to know."

"I know, and I want to, but I also don't want to count the days, okay?"

"You won't be counting the days, but I need you to get ready." She took a deep breath while my entire body shook, unable to contain the emotions racing through me. "Four months, Noah."

"No."

"I have four to five months. If I'm lucky."

"No, nope." I started shaking my head. "I refuse to believe that."

"It might be more, but this is their prognosis."

"No, absolutely not."

"Noah!"

"I don't wanna believe in that, Sophie!" I pulled back from her and stood up, then walked toward the edge of the pond, and looked up at the dark sky. "I can't believe in that."

"Babe," she said as she approached.

I turned around and roared. "And how can you be so calm about it?" I couldn't breathe. God, I couldn't fucking breathe. "How can you be so calm, telling me that your life has an exact expiration date? Huh? Because I can't be calm about this. I can't accept that in a matter of months, I will never be able to see you smile. I will never again hear your voice. I will never be able to hold you close. How can you be so fucking calm when life decided to tear my heart out? When it decided to take you away from us?"

"I'm not calm!" she thundered back. "I am not calm, but I also know that there's nothing I can do."

"You could fight!"

"For what, Noah? For months in a hospital bed? For the rest of my life to be spent on IV drips and endless surgeries, and we all know that none of them would do me any good."

I laced my fingers on the back of my head and closed my eyes, trying to think of anything, something. Just fucking something. I needed a miracle, and miracles weren't exactly getting handed over on a silver plate.

"I can't lose you, darling," I murmured, letting the tears flow freely. "I can't fucking lose you, and I know I will."

"Noah——"

"I wanted us to be together forever, you know?" I opened my eyes and looked at her. "I wanted to put a ring on your finger one day. I wanted to see you with our kids, running around the garden. I wanted you to accomplish all your dreams while I held your hand through it all. Good and bad, I wanted it all with you. Only you."

"I wanted it as well. Don't you think that I did?"

"I know you did, but I don't know what to think anymore. I don't know what to feel anymore. For the first time in my life, I'm feeling lost, and no matter what I do, no matter what I say, the outcome will always be the same."

"But you said it yourself." She took my hands into her own. "We can still live in the moment, and I want to spend these last few months I have left with you. I don't want to fight with you over things that can't be changed. I don't want to leave this world, knowing that I didn't do everything in my power to have an amazing time. I made a bucket list, just like I promised."

"You did?"

"I did. And if you want to, or if you have time, I want you to help me with it." She pulled a paper out of her back pocket and held it in front of us. "Wanna read it?"

I nodded my head, not trusting my voice anymore. Something heavy was sitting on top of my chest, something else was scraping all over my throat, and holding it down was getting harder and harder.

She placed the paper in my hand. "Read it." I opened it up, unfolding the piece like it was the most precious thing on the earth, and wiped away the tears still coating my cheeks.

Sophie's Bucket List

Go skinny dipping
Dance in the rain
See Northern Lights
Visit Grand Canyon
Ride on a motorcycle
Have sex in public
Have breakfast in bed
Get a tattoo
Attend a music festival
See Colosseum

"This is—"

"Is it too much? Do you think we can do it?"

I stood there, staring at the fucking paper. A paper... that's what we resorted to. A paper with her final wishes.

A paper that I wanted to crumble and throw into the pond, because my brain wasn't anywhere near rational thoughts.

"Noah?"

I cleared my throat. "We can do this, darling. We will do everything you wanna do."

"Really?" Her face lit up with the question and I couldn't stop myself from claiming her lips again.

I closed the distance between us and placed a hand beneath her chin, lifting her head up. "Really."

My body burned from the need to take her away and hide her from this ugliness, but I could do none of those things. I couldn't rob her of her time with her parents and her other friends.

So I put my hand on the back of her head and pressed my lips against hers, tasting the saltiness from our tears, from our pain, from the anguish tearing our world apart. But I made a promise, and this was one promise I intended to keep.

Years ago, I vowed that one day, this beautiful girl with the prettiest smile and the brightest eyes would be mine. Now I vowed that if these were the things she wanted to do, we would do them all.

I would do anything to put back the smile on her face.

SOPHIE

I woke up with a start, my heart beating erratically in my chest, until I remembered where I was.

Those few seconds after you woke up, where your mind was completely empty and your body free, were the only moments of bliss these days. Those passing seconds felt heavenly, and just for a moment I could pretend that all these things that were happening were just a bad dream.

And I was getting better and better at pretending.

A heavy arm laid freely over my middle, holding me close to a big body that belonged to a person that still made me smile. Even after all these years, after all those reservations, he still held me like a priceless piece of porcelain, and over the past couple of weeks he never let go.

They said that actions were what mattered and not words, and Noah did his best to show me why it was always only him for me. Countless other guys, opportunities missed, yet none of them came close to what I felt for him.

I wiggled my ass against him, feeling his dick twitching against me. I smirked as his hips started moving, his dick rubbing over my ass, while the small puffs of air escaped from his lips, playing with the hair on my neck.

He tightened his grip against me, pulling me closer to him until his chest became plastered to my back.

His honey-laced lips dropped to my shoulder, quick, sloppy kisses going from my shoulder to the sweet spot behind my ear. My eyes closed while his teeth nipped at my skin, and that hand around my waist started going lower and lower, until his fingers reached the hem of my shirt.

Sneakily, almost too carefully, he pushed my shirt up and spread his fingers over my belly, holding himself there as if he too was trying to savor this moment.

"You're a wicked witch, Soph," he murmured against my neck. "But I like this kind of morning." I could feel his smile on my skin rather than see it, and before I could even answer or say anything at all, he flipped us over, with me right beneath him and him above me.

His sleepy eyes held a brightness that wasn't there two days ago when I told him about my prognosis, and that dark hair fell over his forehead. He grabbed my hands and pulled them above my head, holding me hostage, while his hips held mine locked onto the bed.

"Good morning, beautiful," he croaked and dropped his head down, pressing his lips against mine. "You've been awfully loud last night."

That smirk—that knowing little smirk. "No, I don't remember anything."

"Because you slept like a newborn baby, but the noises." He dove and bit one of my nipples over my shirt. "My name on your lips." He bit the other one, pulling out an involuntary moan from me. "I almost woke you up right there and then. You drove me insane."

"Why didn't you?" Panting, needy, with lava burning through me, rushing through my veins, I needed him to do a lot more than just press those wicked lips against mine.

I lifted my hips, but as soon as I did, he pressed down

on my pelvis with his other hand, his fingers dancing over my belly. "I almost did, but I didn't want to scar your parents for life. I also didn't want to have your brother barging in here while I was balls deep inside of you."

"You're such a romantic, you know that?" I laughed. "Balls deep? Really?"

"And what would you like me to say? While my member penetrated the hard walls of your tunnel?"

"Eww, no." I pushed against him, but he wasn't budging. "Please don't ever utter those words in my presence again. That sounds like construction work."

"Does it?" His hand went to my back and dipped inside my panties. He grabbed a fistful of my ass, pushing his dick up and down, slowly building up the tension I craved even without him properly touching me. "Maybe I should tell him that I deflowered his baby sister in the middle of the night in the forest."

"Oh, no." I grinned. "Do you wish to end up with a broken arm or something?"

He shook his head. "No, but since you don't want me to use that word, this is the next best thing."

"Just don't talk about the two of us having sex, or kissing, or touching each other... You know what, just don't talk to Andy at all." I laughed. "He's been giving you the stink eye for a couple of days now."

"He loves me, trust me. We have this real bromance that you wouldn't understand."

"Oh yeah?"

"Yeah." He grinned. "Besides, he told me that he always thought you and I are going to end up together one day."

"No fucking way." I pulled myself up and moved toward the headboard. "He's been teasing me so much over the years, even though I never confirmed what I felt for you."

He sat up and pulled my feet into his lap. "I mean, it was obvious to everybody else but us. To be honest, it was obvious to me as well, but you were just so stubborn and—"

"I was stubborn?"

"Yeah." Noah nodded. "You never told me how you felt."

He dug his thumbs into the soles of my feet, eliciting a long moan from me.

"You like this, don't you?"

"That, right there." I closed my eyes while he massaged. "But for the record," I opened my eyes and looked at him, "I was not the stubborn one, Mr. Manwhore."

"Who? Me? I'm not a manwhore."

"That's not what half of our school thinks."

"What they think and what really is the truth are two separate worlds, Sophie. Yeah, I never had a girlfriend because I didn't think that it would be fair for them to be with someone whose heart already belonged to another girl."

I shut up after that.

I knew I should've talked to him about how I really felt but telling him everything that sat on my chest never felt right. Even now, even after he told me how he felt, even after everything that has happened in the last month, I still had a hard time expressing all these feelings swirling through me.

I loved him. I loved him since we were kids, but telling him all of it now seemed useless. I had a feeling that telling him how much he meant to me would just cement his decision to stay glued to my side, when that was the opposite of what I wanted for him.

"Noah," I started, knowing that we had to talk about this. "When are the scouts coming?"

Before, he used to talk about hockey more than about anything else, but these days, hockey seemed to be the furthest thing from his mind. He shrugged and looked down at my legs, spreading his fingers over my muscles, avoiding my eyes.

"Babe." I moved myself closer, and he had to stop massaging for a minute. Placing my hands on his cheeks, I lifted his head, forcing him to look at me. "When was the last time you went for a practice?"

It's been days. Maybe even a month since he went to the rink, and this was exactly what I didn't want to happen.

"I don't know," he murmured.

"You can't keep doing this, Noah. You can't stop living."

"But what is the point of living and doing all these things when you won't be there with me? What is the point of fighting for the life I once wanted to have, when the person I love the most in this world is going to be taken away from me?"

"Noah, just because I won't get the chance to do all these things, it doesn't mean that you can't. And I want you to do them. I want you to live life like we once talked about. I want you to fulfill your dreams."

"But what about your dreams?" He placed his hands over mine, pressing them against his cheeks. "I know we keep talking and talking about these things, but I just can't comprehend it. I can't accept it, Soph. And I'm trying to be positive—for you. I'm trying not to let these things overcome me, but it's fucking hard."

"I know it's hard." I dropped my hands to his shoulders

and climbed on his lap. "Trust me, I know. But let me tell you one thing, Noah."

"What?"

"When the day comes, I will still stay with you. I will always be here," I murmured and pressed my hand against his heart. "I will be happy knowing that at least one of us gets to do all these beautiful and magnificent things. I will be thrilled to know that my best friend, my favorite person, the love of my life, will get to live and will get to enjoy life."

"But that's not how I'm feeling. How can you be so positive about everything? I just…" His chest expanded with the deep breath he took before he buried his face in my neck. "I just don't know what to do."

"I can't tell you what to do." I rubbed his back. "But I can tell you what I would love to see you doing."

"Then tell me."

"I want you to pretend none of this is happening, Noah."

"But—"

"Wait," I warned him before he could argue with me. "I know it might not be healthy, and it might not be the best thing to do, but I still wanna feel like me, you know? I don't want this sickness to define me, because I am so much more than that. And I don't want it to define your life. It's a terrible thing, it's a tragedy, I know, and trust me, I am not okay with it, but I made peace with the fact that I'm dying. I am loved. I lived an amazing life. I fell in love. I did all these things I loved. I was lucky, Noah. Lucky to have this family, to have you, to have my other friends and to have skating. Do you know how many people go through their life trying to find that one thing they're passionate about, and they never find it? Thousands, Noah. Yet I managed to find mine when I was a small child."

"But that doesn't make this all better."

"No, it doesn't. Nothing would make this situation better, but I had a wonderful life, babe. Wonderful, happy, and fulfilled life. I lived, I loved, and I was cherished. And I want you to carry that vision of me when you continue without me. I want you to take this version of me that you're seeing right now and take it with you through the rest of your life. That's what I want you to do. I want us to have an amazing time together, to graduate, to laugh, and to love each other until the end of my days. And once I'm gone—"

"Can you please stop talking about it?" he cried out.

"No, I can't until you listen to me. Once I'm gone, I want you to go out there and be happy. Live, love, smile, and cry, Noah. Life is too short for us to be stuck in the past. One minute we are here, and in the next one we're gone. Forgive and forget, you know? I wish for you to be loved again. I wish for you to have kids, to have a family. I want that for you, I truly do."

"But all of that was supposed to be with you, Soph," he murmured against my neck. "All of that belonged to you. That future you're talking about was supposed to happen with you."

"I know. But who's to say that even if this didn't happen, one of us wouldn't get hit by a car and die? Life is unpredictable, and it can be extremely difficult, but it's also the most beautiful thing. We get to wake up in the morning to the chirping of the birds. We get to breathe fresh morning air. We get to do all these amazing things. And who knows, maybe in another life I will survive."

"Sophie," he protested. "Please."

"I promise I will stop talking about this if you do one thing for me."

"What's that?"

I turned my head to the side and pressed my lips against his neck, inhaling the scent of soap mixed with spicy cologne.

"I want you to go to one of the practices. I know you don't have any on Saturdays, but tomorrow's Sunday, and I know for a fact that they're gonna be having one."

A minute passed, seconds ticked away, both of us breathing slowly, waiting for the other one to start talking. I couldn't exactly tell him that most days I woke up with a panic attack waiting for me at my doorstep. I couldn't tell him that dying terrified me more than living, and that the mere thought of not being here in four months scared the crap out of me.

I didn't want him to know that I spent hours during these days trying to memorize their faces—his, my mom's, my dad's, and Andrew's. I didn't want him to know that my headaches started getting stronger and stronger since I came back from the hospital, and that the pills they gave me weren't doing anything for me anymore.

I cleared my browsing history every time before he came over, because I didn't want him to see all these websites I visited.

Stage four of glioblastoma was not something I ever expected to have. I didn't expect to be browsing through forums where people who had the same disease as me discussed how they wanted to be cremated, or buried at their local cemetery.

I was supposed to be thinking about the dress I would wear on our prom. Instead, I was writing down all the things I wanted to do in this short period of time, afraid that I wouldn't be able to finish it all.

Most days, waking up felt like a chore more than a regular thing, and I just didn't have enough power in my body to keep on moving. But then I would remember all of their faces, their tears, their fear, and I would get the fuck up.

The internet wasn't helping. Reading comments from people who lost someone that had the same thing I did, or the ones that were on palliative care terrified me. Cold like nothing I felt before slowly crept into my bones, and no matter how much I tried to push it away, how much I tried to let the blood roar through my veins, it just kept going deeper and deeper.

Some days it was in my lungs; others it was in my throat, cutting off my ability to speak, to express these feelings that were driving me mad. And with each day, it was getting closer to my heart.

"Okay," Noah finally murmured as he placed a hand to the back of my head. "I'll go, but I need you with me, at least one day. I need to see your face behind that Plexiglas around the rink."

"I'll go. You know I'll go. I would go to the end of the world with you if you'd have asked."

"I should've." He smiled, but it looked anything but happy. "I should've taken you away a long time ago."

"Yeah, but even taking me away wouldn't have prevented this from happening."

"I have to imagine that it would've, Soph. I think that part of human nature is imagining the scenarios of things that would have or should've happened. I like to imagine that we never fought. I also like to imagine that we told each other how we felt years ago."

"I like to imagine that too, you know? And before... Before you finally got your head out of your ass—"

"Hey!"

"Shhh. I used to imagine what it would feel like having you with me."

"But you always had me with you."

"Yeah, but it wasn't the same. I had you as my friend. I had you as a person I could call at three in the morning if I needed help, but I never had you as my lover, Noah. And those dreams are dangerous if they never become real. Those dreams eat you alive."

"I'm sorry."

"It's okay. I just… I need you to know, okay? I used to lay right here," I patted the spot behind me. "With tears streaming down my cheeks, staring at the ceiling, wishing for things to be different. I used to drive myself crazy with all these scenarios, all these possibilities. Then I would start thinking about what it was the other girls had that I didn't."

"It wasn't like that," he argued. "It was never about those things."

"I know it wasn't, but it still hurt like a bitch seeing you with them."

"But it'll never hurt again."

No, it wouldn't, because I would be dead, suddenly ran through my head. Jesus.

I needed to book an appointment with my therapist again. This was exactly what I feared would happen.

"The reason why I'm telling you about this is not to make you feel bad. I'm sure you had a fair share of sleepless nights and whatnot. But the point of the story is—try to steer clear from those scenarios and what-ifs. There's a whole life in front of you, Noah, and it would be such a shame if it gets spent thinking about the things that could've been."

I thought he was going to argue with me again. I thought he would try to tell me that it was the only way for him to cope, but instead, the brightest smile appeared on his face, assuring me that maybe, just maybe, we would be fine.

"Why are you looking at me like that?" I asked, unsure where he was going to take this.

"I'm just memorizing your face."

A snap, like a branch breaking from a strong wind, something broke inside of me and the tears I fought so long pushed to the surface, one by one rolling down.

"Hey, hey, hey," Noah whispered, wiping them away. "What's wrong?"

"I-I can't do this," I sobbed. "I can't do this to you."

"What are you talking about?"

"God," I moaned and dropped my forehead to his chest. "I'm gonna break you and you're gonna end up depressed and sad, a-and—"

"Sophie, hey." He lifted my head and pressed his thumbs against my cheeks, my tears hitting him. "I won't end up depressed and sad."

"Yes, you will. This is why I didn't want you to know. You're not going to your practices, you're not thinking about your future. Basically, you put a stop to your own life because my own is ending. And I keep talking about death as if it's as simple as having cereal for breakfast, when I know it's not. And I can't push you away, because I love you too much and I want you with me, but I also don't want you to go through life with a scar on your heart because of me."

"Sophie—"

"And then you look at me like that, and you say those things, and I don't know how I'm supposed to be okay with leaving you. And I don't know what to do or what to say anymore, when all my family's been doing is crying and hiding it from me. I don't know what to do when I can see raw pain shining from every pore of your body, even when you're smiling at me. I just…" I took a deep breath and dropped my head to my hands, my voice muffled when I spoke again. "I don't want you guys to suffer because of me."

A car alarm sounded somewhere on the street and I focused on that instead of his hands that were now kneading the tight muscles on my back.

"Soph," Noah started talking, but I tuned him out, focusing on the sounds coming from outside.

"Sophie, look at me. Please?"

There they were, voices, and the alarm stopped.

"Baby." He hugged me from above, forcing me to push my legs to the side and place my head in his lap. I crumpled down, breaking all the walls I made, one by one. "We're here because we love you. And we cry because we love you, because we're afraid of losing you. I know you're afraid of losing us as well, but no matter what, all of us would rather be here than somewhere else."

"I would rather you all gone, you know? I love you guys, but I'm just so scared. So fucking scared. And it isn't dying I am scared of. It isn't even the pain I am probably going to feel. This fear has nothing to do with me, but everything to do with all of you that are staying behind. That's what terrifies me."

"We're going to be fine." His chest vibrated against my head. "We just need to be sad first."

I knew. And I knew it was always easier for the ones that were dying. Somehow it was. I always felt that the ones that were left behind were the ones that should be mourned. Every one of us carried pieces of other people inside our chest. Our love for them could make us and also break us, but it was undeniable that it often made us who we were.

And because of that, when a person leaves this world, that piece we carried for so long would become like a thorn in our side, reminding us of what we've lost.

"Wipe those tears, baby, and don't mourn us. Yeah, we will be fucked up. We will be sad and depressed at first, and it might be dark for a while there without you, but we're going to be okay. I don't want you to worry about us. And as you said, we're going to make some memories now, starting from today."

"Today?" I wiped beneath my eyes, pulling myself up, and looked at him. "What are we doing today?"

"We're getting started on your bucket list. So get your ass up, go and take a shower, and I'll wait for you down-stairs in thirty minutes."

My bucket list? I almost forgot about that damn thing.

"Noah—"

"No, we're going out, and that's an order. Don't make me drag you out of the house. You know that I can carry you."

My face flushed as the flashbacks of that night replayed inside my mind. How could I ever forget?

20

SOPHIE

RAVEN'S TATTOO stood above the door of the shop while I waited for Noah to pay for the parking ticket.

"You're getting a tattoo?" I asked as he approached me, keeping his hands in his front pockets.

"No." He grinned. "We are."

"We are?" I repeated like a parrot, my eyes widening. "The bucket list?"

"Oh yeah. We're getting tattoos today and crossing one item from that list." He looked toward the side where the entrance to the alley next to the shop was. "Maybe two."

"What?"

"Never mind." He looked back at me. "Let's go inside. They're already waiting for us."

With a hand on my lower back, he pushed me toward the glass door and opened it for me. The little ding above the door rang as we entered and two sets of eyes turned toward us.

A girl stood behind the glass counter containing rows and rows of different jewelry. The first word that came to my mind while looking at her was happiness. Streaks of rainbow colored her hair, while a bright smile adorned her face. Two piercings on her lower lip caught my eye, but her arms... Her arms were filled with ink. Some colored, some black and white, lines and shapes, and it all merged together, creating mesmerizing art.

"Hello there," she called out as the door closed, while the guy we saw came closer to her, stopping right next to the counter. "Noah, right?" She pointed at him, still smiling.

"That's right."

"And this must be Sophie." She looked at me. "I'm Phoebe. And this grump here," she pointed at the guy, "is Leo."

"It's nice to meet you both." I grinned at them. While Phoebe kept smiling, Leo kept the neutral expression on his face and just nodded.

Noah wrapped his arm around my shoulders and kept me at his side as we walked toward the counter.

"Do you guys know what you want to get?"

"Uh—"

I wanted to get a tattoo; I just hadn't figured out what I wanted it to be. I looked at Noah, waiting to see what he was going to do.

"A sun," he exclaimed. "A small sun, right here." He pointed at the area between his thumb and forefinger. "It doesn't have to be too big, but yeah."

"A sun?" I asked. "You never told me that you wanted to have a tattoo."

"We never really talked about it." He smiled. "Do you have something against my choice?"

"No, not really." I shook my head. "I just don't under-stand the meaning behind it."

"Most of my tattoos don't even have a meaning." Phoebe snickered. "In the beginning you think that each and every one of them has to have some special, hidden meaning, but trust me," she walked behind the counter and right toward us. "After tattoo number three, I just started doing whatever I felt was right and whatever I liked."

"Really?" I asked.

"Oh, yeah. People get so concerned that every tattoo has to have a deeper meaning, but they don't. Tattoos are art, and if I see something that I really like, or if one of my friends designs something that really speaks to me, I'll get it done."

"I get that." Noah nodded. "You have some pretty dope tattoos."

"Thank you."

"But this one has a meaning. A very special one."

I frowned, trying to figure it out. "Do you mind enlightening me?"

He dropped his hand and instead of hugging me, he turned me toward him, holding our hands between us. "It's you, darling. You are my sun." *Oh God.* "You're my light, and I figured, why not, you know?"

"Noah—"

"I didn't bring you here to make you feel or whatever. Hell, do whatever you wanna do, or don't. It's completely up to you. I just thought you would like it."

"I do."

"Remember how we used to joke that you were the sun, and I was the moon? What better way to remember you but to get a tattoo that will always remind me of you?"

"Are you sure about this?"

"A hundred percent sure." He leaned down and pressed his lips against my forehead. "I know what I want, Sophie, don't worry about that."

I didn't notice when Phoebe stepped aside, too busy staring at Noah and trying to control my heartbeat.

"I have some designs you could have a look at if you

want to." She held a larger book in her hands, with a white cover. "I would suggest going with something small for the first time."

Noah choked, I snorted, and Leo started laughing behind us.

"Oh, come on." Phoebe laughed.

"That's what she said," I murmured, unable to help myself. As soon as the words left my mouth, I pressed my hand against my mouth, staring at her with wide eyes. "I'm sorry. I just had to."

"I like you, dude. And you," she pointed behind us at Leo, "stop fucking laughing."

I took the book from her, still snickering, and opened it up. Page after page filled with different designs pulled at my attention, and my eyes flickered over each and every one of them, but I already knew what I wanted.

There was no doubt in my mind that I had to get it.

"Actually, Phoebe," I said, and closed the book, placing it on top of the counter. "I know what I wanna do."

"You do?"

"You do?"

Both Noah and Phoebe spoke at the same time.

"I do." I nodded. "I wanna get a small moon." I looked up at Noah as I explained. "Right here." I pressed against the spot between my thumb and forefinger. "A small moon."

"Babe—"

"If I am your sun, Noah, I want you to know that you will always be my moon. This life and the next one, we will always find each other."

He lifted his hand and took a hold of a loose strand of my hair and tucked it behind my ear. "I know we will. No matter what, no matter where we are or what life throws at me, our souls will always be intertwined."

"That was," Phoebe started, blinking slowly. "You guys are the cutest. You really are." She turned to Leo and grumbled, "See, this is how you're supposed to be treating your wife. Then maybe she wouldn't be yelling at you from morning until midnight."

"Well, working with you sure feels like I have two wives instead of only one."

A slap to the back of his head came out of nowhere and he blanched as if he couldn't believe she would do something like that.

"What was that for?"

"For being an idiot." She turned to us again. "Come on, guys. I already have everything ready for you. Leo will do the tattoo for you." She looked at Noah. "And I'll do yours." She lifted her chin toward me. "But just so you know, these might hurt a bit. Hands are extremely sensitive, so if you wanna change your mind about the placement, now's the time."

But both of us just kept staring at her, knowing full well that the physical pain wasn't a match to the emotional turmoil we were both going through.

"Okay, good." She came toward the curtain at the back area of the parlor and opened it up, revealing another room with the massive chairs on opposite sides. Both had what looked like high tables, lined on the sides, filled with all sorts of equipment that I didn't even know how to name.

But what called to me, what spoke to my soul, were the three photos hanging on the wall opposite of the entrance.

"Wow." I came closer. "These are beautiful."

Blues, reds, greens, and grays all danced together, creating a perfect piece of colors, of love, hope, pain, and grief, while the silhouette of a girl adorned only the center piece.

"Did you make these?" I turned around and asked while she prepared her equipment.

"No, it wasn't me," she answered somberly, avoiding my eyes. "It was my sister."

Her voice took a tone that I knew all too well—longing, pain, memories that cut through you every single time you thought about that person.

Wounds were tricky little things; just when you thought that they were healing, they would open up and start bleeding again, over and over. The funniest thing was that the pain always stayed the same. Always the same throbbing, always the same burning sensation, and I worried that the people I loved would feel like that for the rest of their lives once I was gone.

"Are you ready?" Phoebe spoke to Noah who kept quiet the entire time, observing the two of us.

He took off the jacket he wore just as Leo strolled in, wearing a pair of latex gloves already.

"Are you guys allergic to latex, or maybe ink?" Leo asked as he took his place next to one of the chairs where Noah stood.

"Not that we know of," I said, taking off my jacket as well. "Is it okay if I leave this here?" I asked Phoebe while holding my jacket and pointing at the chair in the corner.

"Yeah, of course. Feel free to just drop it there," she said, putting on the latex gloves.

I dropped my jacket and the small bag I carried with me and walked toward the chair that seemed like the type that could be converted into a bed as well. I looked to the side and saw Noah already sitting in his, silently observing me, as if he was drinking every single movement I made.

But that look on his face… That wasn't the look of fear or the look of pity. That was the look of fire, of the little, wicked things he wanted to do to me, and my blood rushed faster just by thinking about it.

Papers rustled as Phoebe and Leo worked on the designs, preparing them to be transferred to our hands, but my eyes stayed glued to Noah's, imagining we were somewhere else at the moment. Somewhere alone, somewhere secluded, somewhere where reality didn't exist and it was only the two of us, hiding away from the world.

"Which hand do you wanna get it on?" Phoebe asked, and like a robot, I gave her my left hand, barely paying attention.

I could hear her voice, but I couldn't understand a thing she was saying, and I had a feeling Noah couldn't hear a thing Leo just said to him.

Phoebe squirted a small amount of what looked like a gel on my hand and rubbed it over the spot where the tattoo was supposed to be placed. Next came a razor, just like the one I used to shave my legs, and as she pressed it down on my skin, removing the small hairs there, I finally looked at her.

"How long have you been doing this?" I asked her.

"Why?" She laughed. "Afraid I'm going to screw it up?"

"No, not really. More like curious to know. Maybe I'll end up being a tattoo artist one day myself." I snickered. "Who knows?"

She started laughing as she cleaned the excess amount of gel from my hand. "Maybe." She lifted the sheet with the design on it and started looking between that and my hand. "I've been doing this for a little over five years. But I can't remember a day where I didn't want to do this."

"Really?"

"Oh, yeah. I drove my parents mad constantly babbling about tattoos when I was a kid. They had to take me every single year to do those temporary ones, because I wanted to have it on my skin. When I got my first one, my mom thought it was the temporary one. Well, the joke was on her when it didn't wash off even after three weeks."

"Was she pissed?"

"A little." Phoebe shrugged. "She thought it was a phase. Turns out it definitely isn't a phase." She pressed the paper on my hand. "Take a look. See if the placement is okay for you."

I lifted my hand, my eyes skimming over the crescent moon colored in purple, involuntarily smiling because it definitely was perfect.

"It looks awesome."

"That's good to hear." Phoebe grinned. "It won't take us too long to finish this one up, but since it's your first tattoo and the placement can be a bit painful, I'll first just press the needle of the machine to your skin, so that you can get a general feeling of how it'll go."

I nodded. "Okay. But I think I have a pretty high threshold for pain."

"You're a figure skater, aren't you? Your boyfriend told us when he came to book the appointment."

My boyfriend. It sounded so weird, yet it also sounded right hearing those words. I'd spent years dreaming of the day when he would finally notice me, and now that it was here... I just couldn't believe it.

"Yeah. I've had more broken bones and sprained ankles than most of my friends."

She picked up a funny-looking machine from the table next to us and pressed on one of the buttons. Almost immediately the machine started buzzing, and weirdly enough, the buzzing did not sound annoying.

As a matter of fact, it was almost soothing as endorphins floated through my body.

Happiness.

I was fucking happy because he brought me here. I was happy that I got to do the first thing on my list. And as Phoebe pressed the needle to my skin, the small smile I had before just grew, even as the pain started spreading through my hand.

I couldn't remember when the last time was that I was this happy.

My eyes were glued to the shape of the moon etched on my skin, while my heart galloped in my chest, both excited and sad. Both elated and terrified, because of what Noah said earlier.

If I was his sun, what would he do once he didn't have it anymore? What would the planet Earth do if its sun suddenly disappeared?

"Noah," I murmured as we exited the shop; his hand in mine and my heart in his hands.

He looked down at me, stopping all of a sudden in front of the door. I expected to see a smile, something that would tell me that he didn't regret getting this tattoo with me, but nothing was there.

"Oh, no."

"What?"

"You regret doing this." I pulled my hand back and took a step backward.

"What? No. Sophie—"

"It's fine. It's okay. You can say it was a bet or some shit like that. I don't want you to have a constant reminder going through your life about m—"

But my words were cut off, because in a matter of seconds, Noah stood in front of me, placed his hands on my cheeks, and pulled my face up. His lips clashed against mine, drowning out all the thoughts, my words, and all my worries.

Our teeth clashed against each other; his tongue licked over my bottom lip, eliciting a moan from me, just as his hand tightened at the back of my neck.

I wrapped my arms around his neck, pulling him down, needing him closer to me.

"Noah," I panted when his lips descended down my throat, all the way to the space between my shoulder and my neck, moving my jacket to the side. "Fuck," I cried out when his teeth clamped down on my skin, followed by his tongue, soothing the bite.

"I need you," he grumbled. "I need you right now."

His fingers tangled with my hair, pulling my head backward, while his lips feasted on my neck.

"Noah," I moaned again, unable to think, only able to feel.

His touch, his scent, his need matching mine.

He grabbed my hand and started pulling me with him, walking much faster than before, all the way to the alley next to the shop. He looked to his right then to the left before taking us deeper and deeper until we came to the large dumpster.

His hands landed on my shoulders, pushing me to the wall, hiding us both from the view of the people passing on the street.

"Noah?"

"Bucket list, remember?"

I frowned at him, trying to recall what exactly he was talking about.

"I don't—" But then it came. "Have sex in public." I laughed. "For a moment there, I thought you went crazy."

"I did. Looking at you in that chair, having to wait because I didn't want us to miss out on our appointments… I almost carried you out of that shop."

"I had to thank them."

"Yeah, I'm pretty sure Leo is telling Phoebe how I am thanking you."

"How are you—" With swift movements, he lifted my shirt over my chest, and placed both his hands on me, playing with my nipples over my bra. "Fuck."

"Are you wet for me, Angel?" He licked the shell of my ear before biting my earlobe. "Should I check?"

"You really know how to drive me wild, huh?"

"It's my specialty."

"Stop talking, Noah, and fucking kiss me."

He did more than kiss me. He bit and scratched; he tore off my clothes, letting them drop around us—and I did the same.

I pushed off the jacket he wore, and then lowered my hands, taking the hem of his shirt and pulling it up, over his head. I didn't wait for him to go first. Instead, I started pressing open-mouthed kisses on his neck, over his collarbone, toward his chest, going lower and lower until I reached the happy trail leading to where I wanted to get.

I dropped down on my knees and started unbuckling his belt, when his hands landed on mine, halting me immediately.

"What are you doing?" I looked up, basking in the heat emanating from him.

"I'm taking what I want, Noah." I shook his hands off of mine and unbuckled his belt. "And it's you. I've been a good girl my entire life." I unbuttoned his jeans and started pulling them down. "But I don't want to be a good girl with you. I want you to dirty me up, make me wild, make me feel how it is to truly be desired."

"Babe," he started just as his dick escaped from the confines of his jeans. Already hard, ready for me. I wrapped my hand around him; smooth, both hard and soft. "Fuck," he cursed as I started dragging my hand up and down his length.

He twitched beneath my touch, and the sounds from him urged me to go faster, harder. I licked my lips, the new need rising in me, and brought my face closer to him.

I opened my mouth wide and took him in. Before this day, it always seemed weird doing this. Some of the girls in school bragged about giving head as if it was the most rewarding thing in the world, and I couldn't understand why.

Until now.

A weird kind of power woke up in me when he wrapped my hair around his fist, holding himself up with a hand on the wall.

"Fuuuuck," he dragged out when my tongue flattened against the bottom part of his dick, licking the protruding vein there. "You're gonna kill me with your mouth," he groaned, slowly pushing his hips back and forth.

I looked up, training my eyes on his, and lifted my other hand to his balls.

"S-Sophie. Fuck. Me."

I grinned around him and fondled his balls, while I bobbed my head in the rhythm of his hips, my tongue dancing around his shaft.

"That's it. That's it, darling." He started increasing his pace. "Fuck, fuck, fuck. I love your mouth."

I hollowed out my cheeks just how Bianca talked about, and he rewarded me with another grunt.

No one ever talked about the amount of power we

possessed when we did this, but as he got louder and more frantic, I figured that this might be one of my favorite things to do.

He suddenly pulled back and lifted me up. Without another word, my bra disappeared, and the pants I wore fell in a heap with our other clothes. My panties were next, and before I could even prepare myself, his hand was between my legs, going from my clit to my opening.

My eyes fluttered closed, and he pressed against me, his dick nestled between us.

"You're dripping, baby." His voice was deeper, raspier, and as he dipped one finger inside, a moan tore out of me. "God, I almost forgot how tight you are."

"Noah!"

"I know, I know." He pressed his lips to my cheek, while his fingers went in and out of me, pressing against that spot inside of me he now knew well. "I love these noises you're making, darling. But I want you to scream for me. I want them to hear you."

"W-Why?"

"Because I want them to know you're mine. You will always be mine, no matter what."

As he removed his fingers and replaced them with his dick, fulfilling yet another one of my fantasies, I had no doubt in my mind that if things were different, Noah Kincaid would be the man I would spend my life with.

21

NOAH

DAYS, hours, minutes, and seconds; they all passed by so quickly. It was as if I had just blinked, and the months passed me by. Time wouldn't wait for us to catch up, I knew that, but every atom in my body wished that it could pass a bit slower.

Just a little bit slower.

Just to give me a few more minutes with her.

But she… She was fading in front of my eyes, and so did any hope I had. Sophie Anderson was slowly dying, and it was obvious to anyone who knew her from before.

Before this sickness took hold of her life. Before it destroyed everything.

I went back to my practices because she insisted, but I wasn't there—mentally at least. My body knew what it needed to do, but my mind was constantly with her, worried that I wouldn't be there if something happened.

Her doctors prescribed medicine to make her more comfortable, to alleviate her pain, but I had a feeling that they were doing more harm than good.

She tried hiding it, tried lying to all of us, but we could see what was really happening. Those four months they gave her were passing too fast, and she was slowly slipping through my fingers.

I'd tried holding on to her. Tried telling myself that things wouldn't be that bad, but every time my eyes landed on her frail form, that courage I tried to build up would crumble down like a house of cards, and the pain would be back.

Sometimes it was easy to forget she was dying, but reality was a harsh bitch who came knocking at my door every time I tried to think positive. And how could I be positive when all of this was happening? Steering clear from the morbid forums where they talked about final days of cancer patients was becoming harder and harder to do.

We were coming to the end of May, to the end of high school, and while I should've been happy, should've been elated about the opportunity that was given to me, I couldn't.

I couldn't feel anything.

"Noah." Sophie stirred next to me, and when I looked down, she started slowly opening her eyes, those dark circles becoming more and more prominent. "What time is it?"

"Around nine, Soph. Go back to sleep."

A storm raged outside, reflecting how I felt.

"I think it's better I get up." She started pulling herself up. "I won't be able to sleep through the night if I continue napping."

Lies, lies, lies, they were all lies she created to make us all feel better.

These so-called naps were full sleeping hours, ranging from four to seven hours during the day, and even with those, she managed to sleep through the night—most of the time. But I could see the way her arms shook when she tried pulling herself up.

I could see her eating less and less, and sleeping more with each passing day.

I could see her disappearing and I couldn't say a thing, afraid I would upset her, when that was the last thing I wanted to do.

It was fucked up being this angry and not having an outlet to direct this anger at. It wasn't her fault, but as the days passed, as her strength weakened, I couldn't stop gritting my teeth every time she wanted to just stay in bed and do nothing.

"Is it raining again?" She looked toward the window and placed her hand on my thigh. Even through the clothes I could feel how cold she was.

Even the warmth started slowly seeping away from her.

"Yeah." I nodded. "It looks like we're about to have a massive thunderstorm."

Just as I said that a thunder boomed on the outside, shaking the entire house.

"You see." I smiled, taking a hold of her hand. "Are you cold?"

"Nah." She shrugged and kept looking toward the window. "I have an idea." She turned toward me, that gleam back in her eyes, and even as pale as she was in that moment, she still looked like the most beautiful person I had ever seen.

"Oh, no." I laughed. "I know that look in your eye. You're thinking about doing something very stupid, aren't you?"

"Not exactly stupid, no. But, I'm not sure if you would be up for this."

"Just spit it out, Soph."

"Well, remember my bucket list?" As if I could forget. Most of those things she wrote there were things that we wouldn't get a chance of doing—skinny dipping, visiting the Grand Canyon and Colosseum, seeing the Northern Lights. All those were things she needed to travel for, and her doctors explicitly said that she wasn't able to travel long distances anymore.

She got tired simply from walking lately, not to mention flying or climbing.

"I do."

"So, it's raining." She looked at me expectantly.

"So it is." I frowned. "Where are you going with this?"

"Noah." She slapped my thigh and smiled. "Dancing in the rain? Remember?"

"Fuck." I dragged my hand over my face and stared at her. "Are you sure that's a good idea? It's freezing outside, and you haven't been feeling very well." And you might only have one or two months left to live, I wanted to say, but bit my tongue at the last second. "I just don't want you to catch a cold or—"

"Noah," she murmured and climbed on top of me, placing her hands on my shoulders. "I wanna dance in the rain, and I wanna dance with you."

"Fuck, don't look at me like that."

"Like what?" She pouted.

"With those puppy dog eyes, and… Yes, that. You know what you're doing."

"I have no idea what you're talking about." She grinned and leaned down, pressing her lips to mine. "Come on. I want to dance with you."

And I wanted to dance with her, but the fear gripped my lungs, pushing my anxiety to the forefront. I wanted to protect her. I wanted to prevent her from getting even worse, and while I wanted to go out and give her everything she wanted, I was terrified that this little excursion could cost us.

"I don't know. What if—"

"Noah," she warned. "If we go through our lives only thinking about what-ifs, we will never get to live at all. And I wanna feel alive. I wanna feel happy. I want the rain to wash away everything from me. Please," she pleaded. "I wanna do this with you. I can do it alone, but—"

"No, absolutely not." She could slip and fall down, hurting herself even more. The other day, she almost fell down the stairs. Apart from her headaches and general weakness, her vision was getting worse, dizzy spells started appearing, and one of us tried being with her at all times. "Get dressed." I sighed.

A high-pitched squeal escaped through her mouth, and before I could react, she threw herself at me, tackling me down on the bed.

"I love you. I love you. I love you," she kept chanting, kissing my cheeks, my eyes, my nose, and then my lips.

Fuck, this is what I wanted for her.

Happiness. Pure fucking happiness.

I wrapped my arms around her, holding her as close as possible to my chest, inhaling the sweet scent of cinnamon and vanilla lingering on the strands of her hair that were tickling my nose.

"I love you, too," I murmured into her hair. "But we'll only go out for ten minutes."

"Ugh." She huffed. "Fiiiine. Ten minutes it is."

I never saw a person dress faster than she did. In less than five minutes, she had a hoodie on, her pajamas stayed with the addition of sneakers on her feet.

"That's how you're going?" I lifted an eyebrow. This might be the worst idea ever.

"Yeah. What's wrong with this?" She looked down at her outfit. "It's not like we're going to the Ritz. We're just going to the backyard."

"You barely have any clothes on."

"All of them are gonna get soaked, anyway."

"Soph," I groaned. "You'll get sick."

"And you'll get gray hair from worrying that much. I'm fine. Can you just move your ass from the bed? Please?"

I grumbled and protested, but I knew that nothing I said would sway her from going out. She bounced on the spot, moving her weight from one leg to the other, smiling the whole time.

I grabbed a hoodie I threw on the chair in the corner of her room and put it on, followed by my sneakers, and before I could even straighten myself up, she was already grabbing my hand and pulling me toward the door.

"Let's go!"

She ran out, with me right behind her, laughing the entire time. Her mom appeared at the bottom of the staircase, while the two of us ran down like two lunatics, with a confused look on her face.

"Hi, Mom." Sophie smiled, going straight from the door. "Bye, Mom!" she yelled out as she stepped out, leaving me behind.

I stared at the spot she just vacated, then looked at her mom, looking as confused as she was.

"She seems to be in a good mood," she murmured, and pointedly looked at me. A flush creeped from my neck, toward my face, and I took a step back, going toward the door.

"Uh—"

"Go." She waved at me. "Have fun. Just make sure that she doesn't spend too much time outside. It's too damn cold and I don't want her to get sick."

In translation, she didn't want to lose her before it was time.

I swallowed down the emotions threatening to come out. None of us ever talked about the end. Even my mom stopped asking me how Sophie was, because every time she did, I ended up in a mood far worse than I was in to begin with.

I simply nodded and turned toward the door, leaving Mrs. Anderson standing there at the bottom of the stairs with the kitchen towel in her hands. These last couple of months were not easy on her, and you wouldn't be able to see it if you didn't look closely enough.

For the entire time that Sophie and I knew each other, I never saw Mrs. Anderson wearing an excessive amount of makeup, but as the days and months passed, her makeup use increased, and I could sometimes hear her coming into the room at night to check on Sophie.

They were okay with me staying over—it was either that or I would be sneaking in—and I was immensely thankful for that. But with me staying over, I could see the toll this sickness was taking over the entire family.

People often forgot that it wasn't just one person suffering when this kind of thing hit. It was entire families, friends, and loved ones. Even the people that weren't too close to the person in question seemed to be affected by it.

You never knew when it could hit someone close to you. Seeing a young person like Sophie going through this hell was enough for everyone involved to slow down and enjoy life.

We tended to go through life as if we were racing through time, never stopping to look around us. We often forgot about people we cared about, trying to chase our goals and dreams, and we never stopped to look at everything we were leaving in shambles around us.

But when things like this happened, you had to slow down. You suddenly remembered that there was more to life than constantly racing and racing and racing and chasing. There were things a lot more important.

A healthy person had a thousand wishes, while the sick one only had one—to get better.

"Noah!" Sophie yelled for me, and I started moving again from the porch of her house, following her voice.

I found her in the backyard just as I passed between our houses. She stood there like an angel, covered in flickering light from the lamp in the backyard, staring at the sky with her eyes closed and hands spread to the sides.

Her long hair was already getting wet from the onslaught of the rain, as well as the rest of her clothes.

But her smile… Her smile was as bright as the sun, and I just stood there, watching her, storing this memory of her in my mind, because I knew that soon enough, I wouldn't have her anymore.

Her voice, her face, her smiles, and her grumpy little expressions that always made me laugh… I would lose them all.

Life wasn't fair, I always knew that, but I just never thought it would be this unfair. Flashbacks rushed through my mind, like a kaleidoscope of memories playing on repeat.

The first time I saw her.

The first time we played as kids.

The first time I held her hand.

The first time we watched a movie together.

The first time she held me while I cried.

The first time we sat at the pond next to that weeping willow.

Our first kiss and our first touch.

The first time we slept together.

Her first golden medal, and her cheering for me from the stands the next day.

My throat started closing, my eyes tearing up. I was supposed to be the strong one. I was supposed to be her anchor, but as I stood here, I knew that it was always the opposite.

She was always the stronger one. She was my anchor, and I feared that the world without her in it wouldn't be the same.

Even now, as she stood there, months, maybe weeks from dying, she was still my anchor. She still held us all together, never allowing us to crumble down. She still smiled, still laughed at my corny jokes. She still had breakfast with her family, and she still spoke of the future she would never have.

I wasn't sure if she was trying to console us or herself, but every time she started making plans for fall, or my games, or the vacations and Halloween, everybody at the table would quiet down.

Everyone but her.

Maybe it was her way of trying to tell us that life still went on even if she wasn't in it. But I knew that my life would never be the same. Not if she wasn't in it.

"Why are you just standing there?" she called out, blinking against the rain. "Come here, silly."

I stuffed my hands into the front pocket of my hoodie and gingerly walked toward her. She was bouncing in the spot, dancing to the imaginary music only she could hear, and she managed to pull a smile from me.

"You seem awfully grumpy, Mr. Kincaid."

"Oh yeah?" I grabbed her around her waist and pulled her closer to me. "And you seem awfully cheerful, Miss Anderson."

"Because I'm happy." She grinned. "I have you, I have my parents and my brother. School is finally over, and you got drafted."

"I did, didn't I?"

"Hell yeah, you did! See, I told you, you could do it. I

don't ever wanna hear any of those 'but what if I don't have what it takes' talks. You were a beast on that ice, Noah. A freaking beast."

"I know. I could hear you screaming from the stands."

"Because I was so proud of you!" She placed her palms on my cheeks, rubbing the raindrops gathered there. "I will always be proud of you, Noah. I hope you know that."

"I do." I cleared my throat. "And I will always be proud of you. Today, tomorrow, a thousand years from now, you will always be here, baby." I placed her hand against my heart. "Always."

She nodded. "I know. I want you to know that no matter where I go or when I go, you will always have my heart, Noah."

My tears spilled over my cheeks, mixing with the rain, and I was thankful that she couldn't see them fully, halfway disguised by the rain and by the shadows falling on our faces.

My lips pulled into a wobbly smile. "You promised me a dance, Soph."

"No, you promised me a dance. Let me just take out my phone."

She took a step back and pulled out her phone from the pocket on her pajama pants, the screen illuminating her face.

"Let's see," she muttered. "What shall we play?"

Minutes ticked by as she scrolled through her phone, all the while rain fell over us, soaking us both to the bone. I knew we should've gone inside at least five minutes ago, but I didn't want to break this spell.

A thunder roared somewhere in the distance, but neither one of us moved from the spot.

"A-ha!" she exclaimed and clicked on the screen. "This one."

I would recognize the song no matter where I went. "Everything" by Lifehouse started playing, immediately sending me back in time to the first time we heard this song. Neither one of us said the words, but we both thought the same thing—this was our song.

This was the song that would always make me think of her, and as she came closer to me, turning the volume to the highest, she placed her hands on my forearms, guiding me to her waist.

"It's our song," she whispered, looking up at me.

"That's exactly what I just thought."

"Why are we whispering?" She snickered.

"Shhh," I murmured and pressed my lips to her forehead. "Just listen."

I held on to her tiny waist, loathing the feeling of her protruding ribs beneath my hands, a clear indication that she wasn't eating as she once used to. My throat started closing as the bridge of the song came closer, leading us to the chorus.

She put her head on my chest, sighing softly, and I leaned down all the way to her ear.

"You're all I want," I choked out. "You're all I need," I sang slowly. "You're everything, Sophie. You're everything to me."

I gripped the back of her hoodie, unable to contain myself anymore. I couldn't hold the pain, the anger, the devastation.

"I don't want to lose you," I cried, my voice breaking while she held me as close as I held her. "I don't want to fucking lose you."

Her body shook, her hands gripping and letting go of my hoodie. Rain started falling faster, angrier, almost punishing.

"I'm gonna miss you so much, Noah." She cried in my arms.

Neither one of us moved. We didn't dance. We didn't do anything but exist for six minutes while the song went on.

"But I'm not afraid anymore." She moved back and looked up at me. "I'm not afraid because I know that I lived my life as best as I could."

I didn't hide my tears anymore.

"Don't cry for me. Don't mourn me, because trust me… I was happy. I was so happy, Noah. And you made that happen. You, my parents, my brother, Bianca. You all made me so happy. I don't think that a lot of people can say that, but I was loved, Noah."

"This fucking hurts," I sobbed. "This fucking hurts, Soph, and I can't make it stop."

I fell to my knees and gripped the grass.

"I know." She came down with me as well, and climbed onto me, wrapping her legs around my waist. "I know it hurts. But I want you to remember that even if I got to do this life again, I wouldn't change a thing. I would like to meet you again. I would again love you, even if you pissed me off. I would still go through all of this if it meant having you with me during the last period of my life."

"God," I groaned and buried my face into her wet hair. "It sucks when you talk about dying like it is going grocery shopping, but I get it. I get it now, even though I don't like it."

"Death is just a part of life, Noah. It's a painful part, but I believe that people who are meant to be together are somehow going to find their way to each other. Maybe in this life we couldn't do all these things we wanted to do, but we will always have the next one. And we will always have these memories."

I knew we would. But reasoning rarely worked when the heart was breaking. Reasoning had no place in my head when it couldn't help me to keep her.

"I will love you forever, Sophie. I want you to remember that." I looked at her. "Always and forever."

She started nodding, her face wet from the rain and her tears. And when her lips came down on mine, I held her tighter, whispering between kisses how much she meant to me.

I wanted us to stay like this forever; underneath the rain and the thunder, holding each other, loving each other. But fantasies were one thing, and the two of us unfortunately lived in the real world.

22

NOAH

Life and death were like two lovers, always dancing around each other, but never touching, missing each other forever, until one day they got to be together again. Like the story of Sun and Moon always yearning for each other, wishing that things were different. Wishing that Fates gave them a better life instead of the one filled with longing and pain.

Unbeknownst to us, we are all nothing but characters in this play Life and Death were orchestrating, and no matter how much we tried to fight against them, how much we tried to resist the pull toward the other side—toward Death—it always ended the same.

They always met each other no matter what we did.

I wanted to believe that there was a reason for all this suffering, all this pain, but as I sat here on the edge of the bed, holding Sophie's cold hand, I couldn't find it in myself to understand why things happened the way they did.

Her once bright face was as pale as the sheet of paper, taking on the streaks of gray over her hollow cheeks. It wasn't even three weeks since that night when we held each other under the pouring rain, mourning the life we could've had, and her condition worsened.

There was no cause, there was no trigger, but when I saw the face of her doctor five days ago, I knew what this was.

It was the end.

But the thing that slammed that final nail into my heart wasn't the sorrow touching the lines of his face. No. It was the tired smile on Sophie's face when I came back to that sterile hospital room. Her eyes told the story I wasn't ready to hear, and she didn't say the words as I sat down next to her and pulled her toward me, begging the forces of the universe to give us more time.

Just a little bit more. A few more days, more months, more years... But no matter what, none of us were ever ready to let go. We tried telling ourselves that when the time came, we would be able to let go—that we would be able to say that we were okay with the final outcome.

But I knew that I could spend a thousand more years with her and I would still not be ready to let her go. My mind understood what was happening, but my heart refused to believe that this beautiful girl with eyes filled with sunshine, and a soul colored with the rainbow, wasn't going to be with me anymore.

She was leaving me.

Since we came back from the hospital I'd spent every waking hour by her side; holding her, loving her, telling her stories about this new life I was supposed to embark on, even when my heart kept breaking.

I was supposed to move to New York in September. I was supposed to be looking for a place to stay already, but it felt as if my entire life got put on hold, waiting for this day to come.

She didn't have to say the words. She didn't have to

show me how much it hurt. I could see it as clear as day—Sophie was tired. My Sophie wasn't fighting anymore because what was the point? One more day or one more week wouldn't make a difference.

A Death Reaper was still going to come to collect his prize, and there was no escaping him.

"Noah?" Her fingers squeezed my hand, but there was no strength left in them. There was no life in her body anymore.

She was here, but she wasn't. Her body was still moving, her chest still rose and fell with the shallow breaths she took, but there was no more spark in those beautiful eyes of hers.

She didn't try to tell me that everything was going to be okay anymore—we both knew it wouldn't. We both knew this moment was coming, but even if I had years to prepare for this, the pain would still be the same.

I started breathing through my nose, my chest shaking, holding the tears at bay. My pain shouldn't be the first thing she would see when she opens her eyes, and I refused to leave her with this broken memory of me.

I refused to leave her with a shattered picture of me.

"Hey, Soph," I murmured and lifted her hand toward my lips, pressing a soft kiss on top of it. "How are you feeling?"

She stirred, fighting to open her eyes, but I knew even that caused her a great amount of pain. Just before the hospital, she told me that her molars felt as if they were going to fall out, laughing about it, but I knew why.

She never told us about the pain she felt. She never once asked me to take her to the doctor, and I knew she kept that pain hidden, grinding her teeth so that none of us would see how much it hurt.

None of the medicine they gave her worked. It did

nothing except for a momentary relief that was replaced by horrendous pain mere moments later.

"Tired," she answered, her voice soft, almost shaking. She pulled herself up into a sitting position and I immediately moved and placed the pillow behind her back. Her tongue darted out, licking her dry lips, but when her eyes opened, the same brightness I knew from before shone through them.

"How are you feeling?" she asked as if it was me lying in this bed, dying slowly.

I swallowed the burning rage that settled in my throat. "I'm okay, Soph. Don't worry about me."

She frowned, her lips thinning into a straight line, and before I could even blink, she moved, settling herself right in front of me, and pulled my hands into her lap.

"You didn't kiss me today." She smirked.

"You were asleep." I tried to smile, but by the expression on her face I knew it looked more like a grimace than a smile. "I didn't want to wake you."

The truth was, I was terrified to touch her. I was terrified that she wouldn't touch me back, that she wouldn't have any warmth in her anymore. I was fucking scared to death that every kiss I gave her would be the last one.

This wasn't the story of a sleeping beauty, and I knew that the moment we were all dreading was already upon us. In this story, my beauty wouldn't open her eyes after she falls into an eternal slumber.

In this story, I wasn't a prince that could wake her by the sheer power of love.

I liked to believe that love conquered all evil, and that it could prevail even in the hardest of times. But this... Love couldn't heal this.

"Are you hungry?" I asked her instead, moving the hair

from her face and tucking it behind her ear. "Your mom was making dinner for all of us."

But she didn't answer. Seconds and minutes passed of the two of us just looking at each other, and just like a child too impatient to wait, she pulled herself closer until our chests touched.

I put one hand on her waist, while the second one still kept touching her face—her cold, cold face.

"I want you to kiss me, Noah."

Her breath washed over my lips, our noses inches away from each other.

"I want to feel your lips on mine, baby." She lifted her gaze and looked at me. "Please?"

I was never one to be able to deny her anything, and without a preamble, without a warning, I pulled her head closer to me and pressed my lips against hers. Her dry lips fought with mine; our tongues collided, while she ran her hands over my body, shaking beneath my hands.

I bit on her lower lip and then soothed it with my tongue, keeping a tight grip on her hair. I pulled her head backward and latched my lips onto her neck, leaving a trail of kisses all the way to her collarbone and back up her neck, back to her lips.

"I love you, Sophie," I murmured. "I love you so much."

"I know." She nodded and pressed her forehead against mine. "And I love you, too. Always, Noah. Don't ever doubt that."

My eyes closed, while her hands played with the hair on the back of my neck.

There was something sitting on my chest; something heavy, something I never felt before. Was this what heartbreak felt like?

Her breathing was much faster now, as if she ran a

marathon. How fucked up was it that one day you were a healthy, young person, and in the next one you find out that there was something inside of you, eating at you, killing you softly?

I had no idea how much time passed as the two of us held each other like that, inhaling each other's air, just existing. But reality came knocking at our door a lot faster than I would want it to, and as the door opened, revealing her dad standing there, I knew that they needed this time with her maybe even more than I did.

I had no idea how much it could possibly hurt, watching your child going through this. Parents should never be the ones burying their children. It was monstrous, unnatural, completely against all the laws of the universe, yet here we were, waiting for the other shoe to finally drop.

"I'll be downstairs," I said and placed a kiss on her cheek. "I think you should talk to your parents."

"I think so, too."

I stood up from the bed and started walking toward the door, looking at her father who kept his eyes trained on Sophie.

He aged over these last few months. Maybe if you didn't know him from before you wouldn't see the difference, but I did.

His hair had a lot more gray streaks now than it did before. Those empty eyes spoke the story of a hollow soul that could only be told by those that found themselves in situations like these.

"Daddy," I could hear Sophie speaking just as I started closing the door. I turned my back to it, when it hit me like a freight train.

Sophie was saying her goodbyes.

I once read that a person knew when they were going

to die. Something came into their soul telling them that it was time, and they just knew.

A weird kind of peace surrounded her, and it felt like… Like she didn't feel pain anymore.

But I did.

My chest tore open, my ribs breaking apart, piercing through my heart, and I ran.

I ran.

I ran.

And I ran.

Down the stairs, through the door of her house, and out to the fresh air. I ran down the street, letting the tears fall.

All the pain, all the suppressed feelings, they all came rushing out onto the surface.

I ran between the two houses of our neighbors, all the way to the back, where our past and future collided, where fairies still danced, but were no longer with her.

I looked up at the sky, loathing the stars for the destiny they gave us. I cursed the Fates, God, everything that might have had anything to do with this.

"Why?" I thundered, coming to a halt right before our tree. "Why her?" I kept looking up, as if they could hear me. As if they could do anything.

"Why didn't you take me? Huh? Why do you have to take her?" My nails bit into my palms. "Why the fuck did you have to do this?"

I dropped down on my knees, pressing my hands against my temples. My entire body shook from the sobs; wrecking me, reminding me. "W-Why her?"

The grass felt cold in the evening, and the soft breeze enveloped itself around me, caressing my skin, whispering her name over and over again.

"Noah!" a voice called from the back, but I didn't turn around.

I couldn't turn around, the grip of reality keeping me frozen in place.

"Fuck, man." Andrew slid down with me and placed his hand on my shoulder. "Are you okay?"

I shook my head. I knew neither one of us were okay, and neither one of us knew what to say.

What could I say to a brother that was losing his sister? What could he say to the guy that loved her more than anything?

There were no words sufficient enough to extinguish this pain. There was no consolation, there was nothing we could do to stop this.

I didn't want him to be consoling me. I didn't want him to be wasting his time tracking me down. He should be there, with her, spending this time talking to her.

"You should be there as well, Noah," he cried out. When I looked up, I saw tears streaming down his cheeks. "Don't run away from this feeling, brother." He clasped his hand around my shoulder. "If we run away from it, we will be running for the rest of our lives. Feel it." His hand landed on my chest. "Feeling it right here."

"I can't, Andy!" I belted out. "I can't feel like this. Why? Why does it hurt so much?"

"Because it's love." He smiled the saddest little smile. "It hurts because it's real, Noah. If it wasn't real, if the two of you didn't love each other, it wouldn't hurt this much."

"But why her?"

"I don't know." He wiped his tears and sat down on the ground. "I don't know why. I would love to, you know? But these kinds of questions won't do us any good."

"I know."

"I know you know. I also know you're strong enough to

go through this, so I need you to get up and come back with me. She needs you. She needs us all."

And I needed her. Even if it was for just a couple of more hours. I would take minutes, seconds, mere moments... I would take anything she was willing to give.

"Okay." I nodded.

"Okay?"

"Yeah." I lifted my shirt and wiped my face, hoping that my eyes weren't that red. "I'll go back with you."

The walk toward the house felt like an eternity, each step heavier than the previous one. I was not a religious man; I never prayed, never went to church, but now I did.

I prayed to all the forces that might exist to give us a miracle. I prayed and pleaded, begging for a miracle to happen. Like walking through a dream, Andrew led me toward the house, all the way to her room.

She was still in the same spot where I left her; sitting and staring through the window. I had no idea how much time passed since I ran out. I didn't have my phone on me, and I didn't really care.

What I did care about was the way her face lit up when she saw me standing there with my hands in my pockets and my heart in my throat.

"Where did you go?"

"I, uh." I cleared my throat. "I had to run home real quick."

"Hmm." She lifted her blanket and stood up, then walked toward me. "Was it the diarrhea?"

"The what?"

"Diarrhea. Did you have to poop but were too shy to do it here in my house?"

"That's... That's not what——" And I laughed.

So did she.

We laughed throughout the evening, and through

dinner with her family. She made jokes, making us all snicker. Her dad recalled some of the first times she skated and how she looked like a newborn foal.

We laughed as I carried her upstairs to her room. And we laughed as we laid in bed, with her head on my chest and my arm around her shoulders.

"Will you stay with me tonight?" she asked, as if that wasn't what I'd been doing all these nights. "Will you hold me?"

I dropped my lips to her scalp, inhaling her clean scent of vanilla shampoo. "Of course, baby. You wouldn't be able to get rid of me even if you wanted to. But tomorrow…" I tickled her side, making her laugh even more. "Tomorrow we will plan that trip to the Grand Canyon."

"Really?" She looked up at me, her lips pulled into a blinding smile.

"Really. We have the whole summer, baby. We need to do something before I go to school."

"Hmm." She bit her lower lip. "I'm gonna have to fight some girls, won't I?"

"You have nothing to worry about, Angel." I pulled her up, right on top of me, and pressed our lips together. "They have nothing on you."

Her fingers danced over my collarbone as her head slowly lowered down on my chest.

"You are the best thing that has happened to me, Noah. Don't you ever forget that."

My eyes shut, one traitorous tear slipping down, falling right on top of her head. "And you are mine, Sophie."

"Always," she started.

"And forever," I finished.

We fell asleep holding each other, talking about the trip to the Grand Canyon, until her eyes closed, and her body went slack on top of me. Small puffs of air tickled my neck, but I didn't dare move.

She was right where she belonged—with me.

Mornings were never my best friends. I could wake up early, thanks to the numerous alarms on my phone, but I still struggled to open my eyes no matter how much sleep I got during the night.

Today was no different.

The morning light slipping through the window of her room irritated my eyes, and I lifted my hand, trying to block it.

I rubbed against my eyes, shaking off the remnants of sleep. My left arm throbbed, sore from the position I was in throughout the night. I looked at her, smiling at the peacefulness emanating from her.

Her blonde hair was spread over the pillow and over my arm, and I couldn't wait to start planning the summer with her, even if we didn't get to do it all.

"Soph," I whispered. "Sophie, wake up."

I shook her with my other hand, but as my palm landed on the soft skin of her shoulder where her shirt slightly fell off, I knew something was wrong.

"Sophie." I shook her harder now and pulled myself upward, letting her head slip off from my arm. She didn't move.

"Sophie. Wake up, Sophie." I pushed the hair off of her face, and that was when I saw it.

Her chest wasn't moving.

"No, no, no." My body started shaking, my hands trembling as I tried to wake her up.

"Sophie!" I yelled at her. "This isn't funny, Soph. Wake up." I pressed my lips against hers. "Come on, open those eyes for me." I pressed my hand against her chest and then moved slightly higher, rubbing my knuckles against her breastbone.

"Wake up, darling. Please." My vision blurred as tears came forward. "Wake up, for me. Please. Please!"

But she wasn't waking. She wasn't moving even when I shook her body.

"You can't leave me, Soph. You can't fucking leave me!" Her hand went over the edge of the bed—lifeless, cold.

"Wake up! Please don't leave me. I'm begging you." I bent down and hugged her lifeless body to me. "I lied, Sophie. I'm not ready for you to go. I will never be ready."

Her hair tickled my nose and started sticking to my tear-stained face.

"You promised me forever, Soph. We were supposed to be together forever. Please. Don't go. Don't go where I can't follow you, baby. Please."

But nothing worked. Not my shaking, not my frantic voice… None of it worked.

She was gone.

My Sophie was gone.

"Oh, God!" I thundered. "Come back. Come back to me. Please."

But her fragile little body didn't stir. She didn't hug me like she usually did.

She didn't open her eyes to look at me underneath those long, light lashes. Her lips were slightly open, her eyes closed shut.

Her skin was as cold as the ice at Alkey Lake.

"Please!"

"What is going o—" The door of her room flew open and through my tears I could see Andy standing there. "No," he shook his head. "No, no, no."

"I'm sorry," I cried. "I couldn't do anything. She just… She wouldn't wake up, Andy. She isn't waking up for me. Why isn't she waking up?"

Two pairs of steps echoed through the hallway outside, and not even a second later her dad and her mom appeared at the door, while Andy held himself there.

"Noooo!" her mom screamed, while her dad rushed into the room, toward us. Andy grabbed his mom before she could collapse to the floor, while I gripped Sophie's body in my arms.

"I couldn't save her, Mr. Anderson," I told her dad, gripping the back of her pajama shirt. "I'm so sorry. I'm so sorry."

Tears fell, his face reddening with each passing second. He came to us and sat down on the bed, right next to my hip.

"It's okay, Noah. It's okay, son."

I started shaking my head. "No. I need her to wake up. Please tell her to wake up."

"It's okay. Come on, Noah. You can let go now. You can let go of her."

"No, no, please. Please don't take her away from me. Please don't."

Slowly, carefully, crying at the same time, he placed his hands on mine and looked me in the eye. "She's gone, Noah. Let her go. We all need to let her go."

"I can't." I buried my face into her hair. She still smelled like my Sophie.

She still felt like sunshine and rainbows and first drops of snow during the winter. "I can't let her go."

"We need to move her, Noah. Help me move her, okay?"

How could he be so calm about this? How was he not breaking down like I was?

But when I looked into his eyes, I could see that he was holding on by a thread. I could see what devastation looked like, and I was sure it looked fairly similar on my face.

With seconds ticking and his hands on mine, I untangled myself from her. I placed one hand on the back of her head and pulled her face toward mine for one last goodbye. One last kiss.

One last time.

"Wait for me, okay? Just wait for me somewhere there." I pressed my lips on her forehead, loathing the icy feeling of her skin.

Her mom sobbed, filling the silence around us, but I didn't dare to look at her. I knew if I did I would break apart again.

With shallow breaths and an empty soul, with her dad's help, I lowered her down on the bed. If I didn't know any better, she looked just as if she was sleeping.

My sleeping beauty.

My almost forever.

NOAH

Dark clouds colored the sky, letting the rain fall on us. Hundreds of black umbrellas surrounded me; hundreds of people. My mom held my hand while her entire body shook from the force of her sorrow, yet I felt alone.

Completely and utterly alone.

Even the sky cried for Sophie. Even nature knew what it lost, not only me.

I trained my gaze on the white casket ready to be lowered down into the ground, but my mind wasn't here. White roses stood proudly on top of it, and I wanted to tear them all off. They didn't belong there. None of these people belonged here.

That girl across from me that couldn't stop crying didn't even know Sophie. That guy in the second row kept blinking and fighting tears, yet he was the one that bullied her over the summer when we were in elementary school, until she confronted him.

He never did it again.

But all of them cried. All of them mourned the young life we lost, yet none of them knew her. None of them knew what made her smile and what made her cry. None of them knew that Sophie feared she wouldn't get to accomplish everything before she died one day. They were all standing there, surrounded by sorrow and misery, and most of them ignored her throughout her short life.

I turned my head to the left and looked at Bianca.

A quiet Bianca who kept staring at Sophie's casket as if she too was trying to bring her back to life. But we couldn't. None of us could.

I could spend a lifetime wishing for it to happen; wishing for the last couple of months never to happen, but no matter what, even if I had to go through this pain all over again, I wouldn't change a thing.

Sophie lived, cried, loved, and laughed, and she shone like the North Star.

Her parents asked me if I wanted to say something during her wake, but as much as I wanted to shout about how amazing she was, I couldn't. The words were there, lodged in my throat, but none of them could come out.

So I refused, hating myself even more when an understanding of sorts passed over their faces. But I couldn't talk about her as if she wasn't here anymore, because she was.

Sophie would always live through us. In my heart, in the reflection of that ice at the rink, in her skates that still hung on the back of her bedroom door... She was in every ray of the sun and every raindrop that fell today.

I thought I saw her yesterday. I almost crashed my car when I pressed on the brakes in the middle of the busy street. Cars honked, people yelled at me, but when I tore open the door of my car and started running after the girl that looked exactly like her, something I didn't think I would feel this soon blossomed inside my heart.

Hope.

Fucking hope, even though a rational part of my brain knew it couldn't be possible.

And stopping that girl that wasn't Sophie felt like heart-break all over again. And every single song carried her soul in them. Every fucking day I woke up, rushing to get out of my bed to head over to her place, only to remember that she wasn't there anymore.

She would never be there again.

And could one continue living when every single thing reminded you of that one person you lost? How could I eat and drink, and live and laugh, when she would never be able to do the same?

It felt wrong living my life, when she lost hers so young. It felt wrong moving forward, putting one foot in front of the other, without her hand in my hand.

We were supposed to do so many things together. We were supposed to conquer the world together. What was I supposed to do now, when I didn't have a direction anymore?

She was my compass, and living without her felt like living in a world without a purpose.

"Noah," my mom called out to me, and it took me a moment to realize that she was tugging at my hand.

"Sorry, Mom." I shook my head, trying to get rid of the fog encompassing my entire being. "What did you say?"

She was worried for me—I could see it in every inter-action we had, in the careful way she spoke about things. Not once did she mention my future or the time when I would have to leave for New York. I had unread messages and emails waiting for me to confirm my apartment, to confirm my classes, but I couldn't find it in myself to do any of those.

"I am going to go with Davina, okay?" I looked over her head at Sophie's mom staring blankly at one spot, and Andy and Sophie's dad holding her on both sides. If anybody ever asked you what devastation looked like, this was it.

Mrs. Anderson was always cheerful, always so full of life; just like Sophie. But this hollow, dark version of her was the complete opposite of who she usually was.

People often spoke about healing and the fact that with time, even the most painful experiences would turn into dust; I didn't believe them.

Those dark circles barely hidden by makeup, and the loss of life surrounding us were not things that could heal with time.

"Does it ever stop hurting, Mom?" I asked and looked down at her. Tears were already gathering in her red-rimmed eyes, and I knew she loved Sophie as if she was her own daughter. "Does it ever stop feeling like my soul is splitting?"

"I don't know, darling," she choked out and pressed her palm against my cheek. "I don't know. I don't think it ever does, but I do believe that it will become easier."

"I don't think so."

"I do. She will always be here, Noah." She pressed her other hand against my chest. "She will always live inside your heart, in all those beautiful memories you two made. And I think it will always hurt remembering all those beautiful times, but it will get better."

Taking a deep breath, I looked up at the sky, at the pouring rain. My mom's umbrella almost hit me in the nose, but it would've been a welcoming pain. At least it would be physical. It could be located.

It was as if somebody pulled my chest open and started scratching over my heart, making me bleed over and over again. It was as if my soul shattered that day when I woke up with her in my arms, only to realize that she wasn't here anymore.

Her body was, but her soul was somewhere far away from here.

"Are you gonna be okay going home alone?"

I knew my mom well enough to know that she wasn't asking only that. She knew I wouldn't be going back home. She knew I wasn't okay. I would never be okay, but she still wanted to know.

"Yeah." I nodded. "You should go. She needs you more than I do right now."

I just wanted to be alone.

Alone to think about all the things we went through.

Alone to cry in peace where nobody could see me, where nobody could comfort me.

With hesitant steps, my mom started walking backward, finally turning around and going over to Sophie's mom.

I knew I shouldn't stay here—no, I couldn't stay here. I didn't want to look at these people gathered here. I didn't want to be reminded that my Sophie laid in that coffin seven feet beneath the ground; all alone, cold and dead.

I stuffed my hands into the front pockets of my slacks and started walking through the crowd, looking at the floor.

I didn't want them to talk to me. I didn't want to look at them. I didn't want to see the grief on their faces.

I just wanted to be angry. I wanted to scream and shout and curse at life. I wanted to disappear.

That first day after she died felt like a nightmare, and I just wanted to wake up.

The wind started picking up, dancing over my face with butterfly touches. I didn't see where I went, I just needed to get away from here. I needed to get away from everybody.

The need to be close to her drove me crazy, and I knew one spot where I always felt the closest to Sophie.

"Noah!" a voice came from behind me, halting me in my steps almost immediately.

"For fuck's sake, slow the fuck down!"

I turned around and was immediately met by Bianca and the grimace on her face. She stopped in front of me, neither one of us talking, just existing.

Bianca couldn't understand my pain, and I couldn't understand hers. Every single one of us hurt in a different way, but we all shared the same sorrow and the same reality.

"How are you feeling?" I asked first, clearing my throat. Her usually stoic face was now marred by the tear streaks on her cheeks, and the eyes that usually carried mischief wherever she went, were now empty.

"I-I." She gulped. "I'd be lying if I said that I'm okay, but I also don't want us to talk about it. Emotions are the last things I want to discuss right now."

I nodded. "Okay."

"I'm here to give you this." She pulled something from the pocket of her suit jacket and extended her hand toward me.

A brown envelope stood between her fingers, and with my heart in my throat, I took it from her, seeing that it had something more inside, and not only paper.

"What's this?" I asked, checking out the small package she gave me.

"It was Sophie's last wish," she choked out. "She, uh… Oh, man, this is hard." Bianca patted her cheeks and squeezed her eyes, while I stood there, unable to provide her with any comfort. "She wanted me to give this to you." Her eyes opened, filled with tears and regrets. "She knew she was going to leave us." A stray tear escaped from her eye, rolling down her cheek. "She gave it to me two weeks ago and begged me to give it to you when the time came." Bianca laughed, but there was no happiness in that laugh. "I told her not to bullshit me, because she wasn't going to die. And she was always stubborn, you know? She was all like, 'Humor me, B.' So I took it... I took it and told her that there won't be a need for me to hand it over to you because she won't die. And she did... She died, Noah!" Her voice raised. "She left us."

"Bianca—"

"I know. I know I have no right to feel like this, or to talk about it with you, because you loved her so much. Even a blind person could see that."

"B." I took a step closer and ducked beneath the umbrella she held and pulled her into my embrace.

"You guys were supposed to end up together," Bianca sobbed. "I wasn't ready for her to leave us. I'm sorry, Noah. I'm so sorry."

"It's okay, B. You loved her too."

"I just don't know what to do anymore. I don't know how to feel."

"I know. I feel the same."

"I'm sorry I'm crying here in your arms. I'm pretty sure you were running away from all this, but I wanted to give you this envelope and then..."

"Don't worry, B. We're still friends, you know?" I pulled slightly back and looked down at her. "We can still go out for a coffee or something if you'd like to talk about it."

She kept staring at me, fighting back the incoming tears and brushing them away from her cheeks.

"You're a good guy, Noah. I'm sorry you've lost her. You have no idea how sorry I am."

"You lost her too. We all lost her."

And as I stood there covered by the huge tree, sharing my pain with Sophie's best friend, a small part of me whispered into the wind.

It's going to be okay.

THE ICE RINK STILL LOOKED THE SAME ON THE OUTSIDE—the same color ice, the same smell on the bleachers, the same faces as I entered the building—yet everything was different.

After I drove Bianca home, unable to just leave her there no matter how much I wanted to disappear, I finally drove to the other side of town, to the place that would always belong to Sophie and me.

This was where some of my worst and best memories were made. This was where I laughed, where I cursed, where I cried, and this was where I loved her. I looked toward the right side of the rink, almost picturing her from my memory during that first competition she had.

Sophie wore the ugliest costume ever known to man, yet she still looked like an angel, with her head tied into a bun on top of her head, and the soft blush on her face. The yellow color of the costume, mixed with the blue tutu skirt, was as hideous as it could be, but she looked like a dream gliding over the ice so effortlessly.

Otherworldly was the only word that came to my mind at that time, and the entire arena watching her knew at that moment that this was a girl meant for big things.

I sat down in the last row, my lips pulling into a small smile when I saw the engraved initials between the two seats.

N & S

A tear dropped on top of my hand as I stroked the old wood. This was where she told me how terrified she was about her first competition. This was where I held her hand, assuring her that she had nothing to worry about. This was where I wanted to kiss her for the first time, not in the middle of the forest.

But I did everything wrong.

I'd wasted time. I'd missed chances, yet she always looked at me as if I put the stars in the sky. She never wavered, never cursed me out for the things I'd done.

She never tried changing who I was. She always understood even when I didn't deserve to be understood.

Even after that fiasco during the carnival, she still took me back.

"How am I supposed to go on without you, Soph?" I asked, but nobody answered. Ghosts of our past hugged me, choked me, squeezed my chest until I couldn't breathe anymore.

"How am I supposed to live when you are not here, baby?"

I knew that if she was here now, she would've told me to get my shit together and keep going, but I couldn't. I couldn't erase the fact that she lived among the clouds now, while I stayed here on earth.

I leaned back, keeping my hand on the engraved letters, and with my other hand I pulled out the envelope Bianca gave me.

I turned it to the other side, seeing my name written in Sophie's cursive handwriting, this time letting the tears flow. I took the envelope with both hands and started tearing at the opening, both terrified and excited to see what was inside.

And wasn't it fucked up that even this small piece of

paper she left for me felt like she was sitting right next to me? The air conditioning kicked in and I could almost smell her vanilla and cinnamon scent in the air.

I could hear her giggling ringing around the arena. I could hear Coach Liudmila screaming at her, but also smiling after she landed every single one of her jumps.

My hands shook as I pulled out the paper and saw something else inside.

Her necklace.

Her snowflake necklace I gave her for her fourteenth birthday. The silver pendant felt cold to the touch when I pulled it out, shining underneath the lights of the arena.

Sophie loved winter. She loved snow more than sunny summer days, while I was the complete opposite.

Every single winter she would knock at my door early in the morning if the snow fell during the previous night. Every single winter she would pull me out of the bed, just to go outside.

Just for a minute, she would always say. *Just to feel the cold.*

I wondered if the place where she went had snow. I hoped she wasn't in pain anymore.

I unclasped the clasp of the necklace and brought it around my neck, clasping it back while the pendant laid at the column of my neck. I would need to find a longer string, but the cold touch of the pendant against my skin felt like Sophie's hands on me.

I looked down at the paper on my lap and picked it up, slowly unfolding it, scared not of what was the content, but of my reaction to it.

The first three words felt like knives slicing through my heart, my eyes unable to move from them.

My dear Noah,

It feels weird writing this letter to you, you know? Especially because I know that any moment now you will burst through my door with the biggest smile on your face, even though I know how much this hurts you. And if you're reading this, that means I'm no longer there with you.

And I know you're angry, Noah. I was angry as well. I was so angry that I wouldn't get to live my life. I was so angry that I finally had you and I had to let you go. But I made my peace.

I know you didn't agree with my decision to not even try any of the treatments, but I knew there would be no point. I would rather have these months with you all over again, then spend them in a hospital bed, only to die feeling more exhausted.

I also know how stubborn you are, and I know that you will try to push away all those people that love you, because you're hurting. But please don't do that. This is one of my wishes for you, and I hope you will respect that. Don't push your mom away. Don't push your friends away. Keep them with you, because these people we have in our lives are the people that could help us to get through the worst things.

Just how you helped me.

I never told you this, but I always believed in soulmates. I always believed that there is a person out there for each and every one of us, and for me that person is you. It will always be you, darling. And I know how much you love me—how much you'll always love me—but here's one thing you need to know about soulmates.

We can have more than one.

And my second wish for you is to go out there, go into this crazy world and find your other soulmate. I'm sure she is somewhere there, waiting for you. She needs you and you need her, Noah. I don't want you to stop living just because I am no longer here. I don't want you to stop dreaming just because I won't get to do the same.

You are so loved, Noah. So, so loved, and I would hate to see you in pain.

I'm sure that the pain would always be there, but please don't let that be the only thing in your life. Pain sucks, I know it does, but it *wouldn't be there if we didn't feel love in the first place. And I love you so much.*

So fucking much, Noah.

You are one of the best things that has ever happened to me, and I wouldn't change a thing. I would go through all of this all over again if it meant meeting you again. So go out there. Go and play hockey, fall in love again, have a family, have kids, Noah. Please live.

I want you to live... For me. Do all those crazy things we talked about. Go bungee jumping. Visit Dubai and Burj Khalifa. Go to Myanmar. Surf in Australia. Do them all. Do them for yourself, because why else are we here if not to live our lives fully?

Don't be sad. I know that's an idiotic request to make, but please don't be sad. I fulfilled most of the things I wanted to do, and more than half of those were fulfilled thanks to you.

If you ever get to visit Rome, like we talked about, please say hi to those marvelous buildings for me. Take pictures. Go wild.

Just don't get arrested.

I'm leaving this pendant with you. I know it sucks giving back gifts, but I wanted to give it back to you. I want you to always have at least a little piece of me with you.

I love you, Noah. I will always love you.

But now you need to let me go. Set me free, darling.

And remember, opportunities are missed only if you let them be.

With all my love,

Your Sophie.

Somewhere in the middle of the letter, I leaned forward, placing my elbows on my knees. The tear stains on the paper made the ink darker against the white surface.

My eyes closed of their own volition, fighting the tears, fighting the pain and joy mixed together. How was it possible to be happy and sad at the same time?

How was it possible that a small piece of paper destroyed even the smallest semblance of calm I had?

She didn't leave me only with memories and love. She left her bucket list with me and when I looked at the bottom, I saw something else written there.

Noah's Bucket List

"My God." I dragged one hand over my face, tears coming out even faster with each passing second.

I dropped the paper on the seat next to mine, trying to calm my breathing. She knew me too well. She knew I would try to downplay my feelings.

She knew I would try to push away the people that loved me, because my world shattered with her passing.

And she also knew that I would be unable to not fulfill her last wishes.

"Fine, Soph," I spoke to the empty air. "I'll live. I'll live for both of us, and one day I'll tell you about it."

One day, we would meet each other again. One day, I would get to take her hand in mine.

But for now, I would live; even if my heart still bled and my soul still cried for her, I would live.

"For you, Sophie. Only for you."

I stood up, taking the paper with me, and with one last glance at the engraved letters between these seats, I started walking out of the arena. Through the rows and to the entrance. I looked back at the rink one last time, because I knew I wouldn't be coming back.

This was our place, and it didn't feel right being here without her.

"Until we meet again," I murmured to my past, and walked out, taking the first step toward the future she wanted me to have. I pulled my phone out as soon as I came to the parking lot and opened the pending emails and messages I didn't dare to look at before, and started planning.

Maybe it was supposed to be the two of us planning a

future together, but I could still live the life she would've wanted me to live. I could still do the things I wanted to do, and by doing them, I would honor her memory.

I would honor everything she wanted me to be.

24

NOAH

Forty Years Later

FRIENDS, family, and random strangers assured me that time healed all wounds. They spoke of it as if it was the solution to all my problems.

But my wounds never healed.

My wounds festered, became more painful, more powerful. Like the bitter taste in your mouth you couldn't get rid of for hours, that's how I couldn't heal my wounds. The worst thing was that they weren't visible.

There was no cure, no medicine, no drug strong enough that could erase the memories.

The memories were the worst.

Not one day passed where they didn't haunt me, where they didn't mock me. The future didn't matter when you lived in the past, when you couldn't move forward, and my future made no sense without her next to me.

I liked to believe that I fulfilled my promise to her. The promise that I would live my life for both of us. The promise that I would be happy. The promise that what happened wouldn't be the end of me.

But over time, I realized that I kept lying to myself, just like I lied to the rest of the world.

I was never okay.

But I survived.

I survived an empty house and a hollow heart. I survived the sleepless nights and life without direction. I survived pitiful looks and women trying to gain my attention without any success.

I survived, but I wasn't living; not really.

My heart was still back there, fifty years ago, in that small bedroom in our small town, dying along with her. It stopped beating the moment I realized she wasn't with me anymore. All that was left was grief and missed chances, and a lifetime of sorrow every time I thought about that period of my life, and I thought about it a lot.

Now, as I stood in the city she so desperately wanted to visit, I wanted to beat myself up because I avoided coming here for as long as I could.

I often daydreamed, especially now in my old age, of what our lives could've been like. She probably would've gone all the way to the Olympics, while I played for one of the teams in the NHL. She would've been a star, the country's favorite girl, because there was no doubt in me that every single person would've fallen in love with that bright smile and the starlight in her hair.

I wondered if our kids would've looked more like me or her.

Andrew had a daughter years after Sophie died, and every time that sweet child spoke to me, I could see pieces of my Sophie shining through her eyes. She had eyes the same color and high, regal cheekbones.

And I was her uncle.

Uncle Noah.

That's the only thing I ever allowed myself to be.

I tried living the life Sophie wanted me to. I tried falling for another woman, but my eyes only ever looked for her in a room full of people, and every time my heart reminded itself that she wasn't here anymore, it hurt just like that first time.

So I gave up trying to patch up the wound inside my chest. I gave up pretending and just went on, reliving our last moments together.

The vibration in my back pocket pulled me back to reality, and as soon as I saw the name on the screen, my lips pulled into a wide smile.

"If it isn't my favorite girl," I said as soon as I put the phone to my ear.

"Uncle Noah!" Ember, my eldest niece, yelled into the phone, her sing-song voice echoing through the line. "How are you?"

Ember was a tiny thing when she was born, but she played such a huge role in my life. In the period after Sophie's death, all of us just went through the motions until Ember.

The first time she wrapped her tiny hand around my finger, tears burst through my eyes at something so innocent, so pure, and I couldn't contain the happiness seeping through the pores of my body. She had her father's eyebrows, her mother's face, but she had her aunt's eyes and her hair.

The first time Ember stepped on the ice, it was as if somebody catapulted me back in time, and I wasn't seeing Ember—I was seeing Sophie.

Sophie in her white skates. Sophie in her pink tulle skirt. Sophie gliding over that ice as if she was born on it.

Andrew cried like a child, while Ember laughed, going

in circles, keeping her arms in the air as if she was trying to fly. And now, years later, Ember looked more and more like what I assumed Sophie would look like.

She had that same stubborn streak in her eye when something wasn't going how she wanted it to go. She had that same grace, same happiness, same light living inside her chest. And she made all of our lives better.

In the middle of our sorrow, the universe gave us a gift.

A gift wrapped in a pink blanket, and none of us could help but fall in love with her.

"I'm good, Em." I smiled. "What are you doing on your phone? I thought you had your practice today."

Ember's love for the ice didn't end that day when we took her for the first time. While none of us pushed her toward it, none of us tried to impose the lost dreams Sophie once had, Ember went on to become a National Champion. And now she was taking on the world, preparing for the Olympic Games with her partner, Damien.

"I am having a practice, but we're on a tiny break right now, so I wanted to call you to see how everything is. Are you enjoying Rome?"

Ah, the million-dollar question. Ember knew about Sophie. How could she not? All of our houses were filled with Sophie's pictures, Sophie's medals and little memorabilia she left behind.

While she didn't share my blood, she was like a daughter I never had. Maybe it was stupid, but Ember was like the daughter Sophie and I were supposed to have.

And she knew about my relationship with Sophie. She knew how she died and who I was. When Ember turned nine, she asked how it was possible that I was her uncle, but she didn't have an aunt.

The entire room went quiet as soon as the words left her mouth, and Mrs. Anderson rushed from the room, unable to contain her tears. My own emotions were all over the place as we tried to explain to her that her aunt Sophie wasn't with us anymore. That she died years before she was born.

So, Ember knew why I was here.

"It's beautiful, Em," I murmured. "She would've loved it. You would too."

The line went silent for a minute while I kept staring at the ruins of the Roman Forum, walking slower than the people around me. But years of being slammed on the ice, years of concussions and broken bones, made my old age unpleasant.

"I'm sorry you had to go there alone, Uncle. I wish I was there with you."

Something squeezed around my heart at the sad tone in her voice. She wanted to come. God, she wanted to travel with me, but her obligations didn't let her. So here I was, all alone in Rome, thinking about the time when we dreamed about being here.

"Actually, I wish she was there with you. I wish Aunt Sophie was with you."

"I do too, kiddo." I wiped the tear that escaped from my eye, trying to calm my racing heart. "But it's okay. She's always with us," I said and placed my palm on the snowflake pendant laying on the column of my throat.

"I never met her, but every time I'm out there, on the ice, I get a feeling as if she's watching over me." My lower lip wobbled. "Maybe it's just my imagination, but it's almost as if I knew her. It's almost as if she never left."

And that was the truth. Even years after her death, I still caught myself rushing back home, smiling, needing to tell her what just happened, or what I just saw. Until reality came crashing into me, and my colorful day once again turned into a bleak gray color.

"I gotta go, but please call me if you need to talk to somebody. Okay?"

"Of course." I smiled, fighting the tears. "Be careful out there."

Her laughter echoed once again. "I'm always careful. I love you, Uncle. Talk to you later."

"I love you, too, darling," I responded a second before she hung up.

For a minute, I just stood there, soaking in the humid evening air of Rome, observing as other people passed by next to me—some were in a hurry, some walked slowly, hand in hand with their significant others, while others, like me, just stared at the ruins of ancient Rome, probably imagining what it used to look like back in the day.

Out of the two of us, Sophie was the one always obsessed with history. But somewhere along the way, after she passed, I became obsessed too. Maybe it was the need to feel closer to her somehow, but old buildings and historical landmarks never ceased to amaze me, and I spent every possible moment traveling and exploring new countries and new cultures, learning as much as I could.

There was so much we didn't know about other countries, their traditions, their entire cultures, and it was such a shame that not every single person had an opportunity to travel and explore. I'd spent a week once in China, going with a friend of mine, trying to learn more about their culture.

I'd spent a month in Dubai, traveling to all seven emirates. The mix of East and West was fascinating there, and while the buildings Abu Dhabi and Dubai had were skyscrapers, the people there still held on to their traditions. And the expats respected the culture as if it was their own.

Two weeks in Bosnia and Herzegovina, and I realized that the terrible war they had a long time ago, didn't steal the hospitality and amazing people. I'd been all over Europe, all over the world, but I steered clear from Rome, afraid that it would be too much for me.

But it wasn't.

Sophie was in every single one of these places. As a young couple took a selfie with the backdrop of some old temple, I could almost see her smiling again, telling me to take a good photo of her.

She was in the air enveloping me as I kept walking down the street, all the way toward the Colosseum. Her scent was in my nose, her touch was on my hand, and I was a fool for avoiding this place this long.

Cars passed on my left and the remnants of ancient Rome stood on my right, fusing together, creating magic in a way that I didn't think would be possible.

I pulled out the map I took from the hotel and then looked up, squinting at the inscription on one of the stones on the side of the pathway.

Via Sacra.

"Almost there," I murmured out loud.

When I looked up, I could already see the majestic building, and with an increased pace, I started going down Via Sacra, the ancient central avenue of Rome, past the ruins, past the history that spoke for itself, and when I came onto the clearing, my breath stopped.

I never thought that seeing a simple building—a ruin, really—would make me feel like this. My lungs seized as my heart picked up the pace.

My palms became sweaty, my vision blurred, and something crawled up my throat—a sob, a creek of elation, I didn't know—but I stood frozen in place, staring at the majestic thing in front of me.

The Roman Colosseum.

Thousands of years of history were hidden between those columns, whispering between those walls, and even half-destroyed it still looked like the king of the world. The lights strategically placed, illuminated each of the windows from the inside, with the blue lights on the ground.

Pictures were a poor representation of the Colosseum, and no matter how much I'd read about it, how much I'd dreamed of being here one day—both for Sophie and myself—nothing came close to the real thing.

And I wasn't the only one staring up in awe. I looked to my left, then to my right, and saw several other people just gaping at the tall building, mesmerized by its eternal beauty. Earthquakes, storms, rain and snow, it all kept hitting it over the years, but it still stood proud, still in the heart of Rome.

"You would've loved this, Sophie," I spoke softly, my words traveling on the wings of the wind. "You would've begged me to stay here forever."

I took a couple of steps closer, folding the map and putting it into my back pocket.

These buildings defied time and human touch, and still stood strong, telling a thousand stories that happened here.

Love and heartbreak.

Pain and happiness.

They were all etched into the walls of this structure, and now the story of Sophie's love for this city was there as well.

I came as close as I could to the wall, my hands itching

to touch the stone, but with the fence separating me from it, I knew I couldn't reach it. Instead, I pulled out the worn-out paper from my front pocket and unfolded it.

The ink faded over time, but I could still make out the letters.

Sophie's Bucket List.

Something clawed at my insides, my hands shaking even more as the first tear dropped on top of the paper, right where her final wish stood.

Visit the Colosseum.

"We did it, Soph." I laughed. "We finally fucking did it."

I looked down at the small tattoo of the sun, faded and more green than black now, and the thing I haven't felt in years started blooming inside of me.

Peace.

"I hope you're happy, darling," I murmured as I started tearing up the aged paper. "I hope you're smiling every single day, because that's how I remember you. Smiling, happy, full of love." Another piece torn, another part of me released. "I still see you in my dreams, Sophie. I still feel you in my veins."

The final piece of the paper stared back at me. "I know you were always there with me, but I think it's time for you to go."

I looked up into the night sky and into the walls of the Colosseum. "I'm setting you free, Soph. I'm letting you go."

And with one final look at the torn pieces of paper, I slowly let them go from my hand, letting them fall on the ground, right next to the Colosseum.

"I am finally letting you go," I smiled. "I hope you're still skating somewhere up there."

I took a step back, then another one and another, putting a distance between me and the building. I turned to the right and started walking toward the entrance, where the rest of the people were waiting to enter as well.

I couldn't wait to tell Ember about it all.

Epilogue

Years Later

A VOICE WOKE ME UP.

Did Ember, Damien, and little Riley stay over? I thought.

Last night, all three of them came to check up on me. Ember played it off as a social visit, but I could see the worry lining around her eyes. Ever since she found me on the floor in my living room after I had a stroke, she'd been begging me to move closer to them.

"*I want to make sure you're okay,*" she said after they released me from the hospital. "*You're my family.*"

So I did.

But eighty-five years on this earth meant that my health wasn't what it used to be. My knees hurt, my back even more, and I had trouble breathing every few hours. She knew all of this, and she made it her mission to visit me at least two times per week.

I wasn't going to get into the numerous phone calls she made during the week when she wasn't here with me.

Maybe they didn't feel like driving? She sent me to bed before they left, promising she would clean up the table, but maybe they stayed.

Yet, when I opened my eyes, it wasn't the darkness of my room that greeted me.

Warm, white light almost blinded me, and I closed my eyes, trying to adjust to the invasion. I slowly opened them up again, squinting against the light, and when I finally adjusted, I realized that I wasn't in my room at all.

And it wasn't ordinary light blinding me—it was the sun.

I slowly pulled myself up, my eyes widening at the sight in front of me.

A meadow was in front of me—a meadow I knew very well—and when I turned around, the breath I was about to take got stuck in my lungs, rendering me speechless.

A weeping willow stood proudly in front of the pond where I fell in love with her—with Sophie. On shaky legs, I pulled myself up and when I looked at my hands, they weren't wrinkly and old anymore.

"What the fuck?"

Birds sang somewhere in the distance, while my mind tried to comprehend what was happening. I haven't had a dream like this one in a very long time.

I looked to my right, then to my left, trying to see if anybody else was here, but there was nothing. Crickets chirped and I ran toward the pond, the morning mist on the grass caressing my bare feet.

"What in the fucking—" I stared at myself in the water, but it wasn't me. At least it wasn't me anymore.

Like looking at an old picture, eighteen-year-old me stared back through the reflection. There were no wrinkles, no gray hair or slumped posture—I looked the same as I did so many years ago.

I pinched myself, trying to wake up from this dream, but I still stayed rooted to the same spot. I tried closing and opening my eyes, but nothing worked.

"Wake up, Noah. Wake the fuck up."

When my eyes opened for the last time, a silhouette walking toward me from the direction of the weeping willow caught my attention.

"No." I shook my head. "It can't be."

"Hello, Noah."

Her voice sounded the same. Her face still looked the same even after so many years. She was still standing there, right in front of me. An angel and a nightmare, because no matter what, I knew I would have to wake up from this.

"Sophie." Her name was like a prayer on my lips. Her smile illuminated her entire face, and as I took a step forward, I suddenly stopped myself. "Is this a dream?" I asked her. "Because if it is, I don't want to wake up."

She shook her head. "No." Closing the distance between the two of us before I could, she kept on smiling as if this wouldn't break my heart all over again. "This isn't a dream."

"You're just saying that because you're a figment of my imagination, and I wouldn't want to hurt myself."

"Always the cynic, aren't you?" She took my hands in hers. "This is not a dream, darling."

"Then how is this possible?"

She kept looking at me, those eyes that always saw more than I sometimes wanted them to see, staring straight to my soul. "What do you think, Noah? How would it be possible for you to see me?"

And it dawned on me. "Am I… Am I dead?"

"I'm sorry, darling."

"Oh." I took a step back. "Wow." I bent down and

placed my hands on my knees, inhaling through my nose and exhaling through my mouth.

"Are you okay?"

"Yeah," I almost squealed. "Just…" I trailed off and stood up, smiling brighter than I did in the past sixty or so years. "I'm finally with you." I turned toward her. "It's really you." I came closer to her and without waiting for another second to pass, I placed my hands on her cheeks and pulled her to me, pressing my lips to hers. Her arms wrapped around my neck, holding me close to her.

She still smelled the same—like vanilla and cinnamon. She still felt the same—all mine.

"I've missed you so much," I murmured between kisses. "I've spent a lifetime missing you."

"I've been waiting for you, you know?" She smiled and pressed her forehead to mine.

"Sorry I'm late. I just had some things I needed to finish." I laughed. "It just took me a bit longer to get back to you."

"It really did, but it's okay." She took a hold of my hand and pulled me down as she sat on the ground. "I'm glad you had Ember in your life."

I went down with her and placed my arm around her shoulders. "You saw her?"

"Oh yeah. She looks exactly like—"

"You," I cut her off. "She looks like a pure replica of you. For a moment, I thought it was you, just in a different life."

"It almost was, but I wasn't ready to go. Not without you. Never without you."

My fingers tangled in her hair felt like the sweetest heaven. "And what now?"

"Now." She bit her lower lip and leaned into me. "Now

we do everything we couldn't do before. Now we live, Noah. Now we love each other."

I nodded. "I'm fine with that." I placed my hand on the back of her neck and pulled her closer. "Always and forever?"

"Always and forever, darling."

THE END

always and forever

Also by L. K. Reid

A Quick Note

I told you at the very beginning of this book that it doesn't have a guaranteed HEA—and it doesn't. At least not in the traditional way.

I am someone who believes that there is a person for every single one of us, living their life, maybe waiting for us as well. I believe that when two people are meant to be together, they end up together—one way or another.

Noah and Sophie are based on some very real people in my life. They are based on me, on a boy I once loved, on every single person this terrible disease that Sophie was fighting took away from me, and on every single person that's still fighting to stay alive. I was in a very bad mental state at the end of 2021, and on some days, I felt as if I should stop writing altogether because it seemed as if I couldn't anymore.

I was trying to write *Temptation*, the second book in the Secrets of Winworth series, and I just couldn't. Every word felt strained. Every single time I would sit down to write, it felt as if I was failing without even starting.

Then Sophie and Noah came. The two characters I never expected. The story that's unlike anything I've written so far.

I was trying to put myself in a box. I tried doing things how others were doing them, but I was so, so wrong to even try. Because art, no matter what it is, cannot be placed in a box. Every single author out there is creating something special, and I am thankful to these two characters for bringing me out of my funk.

Maybe it isn't dark romance. Maybe it isn't conventional or the best book that's ever been written, but it's mine. It's a story that made me cry almost every single time I sat down to write. I felt that it is a story about something that could happen to every single one of us.

The message I wanted to give you with this is not to waste time. Go and do things you love. Take risks, fail, and then get up and try again. Time is a precious gift, and we often forget that it moves faster than we would like.

Go and tell that person that you love them. Apply for that job. Move to a different country—hell, a different continent.

I also wanted to thank some special people for believing in me.

To my Stephanie, who's always there for me and who's always believed in me.

To Julia—thank you for loving them as much as I did.

To Brianna, Zoe and Meredith—without you I wouldn't be able to shape this book into what it is today.

To my absolutely amazing editor, Mary—I promise I'll be sending you fewer books with cliffhangers (in maybe five years).

My amazing Street and ARC Teams—a simple thank-you is truly not enough to express how much I appreciate you all.

My author friends—and you know who you are—I'm so glad I got to meet you on this crazy journey.

My mom and my brother, who I don't get to see as much as I would like—thank you for believing in me.

And last but not least: to the readers. Thank you so much for taking a chance on me and for reading this story. I hope you truly enjoyed it.

L.K. Reid

MAYHEM AND DEPRAVED LOVE

L.K. Reid is a dark romance author who hates slow walkers and people being mean for no reason. She lives with her two cats, Freya and Athena, and she's still figuring out the whole "adult" thingy.

In her opinion, Halloween should be a public holiday, and she also has a small obsession with all things historical—especially Greek mythology. During high school, she wanted to be an archaeologist, and ended up studying law, but obviously neither one of those professions worked out.

If she isn't writing, she's most probably watching horror movies, listening to music, reading, or plotting upcoming books.

Stay in touch

facebook.com/authorlkreid

instagram.com/authorlkreid

goodreads.com/authorlkreid

pinterest.com/authorlkreid

tiktok.com/@authorlkreid

Printed in Great Britain
by Amazon